TRIALS

TRIALS

THE WIZARD AND THE WARRIOR
BOOK TWO

Vivienne Lee Fraser

www.viviennelfraser.com.au

Vivienne Lee Fraser
www.viviennelfraser.com.au

Cataloguing-in-Publication details are available
from the National Library of Australia
www.trove.nla.gov.au
ISBN: 978-0-6482181-2-8

Formatting and cover design by KILA Designs
www.kiladesigns.com.au
Cover image: ©bigstockphoto.com

Illustrations provided by Anna Bazel
www.fiverr.com/annabazyl
Map illustration: ©Jim Simpson

*For Jim and Sam for supporting me
as I follow my muse*

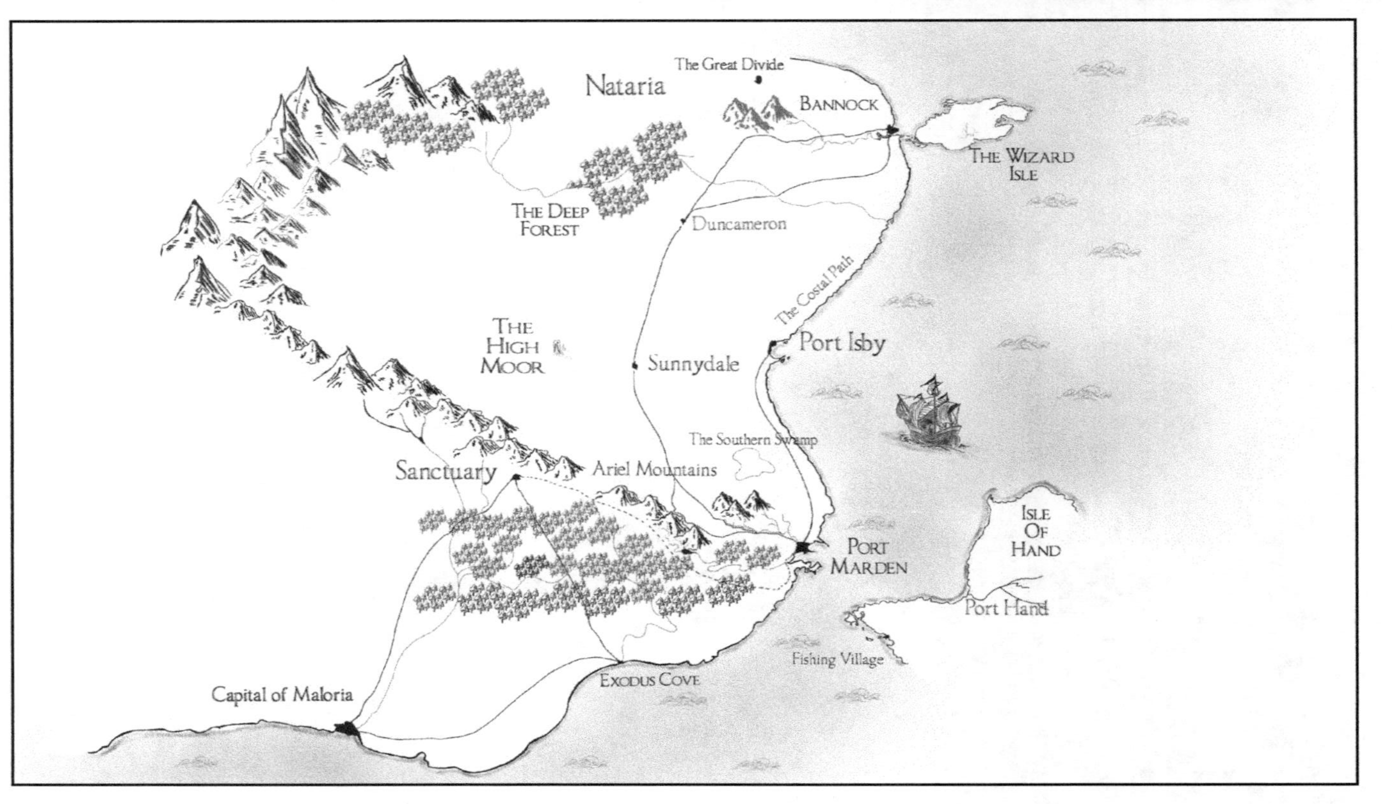

Nataria
The Great Divide
Bannock
The Wizard Isle
The Deep Forest
Duncameron
The Costal Path
Port Isby
The High Moor
Sunnydale
The Southern Swamp
Sanctuary
Ariel Mountains
Isle Of Hand
Port Marden
Port Hand
Fishing Village
Exodus Cove
Capital of Maloria

PROLOGUE

After the decimation and the fall,
When the new power rises
And the Wizard and Warrior meet,
Old and new blood will combine
With the two who are not what they seem
To save one and all.

'Eon,' the elderly seer called. 'Eon.'

'I am right here, master.'

Caraig jumped as the voice came from behind him. He had not heard his apprentice come into the room and for some reason that thought made him uneasy. He frowned and tugged his beard. *What was he thinking? Eon had been with him for years, he had no reason to feel wary in his presence.* He shook his head to clear his thoughts.

'Eon, they are moving closer. If all goes to plan, they will soon be on our doorstep. I would like you to call a Prophecy Council meeting on my behalf. It is time we have this out once and for all.'

'But, master, at the last meeting they asked you bring

more proof that the omens foretold in the prophecy were actually happening now. We have not been able to find anything new.'

'I know.' Caraig wearily ran his hand through his snow white hair. 'Regardless, the ones we wait for are on their way here. At the very least, we need to know what we are going to do with them when they arrive.'

'As you wish, master.' Eon turned to leave the room, but Caraig called him back.

'Can you bring Emer with you when you return? I need to start preparations, and I will need you both to assist.'

'Are you sure we need to involve Emer? I think she is out on patrol.'

'Yes, I need you both. I fear we will not have much support from the others in this matter.'

Caraig caught the sound of Eon's sigh as he closed the door behind himself. In the silence that followed Eon's departure, Caraig mentally reviewed the signs he had seen and tried to decided which would convince the Council he was right—the time of the Wizard and Warrior had arrived.

1
AT SEA

'What the…' Aliah picked herself up off the ground, then held out her hand to help Daniel. She had been practicing her sword fighting with the guardsman in the makeshift arena he and his men built in the ship's store-rooms, when a blast had blown them off their feet.

'Stay here,' Daniel commanded. 'Remember the crew do not know you are aboard, and we are not yet ready to change that.'

He rushed through the door to the stairs that would

take him to the upper deck. Aliah watched him disappear then, unable to stop herself, followed him into the corridor and crept slowly up the stairs. Staying hidden in the shadows, she observed the scene on the deck above, reminded of her escape from a ship a few moon turns ago.

Her initial worry the ship was under attack by someone who had found out she was aboard proved to be unfounded. It seemed the explosion had been caused by Seamus, heir to the Duke of Hand. During their journey Walter, a renegade wizard, had been teaching Seamus to control and use his magical powers. Today Seamus' magic flared out of control when trying to move a barrel from one place to another on the deck. He had obviously used too much force and the barrel, which happened to contain tar for caulking the ship, had exploded. Fortunately, no one was hurt. But there was a large hole in the deck over a cargo hold, and the tar was nowhere to be seen. From the look on his face, the captain was less than impressed. He was yelling at Seamus and gesticulating wildly.

Resisting the urge to go above deck and make fun of her travel companion, Aliah quietly returned to the cargo hold and began practicing the moves she and Seamus had been working on for unarmed combat. Based loosely on the sword forms used to teach attack and defence, it looked rather like a dance. Seamus had started developing the new way of fighting, and lately she had been helping him. Her concentration was interrupted by the sound of slow clapping hands.

'A very pretty dance for a princess.'

Daniel had returned and was clearly amused by what he had seen. 'What is that meant to be? Some girlish form of sword practice without a sword?'

Annoyed, Aliah took a ready stance and faced the son of her father's oldest friend. 'We will see how girly it is, Daniel. Attack me,' she commanded him.

Daniel stopped laughing. 'You have no sword, it would not be fair.'

'I will not always have a sword to hand when attacked. Princesses do not carry swords to balls or state functions. *Attack me.*'

'As you command, Your Highness.'

Daniel readied himself, then thrust his sword towards Aliah. Moving to her right, she allowed the attack to pass her, took a step back, and pushed Daniel's outstretched arm, tipping him off balance. With a kick to his bottom, Aliah almost knocked him over. She laughed gleefully as Daniel rounded on her again.

'I will be more prepared this time, little princess.'

Daniel attacked again and Aliah just managed to move out of the way, feeling the swish of the sword as it went past her head. Maintaining his balance this time, Daniel pushed her back against the hull of the ship.

'Admit defeat,' Daniel commanded, his sword a finger-width from her chest.

Daniel relaxed now he had her cornered, and Aliah ducked below the sword point, turned, and came up on Daniel's left hand side, jabbing her elbow into his stomach. As his balance changed, she swivelled and pushed all her strength behind the flat of her foot, sending him to the ground.

Standing over her felled opponent, Aliah smiled at the figure in the doorway. 'You were right, Seamus. Not having a sword does allow you to use your feet more effectively, and that is very useful in certain situations.'

Seamus walked over to help Daniel up. 'I am pleased it worked so well, but I suspect poor Daniel is not.'

'You caught me by surprise, that is all.' Daniel rubbed his bruised bottom. 'Anyway, what was that?'

'I am so pleased you asked,' Seamus said. 'When I was hiding out in Walter's cellar while making my way to Bannock, I had time on my hands. One evening I came up with this form of fighting. It is based loosely on sword moves, but also on something I remember seeing used by some visitors to my father's palace.

'It allows you to fight when you do not have weapons, and also benefits from using what you have already learnt training as a soldier. Aliah began practicing with me when we travelled from Duncameron to Bannock, and we have continued to work on it aboard the ship. We added feet yesterday, something you cannot do as easily when weighed down with weapons. It seems to work quite well.'

'How long have you been doing this?' Daniel asked Aliah.

'As Seamus said, I have not been doing this very long,' Aliah answered. 'If you have learnt sword work then you can pick it up quite quickly.'

'Impressive.' Daniel nodded.

'Yes, she is,' Seamus admitted. 'I am better at this than I am at using a sword, but I am still not at her level. She has better natural instincts when it comes to combat.'

'No. I mean, yes, Aliah is a good fighter, always has been. I meant the idea is impressive. It uses sword forms, but also uses your opponent's momentum and balance against them. The applications… the ability to fight when you have lost your sword, or are in a situation where you do not have one… very interesting.' Daniel's eyes gleamed as he silently contemplated this new form of fighting.

'You will have to excuse Daniel,' Aliah told Seamus. 'Even as a child he would follow his father around, trying to learn as much as he could about being a soldier. It was all he ever wanted to be. And we have just handed him a very special gift, something new to learn about fighting.'

'Could I join you? Next time you practice, I mean,' Daniel asked.

Aliah looked at Seamus, who nodded. 'Sure. Besides I may need you, Seamus may not get much time to practice over the next two days before we make port. Did I overhear the captain say something about you fixing that hole you made single-handedly?'

'He may have,' Seamus mumbled.

Daniel laughed and clapped the younger boy on the back. 'Never fear, the captain would not let such a rank amateur touch his prized possession. We will be in Port Isby tomorrow. One of the shipwrights in port will be set to fix the deck. We had planned a day there to get supplies anyway.'

Seamus still looked sheepish. 'I really do not seem to be able to get this magic thing. Some days I can do exactly as Walter asks, other days I cannot control anything. Maybe it would be better for every one if I had my magic removed.'

'I am sure you are doing fine.' Aliah put her hand on his arm. 'It is just like learning anything new, we all have off days. You must also remember, you really have only been learning for a short time. Walter said some of the boys he taught on the Wizard Isle took years to get full control of their power.'

'I guess that is true. Anyway, I actually came down here to tell you the captain wants us all in his cabin.'

'We will just tidy up down here and join you.' Aliah turned to pack up her weapons, and Seamus left to meet up with the others.

Aliah oiled then sheathed her sword. While Daniel was finishing up, she gathered her cloak and put it on so the hood covered her face, grimacing as she did. It annoyed her that she had to travel hidden away, even if it was for her own protection. Daniel picked up the two swords, then pulled the hood of the cloak down even further, almost covering her eyes.

'It would not do for anyone to recognise you.' He winked at her.

Aliah frowned and tugged the hood back off her face a little, mentally cursing the traitors on the Wizard Council who wanted to send her to Carsten to marry a king she did not know. It was to ensure when something happened to her father she would not be there to take the crown. Those very same wizards had been working with the King of Carsten to set up an invasion of Aria, causing her father to be in danger, which made her even more annoyed.

'Curse them all,' Aliah mumbled as she followed Daniel out of the hold. He promptly stopped and looked under her hood.

'Curse who?' he asked, obviously bewildered.

'Wizards. If they were not plotting, there would be no invasion. If there were no invasion, I would not be on a secret mission to negotiate military support from the Duke of Hand. Then I would not have to hide myself away.'

Daniel laughed out loud. 'I may only be a mere soldier, not able to fully grasp matters of state, but it seems to me if it were not for those wizards you would not have been on your way to Carsten. You would not have found out what they were planning, and you would not have escaped and travelled home in time to warn your father.'

'But...'

'... What is more, you would not have met Walter and found out about the wizard's plot in the first place,' Daniel continued as if she had not interrupted him.

'Humph,' Aliah commented.

'And, if I remember correctly, you did not have to come with Seamus to meet with his father. You were given the option of hiding with my mother, or your uncle in Nataria. But you got what you wanted—a chance to prove to your father that you are ready to take on the responsibilities of heir to the throne.'

Aliah swirled her cloak around her as she stalked past Daniel, now more annoyed with him than the wizards. 'Mere soldier indeed,' she muttered under her breath as she made her way to the captain's cabin.

The others were all assembled when Aliah and Daniel finally made it to the captain's cabin. The captain sat behind a large desk covered almost entirely by a sea chart. He was a burly man with a sea weathered face that often wore a frown, and had the air of someone used to barking out orders and having others jump to follow them. Aliah had known him all her life, and knew his bark was definitely worse than his bite.

'Highness.' He nodded. 'Young Pup.' He acknowledged Daniel using the name he had called the guard since first meeting him as a child, when Daniel had followed the Captain round the ship like a puppy dog. 'As we are all here, let us make this quick. Barring any further internal attacks on my ship,' he said, glowering at an embarrassed Seamus. 'We should make Port Isby in the early hours of tomorrow morning. We will be there for one night, taking the tide on the following morning. I have to give my men shore leave as it will be expected. They will talk as they do. I am concerned as there are already mumblings on deck about the mysterious woman travelling with us. Dominic, perhaps you can take it from here?'

A tall, brown haired man with a trim goatee and shoulder length hair tied back tidily, moved from his position behind the captain to stand in front of the desk. Even though his guard's uniform suggested a lower rank than Daniel, in this room he was clearly the one in charge. 'What do your men know, Daniel?' he asked.

'My guards were told the princess travels with us. But I have known each and every one of them since boyhood, and all of them would go to the grave rather than tell a soul she was here.' Daniel looked at all of them one by one to make sure they understood they could trust his men as thoroughly as he did.

TRIALS

'I wish I could say the same for all of my crew, young Dominic.' Captain Hank shook his head. 'We took on some new men in Bannock and, while each was vouched for by an existing crewman, many are only known as workmates. They have all been told we have a lady travelling with us who is of a nervous disposition and prefers privacy. I am sure there are some on board questioning this. My first mate has already caught a couple of them trying to sneak into the cabin area.'

'Can we continue without having that hole in the deck fixed?' Dominic asked the captain, who thought for a moment before answering.

'If young Seamus, along with Daniel's men, could help fashion a makeshift cover we should be fine so long as we do not hit any rough seas.'

'And this time of year would we be able to make it directly to Hand without encountering any bad weather, and without running out of supplies?'

Again, the captain weighed his thoughts before answering. 'If I put us all on rations from today, and we dip into some of the cargo we are carrying, I believe we could.'

Dominic looked at Daniel, who nodded his head. Walter also nodded when Dominic met his gaze.

'All right then, we head straight for The Isle of Hand.' Dominic turned to leave the room.

'Good of them to let us listen in on their Council,' Seamus whispered to Aliah as they entered the hallway.

Before she could reply, Aliah lost her footing as the ship lurched and she stumbled into Seamus. He steadied her before holding up both hands and exclaiming, 'That was not me.'

They rushed for the deck, Aliah included, unwilling to wait in her cabin until someone remembered to tell her what was going on. She wanted to see the cause of the second explosion of the day, first hand.

The captain, Dominic, and Daniel headed straight for the bridge, while Walter led Aliah and Seamus slowly after them.

'Pirates?' the captain asked his first mate as they arrived.

'No, sir, but I do not recognise the flag they sail under either.'

Captain Hanks picked up a spyglass as another missile hit the water beside them, rocking the ship and spraying the deck with water.

'They are in range and nearly have their eye in, sir. Orders?'

This time the captain did not hesitate. 'All hands on deck, full sail. We will have to try and out-run them.' He turned to Walter. 'Wizard, is there anything you can do to speed us, or slow them?'

Walter nodded his head. 'I certainly can, Captain. Just let me know when you are ready to go.' Walter headed to the stern of the ship and Seamus followed to see what he was going to do. Aliah drifted behind them, also interested to see what a wizard could do in battle without actually attacking a person, which they were forbidden to do by law on pain of being quietened. This process prevented them from ever using their magic again.

TRIALS

Walter stood silently, waiting for the sails to be raised, and when the first mate confirmed the sails were full, he started a complex series of hand movements as he wove his spell. Beside her, Seamus exclaimed in wonder, 'He is making an air bubble around the other ship so it will have no wind.'

She sensed rather than heard a presence to her left, and turned in time to see a sailor lunge at her, sword in hand. Instinct set in and she ducked away from the blade, kicking the sailor off balance, only to find another set of arms around her and a knife at her throat.

'What...' she started to say, before realising her life was actually in danger. While her mind whirred around, trying to make sense of what was happening, instinct honed from years of training took over. She went limp and, as her assailant relaxed, she simultaneously bit into his hand and elbowed into the soft flesh of his stomach. He dropped the knife and stumbled backwards.

'Who are you? What do you want?' Aliah gasped, still trying to understand what was going on, but her attention was drawn back to the first sailor. He was again coming at her, sword at the ready. Before she could react, he dropped the sword and began screaming and shaking his hand.

Her view was blocked by Daniel's body as he stepped between her and her assailant and pushed her back towards the stern. Two of his men appeared beside him and disarmed the two sailors. With hands held behind their backs by the guardsmen, her attackers struggled, desperately trying to break free as they were marched towards the lockable storeroom below the bridge. The ship lurched in the water and the first sailor escaped his guard while they were all off balance. He grabbed hold of a sword and turned to face them all, daring them to come closer.

'We will not be taken alive, there are some fates worse than death.' Still being held by a guardsman, the second sailor's voice was defiant, but his face was sad, as if he were resigned to his fate.

Then, surprising them all, the first sailor plunged the sword into his companion's heart and, before anyone could react, he withdrew the weapon and fell on it, taking his own life. Aliah froze, staring at the bloody scene on the deck.

'Why?' she started. 'Why would he do that?' Shaking her head, Aliah tried to comprehend what she had witnessed.

'Sometimes the punishment for not fulfilling a contract is worse than death,' Daniel told her as he took her by the arm and swung her round to face him, forcing her to look at his face rather than watch his guards clear away the bodies. 'Are you alright?'

'Yes,' she answered shakily, then took a breath to steady her nerves. Although her father's sword master had often trained her on how to handle herself under attack, this was the first genuine attempt on her life and she was a little shaken, as much from the fight as having seen men die in front of her.

Still trembling, Aliah focused on the captain, who walked up to Walter and tapped him on the shoulder. As Walter turned to the captain, the spell he had been holding to slow the other ship fell apart as his concentration wavered.

'Can you make wind as well as take it away?' he asked

Walter, who nodded.

'It is a little harder, but it can be done.'

'Good, we need to make it to Hand with all speed now, even if it is a little risky. If you could give us some help, we will head out from the coast and catch the main trade wind to speed our journey.' He turned to Aliah and Seamus. 'I need you two confined to your cabins under watch until we dock. The most important thing now is to deliver you both safely with all speed.' With that, he was off to make sure his crew were ready for the impending race to Hand.

Before they could even speak to each other, Dominic had Aliah by the arm and Daniel took hold of Seamus. They were marched down below to their respective cabins before they could even voice a word of protest.

'Great,' Aliah forced through gritted teeth to Dominic. 'I am now to be treated like more of a prisoner, even though I have demonstrated I am perfectly capable of looking after myself.'

Dominic flashed her a smile in return. 'Not a prisoner, princess, just precious cargo. Your father will have our heads if we do not deliver you safely,' he said as he opened the door to her cabin and steered her through.

Jerking her arm free, she turned to find him planted firmly in the doorway, an amused look on his face as if he was daring her to try and leave. Balling her hands into fists, she resisted the urge to punch him.

'Thank you for escorting me to my cabin, I think I will be able to look after myself from here.' She forced her voice to an even pitch, disguising her anger. If she wanted to be treated like an adult, acting like a spoilt child would not help her cause.

Maintaining her calm until Dominic closed the door behind him was all she could manage. As soon as she was alone, she plonked herself down on the bed and punched the pillow, letting out her frustration at not being able to control her own life. Sinking back on the bed, suddenly weary now the adrenaline from the fight had left her body, she had to admit, if only to herself, it was comforting to be safe and secure in her cabin.

2
HOMECOMING

'Seamus, I am really not sure that is what the king had in mind for you to wear as his representative.' Walter shook his head and looked to Dominic for support. Dominic was busy doing up the buttons on his dress uniform, but paused for a moment when Walter spoke to him.

'Do not look at me. I am with Seamus on this. The clothes King Terion sent for him to wear would outshine any princess. They would not be my choice either. I say let him wear what he feels comfortable in. After all, this is just an initial meeting. The real fun will not begin until tomorrow.'

Seamus finished doing up the silver buttons on the midnight blue coat he found in the stash of clothes Dominic left on board for emergencies. The final button at the neck was low enough to show a little white of the dress shirt he wore underneath. It was straight cut and came down to the middle of his thigh. Black fitting dress pants and plain black dress shoes with a slight heel finished the outfit.

'At least wear the shoes with the silver buckles.' Walter pointed to the pair on the bed that sat beside the sky blue coat and blue brocade trousers he had set out earlier for Seamus to wear. 'You are representing a king today, you really should dress for the part.'

Angrily, Seamus turned to take his wardrobe frustrations out on Walter, however the expression on the older man's face showed his genuine concern. He sighed, allowing the tension to leave his body, and his voice as he responded to the wizard was calm.

'Walter, this finery may be suitable for court attire in Castle Bannock.' He gestured to the clothing Walter had laid out on the bed. 'But it would make me stand out like a sore toe here in Hand. I appreciate I am indeed representing the king today, but at my father's court a person is judged by the quality of their contribution, not their clothes. If I enter the court dressed in that at best I would be seen to be showing off, at worst I would be seen to be hiding something or setting myself up to be something more than I am. Believe me, today will be difficult enough without people drawing unfounded conclusions from my clothes.'

He took a deep breath, walked to the table, and picked up the leather bag that contained his and Aliah's letters of introduction as ambassadors for King Terion to the Duke of Hand. The pouch shook as he rechecked he had everything, then buckled it closed, fumbling a little with the clasp. He passed the bag to Dominic, who was acting as his aid today, and asked him to make sure Aliah was ready to depart.

When he left his home a little over two moons ago, he had not thought he would ever be able to return. Magic was outlawed on Hand, and practitioners had their magic removed, or had to leave forever. Seamus had chosen to leave, knowing he could never return if it was found out that he had magical abilities. Now he was going back into his father's court not knowing how he would be received. As an ambassador from the king he would not be dismissed or harmed, but that did not make him feel any safer. Nor did it loosen the knot that had been growing in his stomach since they sighted the island.

He took another deep breath. 'We can go up on deck now,' he said as they were interrupted by a knock on the cabin door.

Walter opened it to admit Daniel, who also wore his dress uniform to mark the occasion. 'I am heading up on deck,' he informed them. 'Aliah is already up there with the others. She is very excited.'

Seamus smiled wryly. 'I am pleased she is enjoying this.' Clasping his hands nervously in front, he walked passed Daniel on his way to meet his fate.

Aliah was resplendent in a sky blue gown over a cream

under-dress. Her honey blonde hair was in a single plait down her back, and she wore a circlet of gold to denote her royal heritage. 'Will you be able to find out who sent those ships after us?' she was asking Dominic. 'I know they gave up the chase when we were in sight of Hand, but we need to know if they are going to continue to be a problem.' She frowned as Seamus walked into her line of sight, and he steeled himself for her scolding.

'Sky blue, I told you,' she growled at him. 'I even gave Walter a specific set of clothes for you to wear.'

'Now, now, princess.' Dominic draped his arm over Seamus' shoulders. 'Blue is the royal colour, no matter the shade. Give Seamus a break. If he is to build a bridge between the Arian Court and the palace of Hand, then you have to let him do it his own way.'

Aliah's azure eyes looked from Dominic to Seamus. Seamus was about to speak in his own defence when she smiled. 'You know what? I am too excited to let this ruin my day. We have out-run those pirates and are about to embark on an important mission. I am not going to let anything spoil that. Seamus, you do look very formal, and I am sure you know what you are doing. Shall we go watch the ship dock? I cannot wait to meet your family.'

Seamus grimaced at Dominic who winked back in sympathy. 'It is going to be a long day for you, I fear.'

'Any tips?' Seamus asked. As a spy for King Terion, Dominic had been in many difficult situations, and he understood this was the first time Seamus would be entering his father's court as an adult, let alone as a representative of the man the duke owed his position to.

Dominic turned to answer. 'The reception today will

be short. We sail under the King's banner, but they have no official word of who is coming because we travelled in secrecy. Today we will be introduced, and the letters will be handed over. It will be a full court, so nothing personal is likely to be said. My advice? Just stick to the formalities. Say as little as possible. Be polite. No doubt Aliah will do most of the talking anyway because of her more senior rank.'

'You make it sound so simple.' Seamus looked out over the port of his hometown as the ropes were thrown down to tie the ship to the wharf. 'If it is that easy, why do I feel like I want to be sick?'

Dominic laughed. 'It is anything but simple. There is a likelihood your father's spies will be watching the docks for our arrival, and will report back that you are on board before we get to the palace. Knowing you are coming will create gossip from everyone as you meet with the duke. They will all be speculating on how a runaway returns as the king's representative. Were you sent away to meet with him? Or were you just lucky?

'And I am sure they have all discussed whether or not you were seen to use magic in the Market Square in Port Marden. Many will be hoping your father banishes you to the dungeon—do you *have* a dungeon? But we can worry about all of that later. Today all we have to do is get the formalities over and done with. The rest will come tomorrow.'

Seamus continued to watch the sailors carry out the docking process like a well oiled machine, and thought about what Dominic had said. He could manage the people of The Court, he had been doing it for years—what he was not sure he could do was look his father in the eye and see his disappointment. It had been his inability to face his parents that led to his running away when he had been forced to use his magic in public. Yet he needed to do just that if he was to play a part in helping Aria fight off the impending Carsten invasion.

As the gangplank was set in place, he drank in the familiar dockside scene, stopping in surprise as the Ducal carriage pulled up in front of him. Then he shook his head and grinned. Of course the carriage would never be sent for him, Seamus, Heir to the Duke of Hand, but it would be sent for an ambassador from the king. That was who he had to be now, for the sake of Aria and The Southern Duchy.

Walking over to Aliah, he formally held out his arm. She smiled up at him and placed her hand on it, then said through gritted teeth, 'I hate this courtly "a woman cannot walk anywhere without a male escort" stuff. But I guess we have to look the part for the sake of convention.'

'Just think of it as play-acting, you are Princess Aliahanna now. You can go back to being plain Aliah when we are all alone,' Seamus said as they walked down the gangplank towards the carriage. He smiled and nodded to the dock workers, who had stopped to stare at the royal envoys.

That is strange. For a moment he thought he saw an eagle on the roof of a warehouse, but when he turned to take a closer look, there was nothing there. He must have been dreaming; an eagle would not be this close to the water.

The footman opened the door of the gleaming black

carriage with the Hand insignia on the door. Seamus allowed Aliah to enter first, as convention dictated, then followed her inside and sat on the ruby, velvet seat beside her. Dominic and Walter both sat opposite, and Daniel took his position outside, beside the driver. After closing the door, the footman took his seat at the back of the coach and they were off through the streets of the Port of Hand.

Seamus looked out at the familiar buildings as they passed, and his stomach churned with fear and excitement over the upcoming meeting with his parents. The warehouses around the dock gave way to the single story buildings of the lower town. Then, as they began to climb the hill towards the palace, these dwellings gave way to the double storied houses set in their own fenced and gated gardens. As they drew closer to their destination, the dwellings and gardens grew larger as the more wealthy citizens of the Southern Duchy had gravitated here to be close to the seat of power in Hand.

Finally the carriage entered a gate in a defensive wall that surrounded the palace precinct. Following the main road through the outbuildings, it swept around in a circle to draw up by the grey stone steps, leading to the main entrance. A blue carpet had been rolled down the steps to stop where the carriage door would open. This meant someone knew one of the ambassadors was royalty, as this carpet was only used when a member of the royal family visited.

Dominic left the carriage first to ensure their safety. When he was joined by Daniel, Aliah was assisted out first as befitted her rank. Seamus followed her, with Walter acting as rear guard. As they walked up the steps, Aliah with her hand on his arm, looking every bit the princess she was, Seamus had to steady his other hand from shaking. He snuck a look at his parents, but their eyes were fixed firmly on their royal guest.

'Welcome to Hand, Princess Aliahanna.' His father bowed and his mother curtseyed, but only just enough to meet required convention for visiting royalty, not low enough to show true deference.

'Thank you, Duke Damon, we are pleased to be here,' Aliah responded.

'We have arranged a formal reception and exchanging of papers for this evening to allow you and your party time to rest from your long journey, if that is convenient for you?' Again the duke looked only at Aliah.

'That will suit us very well. Thank you.' Aliah inclined her head.

'My head of household will show you to your rooms.' The duke motioned to the woman standing behind him. Martha could not help but risk a quick smile of welcome to Seamus before saying, 'This way, Your Highness, sir.'

Seamus was not quite sure, but he thought his father smiled and winked at him as he walked up the stairs and past his parents, but when he turned to confirm it, the duke already had his back to him, deep in conversation with the duchess and his chamberlain. Seamus shook his head—he must have imagined it. His father would be too angry with him for such a private gesture of welcome.

TRIALS

As their party walked through the main entrance hall and up the main staircase, before turning down the corridor to the left, Seamus was vaguely aware Martha was telling Aliah she should let her know if anyone in their party needed anything. His body was tugging him to the right, to the familiar quarters his family occupied in the palace. He was unsure he would be welcomed there, so he followed Martha to the more ornate staterooms, reserved for high ranking guests.

In fact, Martha led them to the suite reserved for only the most distinguished of visitors. As she opened the double doors to the sitting room that separated the two bedrooms, Seamus remembered the first time he had come in here. He had been hiding from his tutor to avoid a particularly boring session going over the Duchy's accounts. Thinking these rooms were empty because there were no visitors at court, he had been surprised to find a rather elderly man sitting by the fire reading. Seamus had stopped just inside the door, and was about to apologise for the interruption when he felt a presence behind him. His mother looked as surprised to see him there, as he had been to see the rooms occupied. The surprise had not lasted long. He left in a hurry, with his mother's scolding voice following him as he hurried back to the school room on the other side of the palace.

With a smile on his lips, he waited as Martha led Aliah to the bedroom on the right, all the while explaining her things would be brought up for her as soon as they arrived from the ship and if she needed anything before then she just needed to say. Aliah stood in the doorway as Martha bundled Seamus to the other room.

'And did you not create a merry dance for us all?' she scolded Seamus, but her smile and the warmth in her eyes took the sting out of her words. 'We are glad to have you back, you little scallywag.'

'Martha, I am surely too big and too old to be called a scallywag.' Seamus smiled down on the short, plump woman who had been like a second mother to him while he was growing up.

'To me, you will always be that boy sneaking into the kitchen to steal hot biscuits from the cook.' Martha laughed. Seamus was sure if she had not had to reach up to do it, she would actually have ruffled his hair.

'Anyway, my Lord Ambassador, this is your room. There are a few of your clothes in the closet, and if you need anything else, you just have to ask. I better go and settle the others in their quarters, but Tom says to tell you there is a horse in the stables needing some attention.' With that she was gone, and Seamus was left looking around the bedroom he was to occupy while he was "home".

The bed was twice the size of the one in his room, and was draped in heavy brocade covers. It all looked very formal and he wished for his own room with the soft, woollen blankets that covered his bed. He sighed and returned to the sitting room to find their trunks arriving, and Sarah, his mother's own maid, taking Aliah into her room to unpack.

The servant carrying in his trunk was followed by Liam, his cousin. 'Would you like me to unpack for you, My Lord?' he asked formally, avoiding Seamus' eyes.

'*My Lord?* Liam, You do not need to treat me like a guest.' Seamus smiled and shook his head.

'My Lord, you are ambassador for the king.' Liam motioned the servant to take the trunk he carried into the bedroom.

'I am also your cousin, and your friend.' Seamus stood in the doorway of the bedroom after the servant had departed. He was angry and hurt by his cousin's manner. He knew Liam had good reason to be annoyed with him for leaving home without a word to the boy he had grown up with, but he had not thought his childhood companion would be so upset with him. Until then, he had not realised how much he had been counting on at least having Liam on his side while he was on Hand.

'Friend?' Liam turned to face him, his anger clearly showing on his face. 'Friends share things. They do not run off without any explanation.'

Seamus' own anger died as he also saw the hurt in his friend's eyes. 'I am sorry, Liam. I really am. It all happened so quickly. I did not plan it. I was scared and did not think everything through clearly.'

'I know why you left,' Liam spat out. 'The fact you did not trust me enough to tell me about it is what hurt the most. You could have talked with me about it any time before you left, but you chose not to. I have no problem with magic. You know that.'

'Was I supposed to guess?' Seamus asked. 'We never talk about magic at all on Hand because it is forbidden. On top of that, if my father knew about me, he would have had to act. And you are sworn to serve my father. How could I have put you in a position to lie to him? Or, even worse, to not lie to him?

'And no one told me about Amelia. No one told me my

father was allowing contact with his sister, even though she uses magic. So how was I to know things were changing here? I really believed I was alone in this.'

Liam stared at him, searching for the truth of his words in Seamus' eyes.

'I guess everyone is talking about how I used magic?' Seamus asked.

'No. Your father told me what the town guards thought they saw in the Market Square. Amelia confirmed it when I visited her after you left. I told your mother about where you were going, and she sent a note to the king. Your father always knew—guessed it, I think—before this even happened. He was sure you would end up with Amelia. But everyone else has been told that the rumours are not true, and you ran off after an argument, as boys apparently will.' Liam's shoulders sagged as his anger drained away. 'What a mess this all is. Do you want me to unpack?'

Seamus laughed. 'Are you kidding? If my father chanced to hear I had not unpacked for myself, that would be the first thing we discuss when I see him later, regardless of who else was in the room.'

Liam's own smile warmed his eyes, 'I have a little time before I am expected back, the least you could do is spend it telling me how you got to be here.'

Relieved the ice was thawing, Seamus turned to answer as the door to the suite was thrown open and some arms wrapped around his legs.

'Seamus! You came back. I told mother you would.'

Seamus turned and picked up his younger sister, and she snuggled into his neck, happy to be back in his embrace. 'I missed you, Cara,' Seamus whispered into her hair. Over her shoulder, he caught the eyes of his younger brother. 'I hope you have not been annoying Jonas too much?'

'I never annoy anyone.' Cara leaned back and Seamus looked into a pair of eyes as dark as his own. 'He is not as fun to play with as you, Seamus. And since you have been gone, father made him do extra lessons, and so Jonas has been far more grumpy than normal.'

Seamus looked at his eleven-year-old brother. 'It has not been so bad. You know Cara, she exaggerates.' The boy shrugged his shoulders, and Cara poked her tongue out at them then snuggled into Seamus' shoulder. Jonas held out the bundle he carried. 'I thought you might like these.'

Seamus moved out of the way so Jonas could put two of the blankets from his room on top of the bed. It reminded him of how he and his brother used to curl up together, and Seamus would teach Jonas everything he had learnt that day, saying maybe one day he would need that knowledge as much as Seamus did, because you could never predict the future. Perhaps even then, he had realised it was unlikely he would be the next Duke of Hand. He carried his sister over to the bed and pulled his brother into a family hug. 'I have missed you both too.'

Tears welled in Jonas' eyes, but he pushed them away with the back of his hand. 'Are you back for good? I mean will you be staying after you have finished with this king's representative thing?'

Seamus gnawed on his lip, unsure what to say to his brother. Taking a deep breath, he started, 'It is complicated,

Jonas. I do not think I will be allowed to stay.'

His brother frowned and looked sad. 'I understand. For what it is worth, I think it is all very silly. Come on, Cara. We must get back before mother notices we are gone. She will not be with the other guests very long.'

'Other guests?' This news superseded Seamus' concern for his brother. He raised a questioning eyebrow, and Liam looked away.

'I am not to talk about them with you. Sorry.' Liam looked sheepish. 'I will say that one of the guests here is someone who will be happy to see you safe and sound.' With those parting words, he ducked past Seamus and left to resume his normal duties.

'We had better go too.' Jonas smiled at his brother. 'You have to get ready for the big banquet tonight. That will be such fun for you.' One of the things Jonas and Seamus had in common was their distaste of state functions.

Seamus placed Cara back on the floor. Jonas reached down taking her hand, and half-led-half-pulled her out of the room.

'Maybe I can sneak away early, and come and see you before bed?' Seamus asked as they reached the outer door.

Jonas looked up at him, his face very serious. 'No, you will not have time. You are one of the grown-ups now, Seamus, and you have a job to do. We can wait until tomorrow. I have been exercising Satin for you. Maybe you could find time for a ride after the formal meetings are over?'

Smiling fondly at his younger brother, Seamus marvelled at how grown up he had become in the few moons since he left home. Jonas really would make a much better duke than he ever would have. For some reason though, the thought saddened him, perhaps because the role he had been trained for since birth was not so easy to give up. Especially as he had not yet found anything else he could do with his life.

'I will see you tomorrow then.' His eyes followed them until the closed door meant he could no longer see his brother and sister. Until he had spent time with his cousin and his siblings just now, he had not realised how much he had missed them.

Left alone in his room, with nothing better to do, Seamus set about unpacking his trunk. He left the totally unsuitable clothes the king had sent in the bottom, and hung up a few linen shirts and another dark blue jacket in the closet. He was pleased to see a collection of his hunting and court clothes already there, along with another pair of indoor boots, and an old pair he used for riding and hunting. He pulled the brocade blanket off the bed and stuffed it in the trunk, shut the lid, then stowed it at the end of the bed. Aliah's voice startled him just as he finished laying out the blankets his brother had brought.

'How did you manage that?' she asked, pointing at the blankets. 'The cover on my bed looks like it might suffocate me in my sleep.'

'A perk for a local you might say.' Seamus shrugged his shoulders. 'I am sure you can ask Martha for some. We have plenty spare in the family quarters.'

'Will she be offended I am complaining about the

decor?' Aliah asked skeptically, and Seamus laughed.

'She will probably dine off the story about the princess who prefers wool for quite a while, but secretly she will think all the better of you for not putting on airs. And even if she did think it odd, would you not rather be comfortable than pay mind to gossip?'

'I will just ask Sarah then.' And with that, she hurried back to her room, her door clicking as it closed a moment later.

As the formal dinner was some time away Seamus decided he needed a snack to keep him going. He hung up his coat and went into the sitting room where he had spied refreshments on a table by the fire when they entered. He filled a plate and went to sit, only to be startled by a voice behind him. Turning, he found an amused Dominic already sitting in the chair he had chosen.

Covering his embarrassment at having nearly sat in his lap, Seamus spluttered, 'How did you get in here?'

Dominic smiled serenely back. 'Seamus, I would not be a very good spy if I could not go about undetected,' was all he said as he continued to eat food from the plate in his hand.

Seamus took the seat opposite, and silently ate, glancing occasionally at Dominic and wondering how he had not seen the other boy was seated in the chair. Aliah joined them not long after, but before she sat, there was a knock at the door. Aliah went to open it herself, admitting Walter and Daniel.

'Ah good,' Dominic said. 'I asked you all to come so we could have a quick strategy meeting before tonight's formalities.' He waited until they had chosen something to eat from the buffet and taken their seats before continuing.

'First thing, there are other guests here. I have not seen them. They seem to be keeping to themselves and I cannot get any of my contacts to tell me anything about them. There is an order from high that instant dismissal will occur should anyone talk to us about them, or to them about us. I do not know what the duke is playing at. I would not be happy to find he was meeting with an envoy from Carsten.' Dominic glanced at Seamus, who shifted uncomfortably in his seat.

'I found out that there were other guests too. My brother and cousin would not talk to me about them, except to say I might know one.' Seamus shrugged, unable to help any further.

Dominic frowned but said nothing, as if hoping Seamus would elaborate, but when there was no response he continued. 'I also overheard one of the servants chatting about your father meeting in the library daily with a strange woman. The woman also meets with your mother and your father's squire. Any ideas?'

Seamus shook his head. 'No, no one is talking to me.' As the words left his lips, a thought flitted across his mind. *Amelia? No, surely not.* As a magic user, his aunt would not be welcome on Hand. Still, part of him wished it to be her as he had not seen her since she helped him and Aliah get away from Port Marden to begin their journey to Bannock.

'This is all a bit worrying, especially after having been chased here by a ship of unknown origin.' Dominic's gaze swept the semi-circle of people around the fire. 'We may need a slight change of plan until we know who the other guests are. Normally we would announce the intent of our visit at the banquet tonight while presenting our papers. I suggest we hold off until we know who these other guests are. Agreed?' The last was more of a statement than a question, as if they would all follow like sheep.

'No,' Seamus said. 'I do not agree. We do not have time to play games. We need to talk with my father as soon as possible about getting help from Hand to fight off the Carsten invasion.' He silently willed Aliah to come to his support.

Aliah closed her eyes, then opened them as she tucked a stray hair behind her ear. 'It is true we only have a few days, maybe not even a full six-day, to get this sorted.' She looked directly at Seamus. 'However, we do need to be careful what we say and do when we know nothing about the other guests. Perhaps there is a compromise. We could say we have come to talk about the Carsten ships heading this way, and request an audience on that matter as soon as the duke is able to fit us in. We might be able to glean something from the way he responds to the request.'

Seamus studied at the princess in front of him, so sensible and regal, and tried to remember the girl he had travelled the length of Aria with. It was almost like with her change of clothes, she had changed her personality. On that trip, when she had not agreed with his plan, she took off on her own without saying a word. Now as her father's representative, she was listening to all sides, taking everything into consideration, and coming up with a reasoned solution.

'You look surprised, Seamus,' Aliah laughed. 'Although I have fought against it, my father has been training me for just this sort of situation all my life.'

Seamus nodded in response. 'I think that might just be the best course of action. Do you want me to take the lead on this, or shall you?' Compared to Aliah, he had little experience with formal court life. Yet another reason why his more studious younger brother would make a better duke than he ever would have. Jonas would have been watching and learning so he was prepared for just this sort of occasion.

Dominic interrupted. 'If my experience would be of help here?' His blue eyes sparkled with merriment, as if he somehow found Aliah taking control of this situation amusing. Aliah tensed, then seemed to get herself under control, causing Seamus to wonder whether it was the interruption, or the person, that annoyed her most.

'Of course, Dominic, I am sure you have learnt much as you secretly spied on many courts.' Aliah's tone dripped syrupy sweetness.

Dominic appeared to ignore the barb, but having spent time in a cabin with him, Seamus found the spy was not as hard as he appeared on the outside. He could tell from a tensing around his lips how much Aliah's words hurt him. Unlike other younger sons of the nobility, Dominic had a certain pride in the fact he was able to provide a service to his king. He wanted to do something for his country, and he did not consider marrying a wealthy woman to be the limit of his contribution. For some reason though, Aliah seemed disturbed by the fact Dominic spied for her father.

A firm knock on the door saved Dominic from having to respond to the question. Daniel opened it to Martha, who had a jacket in Hand Green over her arm, along with a pair of formal dark brown trousers, and some shiny new indoor boots. 'Your mother asked I deliver these for tonight.' She entered Seamus' bedroom and laid the clothes out on the bed.

On her return, she spoke to Aliah. 'One of the maids will change your bed for some Hand woollen blankets while you are at the reception this evening, Your Highness.' Martha curtseyed and then left.

'We are very proud of the wool produced on the island,' Seamus said as the others stared at him with raised eyebrows.

'I asked for them,' Aliah helped him out. 'Everything else is so formal, I thought it would be nice to have something comforting in my room.'

Ah, Seamus thought to himself. *There is the girl I travelled with.*

'I think your Martha may have a few more requests for those blankets,' Walter surmised.

'Back to the problem at hand.' Aliah gestured to Dominic to continue.

'Well,' Dominic resumed. 'In terms of seniority, the princess should take the lead, but I know what the king put in the documents and Seamus' name is first, in an effort to win favour with the duke.'

'Ha.' Seamus snorted. 'I am unsure how much favour I can bring, when my father will not even look at me.'

'Obviously court intrigue is not your strong suit.' Dominic's tone was measured to ensure Seamus did not take offence. 'Your mother has sent you formal Hand court attire hoping you will wear it tonight.' He met

Seamus' eyes, as if willing him to make the connection. The sound of the fire crackling filled the silence as the others waited for Seamus to catch up with them.

'Ah.' Seamus could not help grinning as understanding dawned. 'So I will be petitioning on behalf of the king in the colours of Hand, showing there is already a strong relationship. My mother sending the clothes shows my father is not against our approaching him for support, and that I am not totally out on a limb as she would not have made so public a statement without first discussing it with him?' He looked to Dominic for approval.

'You will never be a natural at this, but there is hope for you yet.' Dominic winked, taking the sting out of his words. 'Princess, after the introductions you will request the audience as it will hold more weight coming from you.'

Tugging at her braid, Aliah appeared to be mulling over the plan in her head, when really, Seamus could tell by the little smile playing at the edge of her lips she had already agreed to it. 'I have one small change.'

'Of course, princess.' Holding back his own smile, Dominic played her game, knowing she would not be able to accept his plan without tweaking it a little.

'Seamus, you must wear some blue as you are a royal representative.' She thought for a moment. 'I have a blue scarf you can wear as a cravat.'

Seamus wrinkled his nose. 'Really? Are you sure it will not be too much?'

Dominic and Daniel laughed at his discomfort. 'Just go along with it, or she may think of something worse.' Daniel wiped the tears from his eyes.

Walter, who had been silent for most of the meeting,

stood. 'I suppose we must all dress now or we will make a bad impression by being late.' His movement signalled the meeting was over and they should retire to their rooms to get ready.

Seamus walked slowly to his bedroom, wishing he could put off the evening for as long as possible. Even though he now believed his parents were happy he was there, his nerves still caused flutters in his stomach.

As he began to undress, two servants brought in a bath and a procession of servants began to fill it. *Private bathing, what a pleasure.* He had always had to bathe in the room by the kitchen as the duke took pride in his children not having to be waited upon. As he stepped in the water, he tried to relax and prepare mentally to meet with his father in front of the assembled nobility of the Southern Duchy, who would be hovering ready to pounce at any mistake he made.

<h1 style="text-align:center">3
FORMALITIES</h1>

'If Seamus fiddles with that collar one more time, I may just have to cut off his hands,' Aliah whispered furiously to Walter as they walked through the halls of the duke's palace to the formal reception room.

'He is a little nervous,' Walter whispered back, trying to show some support for his young friend.

'So am I. But it really will not do to let other people know we are new to this. They might not take us seriously, and we cannot do our job if they do not think we are capable.'

Aliah frowned and tugged at a loose strand of hair.

'You know I can hear you.' Seamus turned and stared at them. 'It is this scarf you made me wear. It will not sit properly with this shirt.' He tugged at his collar again, then sighed and gave up.

Aliah had to admit that he did look the part of an ambassador, dressed in his thigh length, green coat, buttoned up with just a hint of white and blue at the collar. She herself had dressed in a simple blue gown that was fitted and fell gracefully from her hips. The only jewellery she wore was the royal gold circlet.

'I will pull myself together before we reach the hall,' Seamus assured her. 'But no one can see us here, so I do not see how it matters.'

'I should hope you will be on your best behaviour at the reception.' Aliah was surprised at how much she sounded like her mother when she scolded Seamus.

Their small procession stopped at the sound of a new voice. It came from a petite, dark-haired woman, sitting on a sofa facing the windows overlooking the castle's inner-courtyard. The woman rose and walked straight to Seamus, her beautiful face lit with a smile as she took his hands.

'Welcome home, my son. I have missed you.'

As Seamus wrapped his arms around his mother, some of the tension he had displayed since leaving Bannock left his body as he once again connected with his family. Aliah understood just how much this meant to Seamus as he had feared those closest to him might be forced to reject him because of his magic.

'Mother, it is so good to see you.'

TRIALS

'I would so love to hear of your adventures and how you managed to worm your way into Terion's graces and become one of his ambassadors, but I have to get to your reception. We can talk of family things later. I just wanted you to know that even though your father may not show it tonight, you are welcome here. Tonight is not the night for family issues, it is all about the threats facing Hand and Aria.' Duchess Elise pulled her son's head downwards and kissed him on the cheek. 'Do us proud, son.' Then, with a swish of her green skirt, she left them all standing there.

Seamus brushed a tear from his eye and turned to continue their journey. Dominic put a restraining hand on his arm. 'We should wait here for a bit.'

Aliah's eyes widened as a sign of her surprise. 'But we cannot be late to a dinner held in our honour.'

'They will not start the proceedings until the duchess is ready to welcome us, and Seamus needs to take a breath and steady himself for the reception to come.'

They all looked at Seamus, who had clearly been affected by his mother's sudden appearance. He was still wiping tears from his cheeks. 'I am all right,' he told them. 'I just want to get this public bit over and done with so we can get on to the real work and start preparing for the coming war.'

Aliah sighed. 'You know this public bit is as much a part of the real work as the private meetings?' she asked. 'Tension between Hand and the other Duchies has always been high. What happens tonight will go a long way towards making people's minds up about whether they should support the rest of Aria in this war.'

It was Seamus' turn to raise an eyebrow. 'Really? I

had not thought of that.'

Aliah smiled. 'Sorry, Seamus, I did not mean to preach. I am nervous too. I want to make my father proud, and I am worried if I muck this up, he will never let me do anything like this again. Then I will be relegated to sitting at home and doing needlework with the other ladies.'

They all laughed, as if the idea of Aliah sitting sewing with other court ladies was something they could never imagine.

'I think that would frustrate the other women, as much as you. I really cannot see needlepoint being something you are good at.' Dominic smiled.

'Actually, I am disgustingly good at it, mores the pity.' Aliah grimaced. 'Well, we have dawdled enough. Shall we proceed?'

Aliah nodded at Seamus, who held out his arm. Aliah placed her hand just above his elbow, squeezing his arm lightly in a show of support. Dominic and Walter moved in behind as Seamus nodded at Daniel, and he led them forward, round the corner into the main hall. There they were met by a rather tall, gaunt looking man, in the formal robes of the Duke's Court.

'Princess Aliahanna, Lord Seamus, if you would follow me.'

'Thank you, Robin.' Seamus smiled at his father's chancellor and right hand man.

The small group followed him to the double wooden doors of the formal hall. Before they reached the doors, two guards opened them wide to admit their group. Just inside the doorway, Robin stopped and stepped to the side.

'Princess Aliahanna, Heir to the Throne of Aria, Lord

TRIALS

Seamus, Heir to the Duchy of Hand, and their party, request permission to enter the court and petition the duke on behalf of Terion, King of Aria.'

The hall was packed with well dressed people who had made an isle down the middle of the room between the main doorway, and the dais at the other end, where the duke and duchess stood on a raised platform. Below them stood the duke's squire, a boy Aliah had first seen at Seamus' aunt's house, when she was helping them get ready for their journey from Port Marden to Bannock, and who had been in Seamus' room earlier on.

'The Court of Hand recognises the envoy from King Terion, and asks them to approach.' The squire stepped forward to say the formal words that confirmed their status in the duke's court.

Seamus and Aliah walked towards the dais. As they walked, the people on either side curtseyed, not as low as they would have elsewhere in Aria, but the mark of respect for the crown was there. At least she supposed it was for the crown and not because Seamus was the duke's heir.

They stopped in front of the duke and duchess. Aliah stole a quick glance at Seamus and then at his father as Dominic came forward and handed their formal papers of introduction to the squire. The squire handed the papers to the duke, who opened them and read them through quickly. 'You are welcome in my court, Princess Aliahanna, Lord Seamus. And you are also welcome, young sir.' Duke Damon looked pointedly at Dominic. 'I am sure you have been here before, in some other capacity perhaps?' There was a smile playing around the duke's mouth as he let Dominic know he was aware of exactly who and what Dominic was. 'But you, sire, I do not know.' He glanced at Walter questioningly.

Aliah stepped forward. 'This is Walter Ivanson, my advisor, and tutor to Lord Seamus.' She then nodded to Seamus, who also took a step forward.

'Thank you for your kind welcome, we hope our visit will be fruitful for both Hand and Aria.' Seamus spoke the formal words they had agreed upon. That was her queue. Aliah took a deep breath and looked Duke Damon in the eye.

'As you know, we come here on behalf of the king to discuss a grave danger all the people of Aria will face not long from now, and we request a meeting with you, and your advisors, at your earliest convenience.'

Aliah swore the duke's eyes were twinkling, as if he had known how much courage it had taken for the two of them to walk through the hall to face him. There appeared to be pride mingled there as well. As she looked at him, Aliah realised this was a glimpse of what Seamus would look like as he grew older, so alike were he and his father.

'Ah, the impatience of youth.' The duke beamed at his court as if sharing a private joke with them. 'I will need to fully read the letters sent from your father, and discuss them with my advisors before there is any meeting. I will let you know when we can arrange such a discussion. I promise the wait will be short. In the meantime, we have prepared a welcome dinner for you, if you would be good enough to join us.'

Aliah quickly glanced at Dominic, who inclined his

head slightly, acknowledging this was the best they could do tonight. Thanking the duke, she confirmed the formalities were over, and allowed Seamus to lead her into the formal dining room to their left. They followed the duke and duchess, and were in turn followed by the other people present.

There were two long tables down each side of the dining room, and at the top was a table set crossways between them, where the duke and duchess were seated. Aliah and Walter sat to one side of the duke, and Seamus and Dominic to the other side of the duchess. Aliah relaxed when Daniel took a place beside the duke's squire behind the main table. From there, Daniel would be able to keep an eye on everything that happened during the meal.

As with all state occasions, it was a long meal with many courses, and filled with small talk about nothing of consequence. After they had discussed their journey, and the weather, and the state of the Hand economy, there was a lull in the conversation. Aliah took a quick look to the other end of the table where Dominic and the duchess seemed to be having a lively conversation.

Just my luck to get the dull end of the stick, I wish things were more lively down here, Aliah thought to herself, and was immediately reminded why you should always be careful what you wish for.

'So, you have been tutoring my son?' The duke leant forward to look at Walter. 'I thought his formal education long since finished. I would be interested to learn what you have felt the need to tutor him in?'

Oh no, just the topic of conversation we wished to avoid. Aliah's brow creased with a frown. She need not have worried though. Walter had spent many years around her father's court, and was more than capable of answering the trickiest of questions.

'Well, sir, I would not like to bore you with the details on such an important occasion as this. Suffice to say, I have a unique set of skills that allow me to teach your son some things that will enable him to better survive in life.'

The duke stared at Walter, almost as if he was looking into the wizard's very soul. Then he smiled, the same slow smile Seamus had when it had taken him a while to realise something. Quickly he looked around, aware that others were listening in on their conversation. 'There is always something to learn in life, and I would be a fool to think Seamus learnt all that he needed here on Hand. I am sure there are many things an envoy needs that we would not have been able to teach him.'

With disaster deftly averted, Aliah was able to relax again. Walter, taking the duke's lead, continued the conversation. 'With that thought in mind, sire, during our studies, Seamus told me about the extensive library here in the palace, part of which date back to before your people came to Hand. With your permission, I would like to take a look through it while we are here?'

The Duke stopped for a moment and frowned, putting Aliah immediately on alert. A common request such as Walter's should not have raised any issues. Then, as if he realised this himself, the frown disappeared from his face and the duke was once again a disarming host. 'Of course. It is in heavy use at the moment by another guest, but I am sure I could talk with them and find some time when you would not be disturbing their study.'

'I would appreciate that.' Walter bowed his head in thanks.

At a gentle touch on his arm, the duke turned to the duchess, bending slightly towards her as she whispered in his ear. While he was distracted, Aliah lowered her own voice to speak to her other dinner companion. 'Surely we will not have time for you to be losing yourself in a library, Walter?'

Walter smiled as if he found her conversation amusing. 'No we do not,' he quietly confirmed. 'Before dinner Dominic told me one of the other guests is spending all their time there and he asked me to request use of the library to see what response I got. An interesting answer, was it not?'

Aliah was saved from adding her thoughts as the duke rose from his seat. While Walter and Aliah had been distracted, the squire had brought him a message and it seemed Duke Damon was being called away.

'I am most sorry, I must apologise to you all, and our distinguished guests, but something has arisen that requires my immediate attention. Please carry on with your meal and enjoy.'

The duke looked regretfully at Aliah. 'Please accept my apologies, Your Highness, but I really must deal with this now.'

Aliah inclined her head, granting her host leave to go.

After the duke's departure, the rest of the meal continued without anything of note happening. Many of the nobility of Hand were either in awe of the princess, or refused to talk to her because of the long-held belief her family had no right to rule over them. That left her with only Walter to talk to, as she watched the people around them sneak glances at Seamus and his mother.

Finally the duchess looked at Aliah for permission to leave, then stood, signalling the end of the meal. Using this as an excuse to depart as well, she and Seamus gratefully followed the duchess, with Dominic, Walter, and Daniel falling in behind. As there were people still milling around the halls, they held off talking about what they had learnt at the dinner until they were back in the privacy of the state room.

'What was that all about?' Aliah asked them when they were back in their rooms and seated comfortably. 'Did anyone hear the reason the duke was suddenly called away?'

'All I know is that Robin gave Liam a message, which he then delivered to my mother. She interrupted my father and he decided to leave. I could not hear what they were saying,' Seamus offered.

Aliah looked pointedly at Dominic, who laughed. 'I have no idea. I am not sure you fully understand what a spy is. It is not someone with very good hearing, or who reads minds. What I do is blend into the background and pick up on gossip. Sometimes I cultivate friends. Normally I start up conversations and hope I can read people's responses, or they might slip up and tell me something they should not have. All I can tell you is the duke was surprised, but in a good way.'

TRIALS

'Well, you have done ever so well at your job given the duke recognised you,' Aliah spat back at Dominic, tired and somewhat irritated by his glib answer.

'Aliah,' Seamus said sharply. 'Do you have a problem with Dominic we should know about?'

'Sorry, Dominic. I should not have taken my frustration out on you,' Aliah apologised quickly, hoping it would be enough for Seamus to drop the subject.

'It is all right,' Dominic answered, although his eyes betrayed he had been hurt by Aliah's outburst. Shame she had lashed out so quickly washed over her.

'No, it is not,' Seamus told him angrily. 'That is the second time today Aliah has sniped at you because of the work you do. We all have to rely on and trust each other, and Aliah seems to have a problem. I am not sure if it is with you, or with what you do. But we really need to get it out in the open.'

'It is with what I do, I am afraid.' Dominic kept his eyes on Aliah as he spoke, but she could not meet his gaze. 'Will you tell them, or shall I?'

Aliah dropped her head, her new-found poise deserting her for the moment. She could feel everyone's eyes upon her, waiting for her answer, but she was not sure she was ready to share the reasons for her unease around her father's spy.

'When Aliah was little, her mother happened on what we believe was a Natari spy in her rooms. She called the guards and there was a fight. During the melee, the queen was stabbed. We are unsure whether it was intentional, or an accident.

'Although she was injured badly she seemed to recover,

but the wound continued to trouble her. A little over a year later, she died from heart strain caused by an infection in the wound.' Dominic spoke as if he were reciting a history lesson.

'How could this have happened without everyone knowing about it?' Seamus asked, his face displaying his shock.

'The king commanded it be kept quiet. He did not want anyone to know his court had been infiltrated so easily. Also, if it were known that someone from Nataria had caused the death of the queen, it would have strained relations with a rather strong neighbour on our borders. So the king ordered the whole thing hushed up.'

'And that is why you have a problem with Dominic?' Seamus asked Aliah directly.

'Yes,' she responded slowly, still not able to meet anyone's eyes. 'It is not Dominic himself, you understand, it is what he does. The logical part of me knows spies are necessary, and I also know my father would not employ anyone as unscrupulous as my mother's killer, but still...' In spite of all her best intentions to be more stately and grown up, Aliah could not deal with this one thing unemotionally.

'I imagine it is very hard to get over something like that,' Dominic consoled her, but still she would not raise her head and meet his eyes.

'I can not even imagine how any decent person can live their life being someone they are not,' she admitted, looking into the fire.

'It is not easy,' Dominic's voice came from behind. 'And sometimes I really want to give it up and go back to being just me. But I have a brain that is able to piece together bits of information and see how it fits into the big picture of what is going on in the world. I also have the ability to get people talking, which helps with gathering information. And it is information your father needs if he is to make good decisions. Also, your father asked me to do this work for him when he recognised my particular talents, and I could not refuse.

'I am good at this, and I can contribute to Aria by doing it,' he told her proudly. 'The alternative for me is to be sold on the marriage market to the highest bidder so I can further my father's ambitions. I am capable of so much more than that. I want to make a worthwhile contribution.'

Aliah sensed for some reason it was important to Dominic that she accepted what he did. Also, some of what he said struck a chord with her. Something she could not quite place her finger on. Then a light blinked on in her head, and she turned to Dominic. 'Funny, for a moment there, you sounded just like me. Trying to escape being a pawn in someone else's game.' She marvelled at how alike they were in that way. Wishing to make some amends, she continued. 'If I am honest, and ignore my feelings about spies in general, I have to admit we could not be doing any of this without your input and advice. I promise I will try harder to see you as a person, and not a spy.'

The room fell silent after Aliah's words. Before anyone else could speak there was a knock on the door. Daniel opened it to admit Liam. 'Excuse me, Your Highness, sorry for the intrusion, but the duke would like a private word with his son if you are finished with him.'

Dominic raised a questioning eyebrow as Aliah tried to hide her annoyance at being interrupted.

'He did say I should tell you it is a family matter, not a matter of state,' Liam assured the company.

Seamus rose to leave, ready to go whether they had finished talking or not.

'Ah… he did also say that if Tutor Walter wanted to accompany us, now would be a convenient time to visit the library.'

Keeping up the ruse about his interest in Hand's book collection, Walter joined Seamus as Aliah attempted to quieten her annoyance at being left out.

4
THE PAST RETURNS

S eamus followed Liam down the dimly lit corridor into the public reception area of the palace, past the doors to the room they had dined in that evening. As they passed the large wooden doors of the reception room, Seamus thought there was a noise on the stairs behind them. He glanced back over his shoulder, but could see no one there.

'Did you hear that?' he asked Liam.

'What? I did not hear a thing. You will be jumping at

your own shadow next.' Liam laughed.

That was the longest sentence he managed to get from his cousin as they turned down another corridor, which led to the library and some other rooms, housed in the oldest part of the building. All attempts to find out why his father summoned him late at night were frustratingly rebuffed with, 'You know I am here as duke's squire now, I cannot tell you anything except what I have been told to say. So stop asking.'

The candle-lit corridor wound deep into the old part of the palace. The walls were dark with age, and years of soot from the candles housed in the sconces placed every few paces. They finally arrived at the large, wooden library door. There was a guard standing outside. Recognising Liam, he opened the door to admit them.

'A guard outside the library? That is a little unusual,' Seamus whispered to Liam as they passed into the room. Liam ignored him. As they entered, Seamus' eyes were drawn to the two figures standing by the large wooden table that dominated the centre of the room.

'Amelia.' Seamus grinned as the woman standing with his father walked towards him and drew him into a hug. 'So this is the secret guest you have been hiding?'

Duke Damon frowned, seemingly confused, but the expression was so fleeting Seamus thought he must have been mistaken.

'Seamus, you have no idea how glad I am to see you again. To know that you are safe and well at home warms my heart.' Amelia stood back and studied at her nephew. She had taken Aliah and Seamus in when they had escaped from Port Marden three moons ago, then helped them prepare for their journey north.

'Amelia, I did not expect to see you in Hand of all places. You know, because of your...' Seamus looked over her shoulder to his father, who stood by the table looking at a large scroll.

'...magic?' Duke Damon turned. 'Well, desperate times call for desperate measures.' He walked towards Seamus and caught his son in a hug. 'I am also pleased to see you are safe and alive,' the duke said gruffly. 'You had your mother and me worried out of our skins.'

'I am sorry, father, I truly am. But surely you know why I left. Amelia...'

'Yes, yes. Amelia told us you wanted to go to the Wizard Isle to train, rather than stay here and take your rightful place as Heir to the Duchy.'

'How could I stay?' Seamus asked angrily. 'If I stayed, I would have faced having all trace of magic removed. That would have been denying who I am.' He pulled away from his father. 'I have magic and that is part of who I am.' Saying the words out loud felt strange, but also liberating.

'Whoa, slow down Seamus.' His father placed a restraining hand on his arm. 'I know why you left, and I sympathise. You have no idea how much I have regretted what happened to my own sister because of her magic. I am most annoyed because you did not come and talk to your mother and me about this. Did you not even consider that we may have been able to help you through? Even after that dust up in Port Marden where you moved some crates. We could have worked to cover that up while we decided what to do.

'Instead, you placed yourself in danger by running

away. Your mother and I had to put on a brave face and deal with all manner of rumours, all the while not really knowing where you were, or what you were doing. Your mother was distraught...'

As if on cue, the library door squeaked. They turned to see Duchess Elise, who had been standing listening. 'Yes, Seamus that really was very thoughtless of you. We worried so much, even after we found out you had been with Amelia. You undertook a perilous journey, travelling to the Wizard Isle with only a strange girl for company.'

'I am sorry you and father worried about me.' Seamus had the grace to look a little embarrassed. 'But as you can see, I am perfectly able to take care of myself.'

'Yes, I can see that. In fact you seemed to have done more than that, given you have turned up here with a princess who is supposed to be missing somewhere in Aria. And on a mission from the king, no less.' His mother's eyes searched his face. 'That must be quite a story you have to tell.'

'I may be able to help with that.' A voice came from the opening door. 'Sorry to interrupt,' Aliah said as she let herself into the library, not looking very sorry at all. She smiled at the guard, and handed him back his sword. 'Your guard thought to stop me from entering, but when Dominic told me he believed the stranger in the library was a female relation of the duke or duchess I had to come and see for myself.' She walked over to Amelia and hugged her. 'I am so glad to see you again Amelia, and to have the chance to thank you for all your help in getting me home.'

The duke and duchess turned to Amelia questioningly,

and she smiled as she responded. 'Well, who would have thought… So that is how young Seamus managed to join forces with a princess.' Amelia put her arm through Aliah's and turned to her brother. 'The young girl I sent off travelling with Seamus turns out to be Princess Aliahanna, not Ali as she first introduced herself.' Amelia chuckled. 'Although I can see much of the future, I did not see that coming. But once you know, it all fits together.'

'What are you doing here?' Seamus asked Amelia. 'I thought you were banished from Hand because of, well, you know…'

'Magic?' Amelia helped him, and he nodded.

'She was, and still is,' Duke Damon interrupted. 'That is why her presence here has been kept a secret, and why we will not openly discuss what your tutor Walter has been teaching you.

'By the way we have been treating your disappearance as a youthful indiscretion. Remind me later I will have to devise a punishment for you, maybe one that involves you moving to Port Marden for a while until we decide what to do for the long term.'

'So things have not changed then.' Seamus had to admit there was disappointment tinged with resignation at the news he would unlikely return to Hand. Seeing Amelia had led him to believe maybe there was a chance, however small, for him to return home.

'I did not say that Seamus.' The duke gestured to the table. 'Come, sit down, all of you. By now, Liam is fetching Lord Dominic. Best he hears this directly from us rather than his usual sources. Do not worry,' he said to Aliah. 'We will only use his true name in this room.

'We have found something, but it would be easiest to explain it to all of you at once. Our original plan had been to ask Walter for his help tonight, and talk to the rest of you tomorrow, but we may as well take advantage of the fact you are all here now.'

'Then why did you need Seamus?' Aliah promptly asked.

'For what we are to talk about tonight we did not, I just wanted to see my son.' The duke gestured for Aliah to be seated and, once she sat down, the others found seats around the table and waited for Dominic to return with Liam.

Liam only seemed to have been gone a moment when he and Dominic came through the library door. 'I did not have to go far,' Liam informed them. 'I found him lurking in the main entranceway.'

As Dominic and Liam took a spare seat each, Seamus had to admit that never in his wildest dreams had he thought to see this group of people sitting down together in his home.

Duke Damon stood and looked down the table at the people assembled in front of him. 'Before we start, I want assurances from all of you what we discuss now will stay in this room.' They mumbled their agreement, except Aliah and Dominic.

'I am not sure we are able to do that, sir,' Aliah said. 'Our first allegiance is to Aria and the king, and we might feel it our duty to pass on something we discuss here.'

TRIALS

Duke Damon nodded. 'Good. Forgive my little ploy, but I wanted to test your mettle. I need to know those of you I am not familiar with will speak honestly. How about we agree that before you pass on any information, you let me know what you intend to do first.'

Aliah and Dominic exchanged a glance before answering. 'That we can agree to do,' Aliah answered for them both.

'I have one more request. While we are in this room, we dispense with titles and politics. I believe we all need to work together to help save Aria from the forces that threaten our peace. I think that can best be achieved if we feel we can speak openly.'

'So you will join forces with my father?' Aliah was quick to ask.

That was too easy, Seamus thought to himself, and he was proven correct when his father responded to the princess' question.

'That is a matter for myself, and my council, and we will discuss that at a later time. Tonight, I want to talk about something a little less... um, tangible. Something I am not really comfortable with, something I am not sure I even fully understand. I believe it affects all of the people in this room, so maybe together we can work this out.'

Seamus had not seen his father so lost for words before. He normally assessed a situation and acted with full authority. Then Duke Damon did something else Seamus had never seen his father do. 'I will pass over to my wife. I believe she and Amelia have a much better understanding of what might be going on here.' And with that, he sat down.

Although his mother was no mere figurehead, sitting

as an advisor on his father's council, Seamus had never seen her lead a meeting. Pride welled up inside as his mother stood to address the room.

'All this started when Seamus ran away. Before he could walk, we were sure he was pulling things he wanted to himself, so we were aware he was likely the child of his generation to have a magical talent. Lately, his father and I had been sure his magical abilities were growing stronger, and we perhaps waited too long to talk to him about them,' Elise's sad gaze turned to Seamus. 'Largely, because we were not sure what to say to him. Magic is outlawed in Hand, and we knew it would be hard to change so many years of prejudice against magic users. We waited, because we did not want to lose our son.'

Seamus blushed and suddenly found the grain on the wooden table very interesting, attempting to hide his embarrassment. He could not believe his mother was speaking so openly of such private matters.

'Then we lost Seamus anyway. Damon thought Amelia was hiding something, so he spent time at the cottage to see if he could wheedle the truth out of her. Eventually, she admitted Seamus had been there, and where he was heading. Damon led a small group over the Ariel Mountains, following Seamus' trail. In Sunnydale, they found he had already left for Duncameron. In Duncameron, the trail went cold, he seemed to disappear into thin air. Damon had no option but to return home. In the meantime, I sent a letter to the king asking him to look out for Seamus, and to let him know we would like to hear from him.

'However, I could not sit at home and wait for my son to be returned. I needed to do more. I wanted to find a way to bring Seamus home, if not to take his place as Heir, then at least to be with our family. So I started looking through the histories and records of our people. I wanted to know more about why magic had been banished in the first place. That is the problem with not talking about a subject, we soon forget why we stopped talking about it in the first place.

'We all believe magic was outlawed completely when the Natari Princess Damon's forefather was forced to marry, turned out to be a witch. The people of Hand were so disgusted they sent her to live in Port Marden. It was then the practice of not using magic on Hand was formalised into law. Before that, magic users had been frowned upon. After that, anyone showing magical abilities suffered the fate of banishment or quietening.

'I found some ancient scrolls in the old library below that told a different story. These scrolls suggested our distrust of magic began long ago.

'The people of Hand migrated here from what is known in Aria as The Unknown Lands. This was already a part of our historic knowledge. The Ariel Mountain range has prevented the people of Aria from interacting and trading with their western neighbours, but on Hand, we occasionally trade with the tribes through their main settlement on the coast. Sometimes we receive visits from their dignitaries. Seamus used to love watching some of their soldiers train in the courtyard when he was younger. These people call themselves the Malorians, and they are distant kin to the people of Hand.'

Seamus interrupted his mother. 'So let me get this straight. The people of Hand migrated here and we were originally from Maloria?' He was getting a little lost in the story, and a little bored as well.

'Yes, son, but Amelia and I found out more than that. Sorry, this is beginning to sound like a history lesson, but it is important you fully understand the background before we get to the really interesting things Amelia and I found.

'Before moving to the coast, the Malorians were an inland tribe, part of the Talagra nation. From what we can make out, they broke away from the other tribes due to some conflict over using magic. At first I could not understand much of what the scrolls said, I have very little knowledge of the branches of magic so I asked Amelia to come and help me.'

Seamus shook his head. 'How could Amelia help? She has been living away from everyone on her farm for years, not even using her magic.'

His mother smiled at him. 'Your aunt may have given that impression to others, but I have always known she is part of a network of magic users who use their gifts to benefit others. She knows more about magic than anyone here, except maybe you, Walter.' Elise acknowledged the wizard sitting at the table. 'Amelia, will you tell them all what we found out?'

As the duchess sat, Amelia stood to take over. 'Not much more to go, and this is the interesting stuff. I will summarise. The Talagra were heavy magic users, but some tribes began to rely on magic too much, to the extent they began using battle magic to expand their tribal holdings. The Maloria tribe were known to have great seers and they foretold this would lead to the destruction of the Talagra Nation. When the other tribes would not listen to them, they walked away from the Tribal Council and Talagra, leaving their traditional lands and family ties behind.

'When they had established themselves near the coast they began setting up a new community. As they debated new laws, they found themselves divided over the issue of magic. Some thought banning the use of battle magic as had been done in other countries would be enough to ensure they did not suffer the same fate as Talagra. This way they could still use magic defensively to keep themselves safe should they need too. Magic had become so much a part of their culture they could not see how they could live without it.

'Others believed magic should be outlawed to ensure no one would be tempted to use it against other people. The latter group were in the minority, but many of them strongly supported the ideal of giving up magic and living by the work of their hands alone. They could not agree a way forward together, so the smaller group broke away and moved to an island off the coast. Naming their new home Hand, they enshrined their commitment to living without magic.'

'So based on our history,' Seamus interjected. 'A hatred of magic has been part of our culture for generations. You and I will never be able to come home.' Seamus' eyes sadly found Amelia's.

'Maybe not anytime soon.' Amelia placed a hand on his shoulder. 'But there is hope for the future, as you will soon see. We found that the marques we have always given our children to identify their families, and to celebrate different stages on their journey to adulthood, have a very different origin.'

'Really?' Seamus sat up straighter in his chair. Now they were reaching the really interesting ideas, they had his full focus. Beside him Aliah fidgeted in her chair, her attention wavering, and he worriedly hoped her new found need to be more statesmanlike would stop her from interrupting Amelia long enough for him to find out more of his history.

'Yes, originally the marque placed on each child showed their family bloodline or clan. The marque was not finished until a child had reached adulthood and had demonstrated a magical skill, and that skill had been tested and confirmed. It appears our family were strong in reading the future, and the marque that we get when we reach adulthood identifies us as being minor seers. We have found many of the other clans within Hand show other types of magic, such as healing, or growth.'

Seamus laughed. 'So you are suggesting there may actually be other magic users on Hand, we just do not know about them? Like the Paster family generally become healers, and the Agrit clan are known for their ability to grow the best produce? That might be magic at play?'

His father smiled at him. 'We suspect so, but we still need to do a little delving into family histories and have some discreet words with a few people before we can say for sure. Then we need to consider what this means for us as a people. Our ancestors abhorred magic, and many in the tribe of Hand still do. We need to decide if we want to change, and then if we do, what that change will mean in practice.'

'This is all very interesting, and I can see for your

family it could be life-changing. But I do not understand why you needed Dominic and me here for this. Or even Walter, for that matter.' Aliah shuffled in her chair as if getting ready to stand.

'Please bear with us a moment longer, Aliahanna,' the duke requested. 'We have only a little more of our tale to go.'

Aliah fidgeted some more, then sat still with her hands folded on the table in front of her. In contrast, Seamus continued to sit rigidly in his seat. Although this was his family history, he could not escape the feeling this meeting was very important to everyone here, but he could not place his finger on exactly why.

'I know it is late, but what Amelia and Elise discovered when they were looking through the old records surprised even me. While my men and I were in Duncameron, rumours circulated that the Wizard and Warrior have risen, and would champion Aria in the coming battle. We have the story here in our archives. I had always thought this prophecy came from one of my ancestors at the time of the Natari invasion. I understand there is a similar version in the histories of Aria. When I returned, I searched through the library to find a copy, wanting to refresh my memory.

'I found it in one of the books here and Amelia happened to glance over my shoulder as I read. She said she had come across a similar prophecy, but worded slightly differently.

"After the decimation and the fall,
 When the new power rises
 And the Wizard and Warrior meet,

Old and new blood will combine
With the two who are not what they seem
To save one and all."

'That is all very interesting, father, but I still do not see where we fit into all of this,' Seamus interrupted before Aliah could.

'No, you probably do not. And I am not really sure either. That is why you are all here. At this moment we have visitors in the castle from Maloria. They also have this prophecy. Their belief is the decimation refers to the fall of the Talagra Nation. They also believe the time the prophecy spoke of has arrived, and they will find the Wizard and the Warrior here on Hand. Representatives came a few days ago to await their arrival, and to take them back to Maloria for some sort of testing. For some reason they have convinced themselves the Wizard and the Warrior are amongst your group.' Duke Damon ignored the rest of the group and stared directly at Aliah, as if he were making sure she fully understood the importance of his words. 'I do not know whether all this is true or not. I mean ,we here on Hand do not deal with magic, let alone the High Magic that is prophecy. I fear we do not have long before they insist on meeting you all and discussing this with you directly.'

'And that would be bad?' Seamus asked.

'Maybe, maybe not. But we need to consider them seriously in light of the fact they have offered to provide assistance with the invasion should the Wizard and Warrior agree to return with them to their Sanctuary. Their warriors could be the tipping point in our favour, should we have to fight a force larger than ours.'

'I can see why this is important,' Aliah now spoke. 'Although I do not fully understand what is going on here either.'

'That is why before we meet with the Malorian Ambassador we should have completed our study of the ancient documents my wife and sister have found, to see if they shed any more light. In the interest of saving time, Walter, I was wondering if you would work with Amelia tonight and see if there is anything else you can find out from our documents? Or perhaps you can contribute something from your extensive knowledge?'

'It would be my pleasure,' Walter responded. 'Although I must admit there is a reason why Maloria is called the Unknown Lands in Aria—it is because we know so very little about them.'

Seamus wondered why Walter was almost glowing with pleasure? Was it because he loved working with ancient documents? Or did it have something to do with the way he had been looking at Amelia since they entered the library?

'That is not very comforting. Well, do the best you can. In the meantime, the rest of us should get some rest. We have a formal meeting with the council tomorrow morning, and I think we will need to have all our wits about us when we face them.' Duke Damon called the meeting to an end.

Aliah, Dominic, and Seamus rose and headed towards the door. Duke Damon hung back and halted Seamus as he went passed. 'I am truly sorry we could not welcome you home as I would have wished,' the duke said to Seamus, as he embraced him. 'But it is fortunate you arrive as the king's emissary as it means we will not have to answer any suspicious gossip at this point.'

'I understand father.' Seamus started to leave, then turned back at the door, 'I am truly sorry I did not trust you and mother enough to talk things through before I left.'

'We know you are, son, but everything happens for a reason. I truly believe that.' The duke turned to go back to Amelia and Walter, who were bringing armfuls of new scrolls to the main worktable. Seamus shut the door quietly behind him.

Liam and his mother had disappeared, but Dominic and Aliah were waiting for him the corridor. Seamus took the lead, heading back towards their state rooms.

'Well, that was all a bit unexpected,' Aliah stated the obvious. 'I wonder if all diplomatic missions are this exciting?'

'They most certainly are not.' Dominic started laughing. 'We have an errant son returning home, a battle on our doorstep, and a prophecy enacted. That is enough for a bard to write an epic song about.'

Once inside their suite, Seamus left the other two with a curt goodnight, and retired to his bedroom. Totally drained after the meeting with his family, and worried about the coming war, he flopped down on his bed, not even bothering to remove his clothes. To find out someone believed one of their group was part of a prophecy written hundreds of years ago, was all a bit too much to take in. Were he and Aliah destined to be plagued by that silly prophecy all their lives? It was not long ago a wizard named Gaius was using it in Duncameron to scare the locals out of helping them.

Mentally exhausted, he just wanted to sleep, hoping that when he woke in the morning he would find it had all been a bad dream.

5
AN AGREEMENT
IS REACHED

Aliah awoke the next morning to the scraping of a chair across the floor, and realised it was probably Seamus moving about in their shared living room. There had been a lot to take in last night and with Seamus heading straight to bed, they had not had a chance to discuss the implications. Arising quickly, she grabbed the dressing gown from the end of her bed and pulled it over her nightgown as she headed for the door.

Seamus was seated at the table to the left of the

fireplace, looking out the windows into the back courtyard. He jumped in his seat at her *good morning*. She joined him at the table as a polite knock on the door was followed by servants bringing in their breakfast.

'Your Highness. Milord.' The girl leading the procession placed a basket of hot rolls on the table. She was followed by another servant with hot tea, and another with butter and a range of honeys and preserves. 'Please accept our apologies for the meagre meal, but the duke would like to see you both as soon as possible,' the first serving girl primly informed them and then led her tail of servants out.

They had no sooner shut the door than it opened again, this time admitting Dominic. 'Ah, I see I am in time for second breakfast,' he said as he joined them at the table.

'Second breakfast?' Aliah raised an eyebrow.

'Yes, I have been up since the crack of dawn trying to find out anything else I can about the other guests.'

'And?' Aliah asked as she buttered a steaming roll.

'Not a thing!' Dominic admitted as he helped himself to the food.

Seamus had not stopped looking out the window for the entire conversation, and had made no effort to eat breakfast. Aliah was worried about him.

'Seamus. *Seamus?* Are you all right?' she asked, and Seamus' gaze slowly focused back into the room.

'What? Umm... Yes, I guess so.' His eyes glazed back over as he returned to whatever he had been thinking.

'Do you want to talk about what went on last night?' she asked him, trying to draw his attention back to the things they needed to discuss.

'There is not really much to talk about,' Seamus answered without looking at her.

'There is *a lot* to talk about,' Aliah corrected him. 'There is the history of non-magic and Hand. There is the prophecy. There is what we will do if the Malorian's want to take someone from our group away in return for their help with the war...'

Seamus looked thoughtful as he turned his gaze on her. 'Yes, there is all of that. But really, what can we do prior to going before the council? You heard the maid, my father wants us there as soon as possible. Besides, we do not know anything more than we did last night. So let us focus on the job at hand: getting my father to agree to working with the Arian Army to stop the invasion.' Seamus calmly reached for a roll.

Remembering her resolve to act more statesman-like, Aliah forced herself not to bang her cutlery on the table in frustration. Yes, their mission was important, but this was a whole new thing. They could bring additional forces into the upcoming battle, and it may just be the difference between winning and losing the war. It was important they agreed a strategy. She turned to Dominic.

'What do you think?' she asked.

Dominic stopped eating the roll he was biting into and looked at her. 'You're asking me for input?' He looked shocked, and she could not tell if he was laughing at her or being serious.

'Yes, I am asking for your opinion,' she said in as level a voice as she could manage when dealing with two frustrating friends.

'Oh, well I agree with Seamus, actually. Your father

wants us to secure Hand's support when Carsten invades. That is our main goal, but if we can get agreement to their navy and guard units working alongside ours under a united command, that would be a real bonus. We need to concentrate on that, rather than some pie-in-the-sky support based on an old prophecy. It would all be supposition anyway, and we cannot plan to cross a bridge when we do not even know where it is.' He calmly carried on eating.

Before she could vent her frustration, there was a knock at the door and Liam opened it from the other side to admit the duke and duchess. Seamus and Dominic rose, and the duke waved his hand. 'Carry on, we have little time for formalities. I have to be in the Council Chambers in a quarter candle-mark.' The duke and duchess were followed in by Amelia and Walter, with Daniel and Liam bringing up the rear.

'Why are you not dressed yet?' Daniel looked appalled at Aliah, sitting there in her nightclothes, hosting the duke and duchess of Hand. 'You have to be in the Council Chambers in a half-candle-mark, you cannot simply throw something on for that. And you have company...'

'Not to worry,' the duke said to the flustered guard. 'We are running a bit late ourselves. Walter and Amelia asked to talk to us all before going to the Council Chambers, so this is a bit rushed. It seems they found out something last night. Is it all right to speak in front of your guard?' the duke asked Aliah.

Aliah briefly considered paying Daniel back for his rude remark by asking him to leave the room, but thought better of it. 'Daniel is head of my personal guard,' Aliah told the duke. 'He knows most of my secrets as we grew up together. He is more than trustworthy, and our word last night extends to him.'

'What word?' Daniel asked quizzically, but the look Aliah sent him stopped his questions short. It also made her take a good look at her friend, and she had to say he did not look at his best this morning. *Too much time spent in a tavern, no doubt.* She had to stop herself from smiling. It was good to see her normally focused and duty-conscious friend taking some time out for himself.

'Fine. Amelia, you may begin.' The duke brought her attention back to the room.

Amelia stepped forward. 'We read a lot of the history of Talagra last night. In summary, there was a major war and the nation descended into a number of warrior groups, who then banded together into a single tribe, located not far from the Malorian boarder. The Malorians and Talagrans have been trading together for some time now. Since their countries have settled down, it seems neither used battle magic again,' Amelia summarised.

'Nothing about the war and the prophecy?' the duke asked impatiently.

'Not exactly.' It was Walter who answered. 'What we did find is the Malorian's had a great seer who is protector of the history and the prophecy. From what we read, we believe it is likely that the Malorians want to take the supposed Wizard and Warrior to be confirmed as such by their Seer.'

'Not exactly comforting,' the duke said. 'In truth, we really know no more than we did before.'

'Do we need to know any more?' Aliah asked. 'We face a great enemy. An enemy that outnumber us and are better prepared than us, if reports are to be believed. If we are being offered a fighting force from a warrior nation for the small cost of allowing two of our number to be taken to meet with a seer, then surely we must do that. At the least, we will lose two people, at the most, we might gain a Wizard and Warrior on top of another army. That could turn the tide of the upcoming battle.'

'Now is not the time.' It was the duke's turn to interrupt Aliah, and she frowned while furiously tucking her hair behind her ear. Before she could say anything, Seamus stood up.

'I agree with Aliah,' he said. 'We must explore every avenue we can to ensure we win this war. The consequences should we lose could be even more devastating than you can imagine. Some of the wizards on the Wizards Isles have been working with the people of Carsten. They plan to seize as much power as they can through this conflict and they must be stopped at all costs.'

Aliah was touched Seamus had come to her defence, but it also dawned on her the duke's face showed Seamus' revelation was not news to him.

'We have known this to be true for some time.' The duke confirmed her suspicions. 'But talking to the Malorians could be risky. We do not know who they are going to take. It could be the two of you.' The duke looked directly at Seamus and Aliah.

'I appreciate your concern.' Aliah stood between Seamus and his father. 'However, as the people in question are part of the Arian Embassy it will be up to us to make the decision whether or not those chosen will go to Maloria. We will of course take your wishes into account, but the final decision will be ours.'

With that, Aliah left the room to dress appropriately for the council meeting. As a maid helped her into her formal clothes, raised voices penetrated the door, but by the time she finished dressing and returned to the sitting room, Seamus was alone, staring into the fire and chewing his bottom lip.

'Aliah, do you think that was wise, cutting my father off like that? We will need him on side today if we are to get Hand to agree to the Arian and Hand armies working together.' Seamus rose from his chair to stand in front of her.

'It was a little risky,' she admitted to Seamus. In fact, she had been cursing herself about that very thing as she dressed. She worried that in asserting her control, she would alienate the duke, but she felt it important he understood that in spite of her age she was not his subordinate. 'I only spoke the truth. The duke cannot order any one of us not to go with the Malorians. But perhaps I could have considered my words a little more carefully.'

'What about me?' Seamus asked. 'What if I turn out to be the warrior they talked of. What master would decide whether I go or stay?'

'You are surely not the warrior.' Aliah burst out laughing. 'I have seen you fight. You can defend yourself, but no one would call you a warrior. Anyway, you are a part of my father's mission and remain so until the king releases you, therefore you are under my power. And I would let you make up your own mind.'

Seamus laughed with her. 'Well, I am definitely not

the wizard. I can make a strong flame, and sometimes I can make things move, but that is the extent of my skills. If we are relying on me to be the great wizard to save Aria from certain doom we may as well surrender.'

Aliah wrapped her arms around her stomach, she was now laughing so much it hurt. 'I am sure one day you will make a perfectly adequate wizard, Seamus, but I am thinking they mean Walter. He always was one of the strongest in magic on the Isle. And Daniel has the best military mind of his generation, I am sure if there is a warrior in our party it is him. Anyway, we should go. They will be waiting for us.'

Seamus shrugged his shoulders and held out his arm so he could formally escort Aliah to the Council Chambers.

Aliah was surprised at how little time it took to persuade The Council of Hand that their interests would be best served by fighting along side the Arian Army in the upcoming invasion. Apart from two aged lords who swore never to work with enemy forces—as they thought of Aria—the rest realised they could not hope to stand alone against a fleet the size of the one sailing from Carsten. After some too-ing and fro-ing, they all agreed Daniel and Captain Hanks would liaise with the army and navy of Hand, helping them integrate with the Arian forces when they arrived.

Many of the council members closely watched Seamus and his role in negotiating the agreement, and Aliah was sure they were all wondering how he had come to be in the position of King's Ambassador. One had even gone as far to suggest how smart the duke had been to send his son to Bannock to make first contact with the king. Lord Damon neither confirmed nor denied this comment, and Aliah had followed his lead. If it helped with their cause, for people to think the agreement to fight together had been initiated by the Duke, then Aliah was happy to oblige.

Back in her bedroom, Aliah asked the maid to help her change out of her state clothes. Aware Seamus was spending some much needed time with his brother and sister, she wondered what she would do with her afternoon. Her thoughts were cut short by a knock at the door. She sent the maid to answer it.

'It is one of your guards, Your Highness. He says there is a man waiting to see you in the other room, and he strongly suggests you meet with him.'

Frowning, Aliah began pulling back on the dress she was half out of. The maid finished doing up the buttons she had just undone, then checked to make sure Aliah looked presentable.

On entering the living room, Aliah acknowledged Dominic standing to attention inside the door in his formal guard pose, but immediately turned her focus to the elderly gentleman standing by the fireplace.

'Lord Ambury, of Maloria, Your Highness.' The man bowed low from the waist. 'I have come on a special mission from The Great Council of Maloria and beg an audience with you.'

'Lord Ambury, this is most unusual, all requests to speak with the king's representatives should come via his staff. And none of my advisors are here.' Aliah paused as if she were considering his request. 'But maybe I can spare you a moment of my time. Please, take a seat.' The elderly man waited until she was comfortably seated before taking the chair directly across from her.

'The Duke of Hand has already told me something of your mission here. He mentioned a prophecy, and that you thought the people from this prophecy were numbered amongst my company?' Aliah started.

'How very direct you are, Your Highness, but you are only partially correct.' Although the man in front of her had to be in his sixties, his brown eyes sparkled with appreciation at her taking control of the situation. 'Let me fully brief you. There is some debate in our council as to whether or not recent events mean this particular prophecy has been activated. This is a very important matter for our people, as we have been entrusted for generations with ensuring the Wizard and Warrior are equipped for their tasks when the world needs them. This is something we all take very seriously.

'So I have been sent here to retrieve the Wizard and Warrior of the prophecy to bring them to the council. This is so the members can make an informed decision about whether or not the prophecy has begun.'

'And if I release them to go to Maloria, you will ensure your army supports Aria in the upcoming fight against the invasion from Carsten?' Aliah asked.

'Again, partially correct. We have no army as such. Each tribal group has their own warriors, and they have pledged half of their men to come fight with Duke Damon's forces.'

Aliah appreciated he was reaffirming their alliance

was to the duke and they would follow his orders. This made her doubly pleased they had already agreed with the duke the forces under him would be working in concert with the Arian Army, as she would have hated to lose these additional troops if they had not been able to reach an agreement.

'So, if I release these people to accompany you, then what exactly will that mean for them?' Although Aliah would agree to almost anything to have the Malorian forces join them, she believed it part of her duty to make sure they knew exactly what Walter and Daniel were getting themselves into before she agreed they could go. Out of the corner of her eye, she caught Dominic nodding his head in approval, and a surprising warmth spread through her belly.

'The Wizard and Warrior will have to travel with all speed to the sacred meeting place of our council, The Sanctuary. The Prophecy Council will then judge whether they are in truth the ones foretold in the prophecy. More than that, I cannot tell you. The workings of the Prophecy Council and the High Seer are a mystery to me.' Lord Ambury folded his hands in his lap, waiting for her response.

'What if it turns out my people are not the Wizard and Warrior you believe them to be? How quickly will they be returned to us?'

'I cannot answer that, Your Highness. They will be entering our sacred grounds and it is up to the High Seer and the council to decide what will happen.'

'So just to clarify, you want me to send people with you, to go through some unknown test they may not return from...at all?' Aliah did not know if she could ask this of anyone, even for a fighting force of the size Lord Ambury was promising.

'It is perhaps even worse than you fear, Your Highness, for the people we want to take with us are yourself and the young Lord Seamus.'

If the aged Lord Ambury had pulled a knife and tried to kill her, she could not have been more shocked. In fact, she was speechless. Looking hopefully at Dominic to help her out, she was disappointed as he simply raised his eyebrows and shrugged his shoulders. This was something he had obviously not been expecting either.

As if he sensed her discomfort, Lord Ambury spoke. 'Surely you have heard the rumours about the two of you being the Wizard and Warrior. They have been circulating since the Wizard's Council sensed you were travelling with someone with magical powers.'

'There were rumours, but we were sure they did not apply to us, and that did not seem unreasonable given the circumstances. We thought it just a ploy to keep people wary of us, as I have only ever raised my sword in a fight once, on the boat on the way here. And to call Seamus a wizard is a little premature, he has only just started his training.'

'Still, many a truth has been said in jest. Our High Seer has been following your progress these last few moon turns. He feels sure you are the ones.' Lord Ambury seemed unmoved by Aliah's protestations. 'And you are the ones the seer wishes to have brought to him. That is why he sent me here to meet you.'

'I understand you arrived here a few days before us. Only a select few people were aware of our last minute plans. So how did you know we would come here?' Aliah voiced her surprise.

'I did mention we have a High Seer who has been tracking you, did I not?' Lord Ambury smiled serenely at her.

'I. Um, I...' Aliah was simply lost for words.

'I can see you were not expecting this, and you will need time to think. I should leave you and perhaps return before the dinner bell?' the lord asked, and Aliah nodded her head, allowing him to retire.

The Malorian lord rose and, after bowing, left the room. Aliah stared at the fire, stunned.

Me, the warrior? Really? Frowning, she ran the idea through her head. *It must be some mad sort of joke.*

'That certainly puts the cat amongst the pigeons.' Aliah was so lost in her own thoughts she actually jumped. She had not realised Dominic had come to take the seat beside her. 'I cannot think what your father would say if we let you traipse off into Maloria. He would not he happy at all, not even if you did raise a considerable fighting force by going.'

Aliah wanted to tell him it was not his, or anyone else's, place to "let" her do anything. But somehow she could not find the energy. She merely rose from the chair and went back to her room to finish changing. Stopping at the door, she turned. 'Can you please go find Seamus and Daniel. I think we really need to talk about this.'

'Not Walter?'

'No, not at the moment. I think he is of more use working with Amelia.' And with that, she closed the door behind her, not able to think through what had happened with Dominic in the room.

Seamus, the wizard? The seer must be out of his wits. The thought popped into her head as she sat on the edge of the bed. Still, even though she tried to dismiss the idea as foolish, she could not help thinking what if she really was the warrior?

Satin nuzzled his nose into Seamus' hand. Reluctant to leave the comfort of his old friend, the boy buried his face into the horse's neck, breathing in his familiar scent.

His ride with Jonas had been liberating because for a time he could forget about the coming war and the fact he would unlikely ever call Hand home again. Unfortunately, all good things come to an end, and soon Jonas had to return for his afternoon lessons.

Waving the groom away, Seamus took care of Satin himself. The rhythmic movement of the brush as he brought Satin's coat up to a brilliant shine had allowed him to forget the rest of the world for a few moments longer.

A prickling between his shoulder blades forced him to raise his head and look around the stable yard. Throughout the ride with his brother, he had had a similar sensation of being watched. However, every time he checked, there was no one around, just forest animals and birds. He did think he saw the same wolf a few times, but dismissed that thought as improbable. Now, as he glimpsed a familiar grey tail disappear around the side of the stable block, he wondered if he had not been right.

Acting on instinct, he trailed after the wolf. When he turned the corner into the yard in front of the kitchen, all he found was one of the maids sitting in the sun churning milk into butter, and a hooded figure heading towards the guard's barracks to the other side of the main palace building. The long grass was standing tall, no flat patches suggesting a wolf had snuck through to hide in the surrounding trees.

Wondering if the stress of the last few days had caused him to see things that were not there, he shook his head and decided it would not hurt to have a look behind the stables, just to make sure. Rounding the corner he found not a wolf, but Daniel, leaning against the wall looking decidedly unwell.

'Are you all right?' he asked worriedly, as Daniel really did look quite ill.

'No, not really,' the guard answered. 'Must have had some bad seafood to eat last night.'

'But the seafood course was left out of the dinner last night.' Seamus frowned, remembering his mother had commented on how cook had complained he did not have enough to serve all the guests, so no one was getting any.

'I was on duty last night, so I did not eat at the formal dinner. I had something later.' Daniel winced in pain.

Unusual, Seamus thought. *The kitchen does not have time to make two meals when we have a formal function, so staff generally eat a plainer version of what is served at the main table.* Then he shook his head. Of course Daniel did not have to eat at the palace, he could have gone out to a tavern for dinner.

'Come with me. Cook has a great remedy for upset stomachs.' Seamus took hold of the guard-man's arm, and led him towards the kitchen.

As Daniel swallowed the last of the tonic cook had prepared, Dominic joined them at the large wooden table that dominated the centre of the kitchen.

'Finally found you. I have been looking everywhere. Aliah wants to see you both. Something rather unusual has happened.'

'What?' Daniel asked, clearly not happy about having to move, although he did look a little less green.

'I will let her do the honours.' Dominic smirked, and they had no choice but to follow him back to the state rooms.

When Aliah returned to the living room, she found Seamus and Daniel sitting with Dominic, engrossed in the details of Seamus' ride through the forest and a stray wolf. Part of her wished she had gone out riding today, then she would have missed the meeting with Lord Ambury, and she would not feel as confused as she did now.

They stopped talking as she took her seat. Instead of beginning, she turned to Dominic and asked him to tell the others what had happened.

Dominic's eyebrows raised in surprise, but he quickly went through wha the Malorian Ambassador had said. Hearing the lord's words a second time did not give her any more clarity, and she was still trying to sort out her jumbled thoughts when Dominic finished.

On the one hand, as Heir to the Throne she could not simply run off on a whim, on the other, it was her responsibility to do what she could for Aria's safety. And what about Seamus? Theoretically she could order him to go, but she really could not ask him to place his life in danger for Aria, and that was if his father did not object to his leaving.

There was a lull in the conversation and her guard, her spy, and her friend all looked towards her as if waiting for her to answer a question. She did not have a clue what they had asked, so she just stared blankly back.

Should she and Seamus go? Looking at Seamus, she realised she did not want to discuss it with everyone and come to a group consensus. If they were to go, it would be Seamus and her making that choice.

'So will we journey to Maloria?' she asked him, wanting to hear him say out loud what he thought on the matter.

'Do we really have a choice?' he asked in response, and she could see from his eyes he was as unsure what to do as she was.

She closed her eyes, unable to bear his gaze, and said quietly, 'Yes we do, and we are the only ones who can decide.'

She opened her eyes in time to see Seamus take a deep breath, as if he had just made up his mind, and he looked her directly in the eye, nodding once. She knew then he was going. And if he was, then so was she.

Then reality struck. They actually had to see this through because they needed to find out for themselves if they were part of the prophecy. Even if there was only a slim chance they were, then they might be the sole hope of saving their homes, and the lives of the people they loved.

6
STEALING AWAY

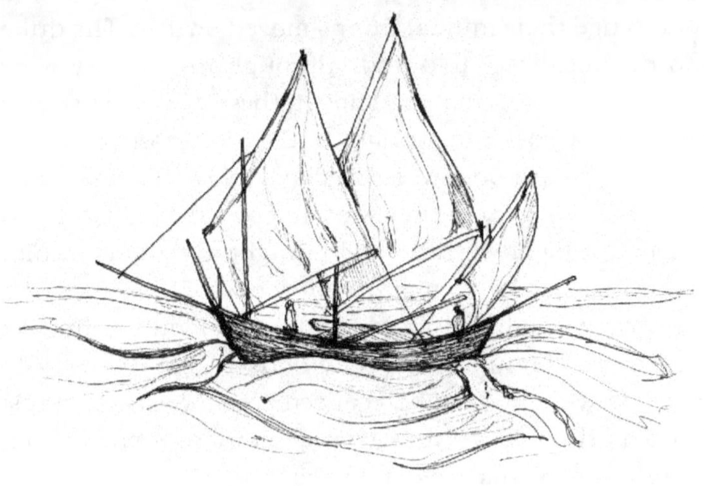

Once Aliah and Seamus had made the decision to go, they calmly sat back and watched the uproar it created. Daniel and Dominic talked over each other, each coming up with new reasons as to why they should not leave. It seemed they were being thoughtless, putting their lives on the line for something so vague, even if it did mean they gained a substantial armed force in return. But Seamus knew deep down in his soul this was what he and Aliah had to do. While the other two argued, he turned to Aliah.

'We have to stand strong, I am sure no one is going to be in favour of us going to Maloria.'

Aliah twirled the end of her plait. 'I know, but we have achieved what we came here to do. Hand has agreed to work together with Aria against the invasion. There is no real reason for us to stay.'

When Dominic and Daniel finally realised they would not change their minds, things moved swiftly. The duke and duchess were told and, although to say they were not happy was an understatement, they agreed to arrange transport across the straight to the Malorian coast.

Then Lord Ambury was called and told of their decision. After informing them they would need to travel light and in secrecy, he advised he had brought a guide with him who would be able to show them the way. It seemed The Sanctuary was hidden and would be difficult to find on their own. He suggested they chose a small party to accompany them. That had caused even more arguments. Sick and tired of everyone trying to talk over each other, Seamus closed his eyes and tried to block out the noise. If anything, the sound was louder, as if making up for the loss of one of his senses. He opened his eyes and sighed.

If Seamus had to go, Duke Damon insisted Liam went as his body guard. Daniel and Dominic disagreed over which of them should go as Aliah's protector. When Aliah maintained she could do well without either of them, as the warrior of prophecy did not need protection, they ignored her and carried on arguing. Finally Duke Damon stepped in and said Daniel needed to remain behind to liaise between the Hand and Arian forces, therefore

Dominic would go with them.

Then there was Walter, who argued he had to go because Seamus would need to continue his magic lessons, especially if he was supposed to be some sort of wizard saviour. His expertise and knowledge of magic would come in useful when dealing with the Malorians, he added.

Then Amelia took a stand. If Walter travelled with them, why should she not go? She had done most of the research and knew about Malorian customs. She wanted to meet the Great Seer and discuss her gift of foretelling with him.

Once the expanded travelling party was agreed, transport became the next issue. Duke Damon wanted them to take one of his navy ships. Concerned about them being attacked at sea again, he wanted them to have extra protection. Dominic assured him his sources in Port Marden confirmed the ships they met on the journey to Hand had been pirate vessels from further north. Bad weather had forced them south and they thought to chance their arm at some booty before returning to the Natarian coast.

Even after he agreed the attack on their ship had been pure coincidence, the duke still would not put aside his concerns and insisted on a full naval escort.

Dominic pointed out they could not really maintain their need for secrecy if they left on a naval ship. Someone was bound to see them. The duke had stood firm. It was only when Lord Ambury impressed on them the need to move quickly given the Carsten forces were close by, did the duke reluctantly offer the use of a fishing boat from a village close to the port to take them to the mainland.

The details were all agreed, and everyone went to get

themselves ready. On the duchess' suggestion, Aliah sought Martha to find out what travelling clothes they might have in storage. Seamus decided although he still had the travelling pack given to him by Amelia for his journey to Bannock, this time he would leave with his own possessions.

Opening the door from the state room he nearly fell over Robin. 'Erh, sorry Robin,' he mumbled, wondering what the man had been doing outside his door. As his father's chancellor, he should have been busy dealing with matters affecting the Duchy, not lurking in corridors.

Surprise flitted across the older man's face, before he composed himself and half-bowed to Seamus. 'I was coming to see if you or your party needed anything. I saw them all rushing out and thought maybe you might require assistance.'

Seamus raised his eyebrows, not sure if it was common practice for a chancellor to personally help state guests, then shrugged his shoulders. He had far more important things on his mind. 'Thank you, Robin, but we are all fine. I think the princess wants to talk to Martha about getting some of our woollen blankets shipped to Bannock, and the others, well I am sure they have things they are meant to be doing. I am going to my room to gather some personal items. I think I can manage that myself.'

The Chancellor gave the briefest of nods required when dealing with a superior, and Seamus smiled in return. He had always had a prickly relationship with the man his father trusted with so many of the tasks required to run a Duchy. For some reason he had taken a dislike to Seamus at an early age, and barely tolerated his presence.

TRIALS

Never rude, he was not quite polite either.

Turning, Robin led him down the corridor and left him at the stairs without another word. Seamus carried on through the door that led to the family quarters—a suite with a large sitting room and three bedrooms branching off it. His parents occupied the main bedroom across from the doorway he stood in, the room to the left of the door was his, and his brother had been moved into the room on the right on his tenth birthday. In the far corner there were stairs leading up to a nursery, school room, and bedrooms for a nanny and a tutor.

He had expected to feel at home walking into these rooms, but instead he felt more of a stranger than ever. Perhaps because he did not believe he would never come back here to live, or perhaps because he had out-grown the need for the security blanket the palace family rooms represented. After all, he was nearly at the age when he could have been moved to his own suite as the Heir anyway.

Sighing, he opened his bedroom door, surprised to see the contents almost as he had left them. A little tidier perhaps, but everything still pretty much in the same place. He ran his fingers over some of his prized possessions; his books, his bow, his set of throwing knives. *Mmm, those are definitely coming,* he thought as he picked them up.

Heading over to his wardrobe, he found his hunting pack at the bottom where he had left it, picked up a favourite pair of sturdy boots, then chose three changes of clothes. Finally, he took his warm, woollen hunting jacket out. Shutting the wardrobe door, he took one last look around before leaving his childhood room.

Daniel carried the clothes, boots, and travel pack Martha had found for Aliah between two blankets to hide them from prying eyes. They were taking the servant's stairs back up to their rooms to ensure they did not come across anyone who might ask questions about what they were doing. Aliah glanced over her shoulder at her childhood friend, who was not doing a very good job of hiding his annoyance at being left behind.

'Daniel,' she started. 'I know you are upset, but I think you are looking at this the wrong way. What guard of your age gets the opportunity to play such a senior role in a war? This is a great opportunity for you.'

'If you disregard the fact I will be failing at my duty to protect you and Seamus, then I guess you could see it that way,' Daniel answered, his words sharp and surly.

'You did what you were asked to do.' Aliah was exasperated. 'You got Seamus and me here safely so we could agree terms with the Council of Hand. Now you are going to work with the people of Hand to thwart the invasion, and we are all starting on a new journey. So your role is different. But better different. Come on,' she tried to jolly him out of his bad mood. 'This is what you have been studying for all your life, to lead an army into battle.'

Daniel did not respond, and so intently was she watching his reactions that she did not hear the duke's chancellor come down the servant's stairs behind her.

'Can I help you with anything?' he asked, and Aliah

nearly jumped out of her skin.

'Um, ah...' Aliah started.

Dominic had appeared behind Daniel. 'It is fine, thank you, Robin. Sorry, Aliah, Martha delayed me with some story or other about woollen blankets. Daniel, I can take some of that from you if it is too much for you to carry upstairs.' His voice as he spoke was polite, but Aliah could see a hardness in his eyes as he almost glared at the chancellor.

Moving to the side, Aliah and Daniel allowed Robin to sweep past them down the stairs.

'What was that about?' Aliah whispered to Dominic.

'There is just something... I cannot place my finger on it, but something about him makes me uneasy. Come on, we have not got much time if we are to be ready for this evening.'

Dominic passed them both, and Daniel followed behind. Aliah paused, frowning at Daniel as he passed. *Speaking of things being not quite right, something is bothering him, and I aim to find out what it is...* she thought as she began to climb after them.

Seamus closed his travelling pack and made sure his bedroll was securely attached to the side. Even with all the arguing and planning, they had managed to get some sleep before their pre-dawn departure time to catch the morning tide. His parents had come and gone, saying one last farewell before the group departed. They were to hold to the story that Seamus and Aliah had been taken ill with a strange sickness and the doctor had quarantined most of their group to prevent spreading the illness. Only Martha would be admitted to their rooms to bring food and medicines. They hoped that would give them a six-day before anyone raised serious questions about their whereabouts.

More relaxed about leaving this time, perhaps because he had an opportunity to say goodbye to everyone, but also because he left for a specific purpose, Seamus whistled a tune under his breath. This new journey allowed him to put thoughts of the future from his mind for a while. However, there was still a sadness surrounding his leaving.

The previous night Jonas had hugged him gruffly. Seamus told him to keep up his studies and he would make a great dukc someday. His brother merely nodded in response, saying Seamus would be proud of him when he returned. His younger sister had given him a chain with a round metal disc showing the sign of The Lady, shyly saying if he wore it, The Lady would protect him.

He touched under the neck of his linen shirt to feel the round metal with the three lines of waves on it; one each for birth, life, and death. He let it fall back in place. His mother had simply hugged him tightly. His father had told him how proud they were of him as he held him close. Seamus had fought to hold back his tears.

Still a little reluctant to say goodbye to his home again, he stared out the window into the courtyard below. Only the outlines of buildings were visible as it would be a candle-mark or so before the sun rose, but he filled in each and every window and doorway from memory.

Although he knew duty called him, it would be so easy to stay here where he felt comfortable, and try to rebuild his life.

'It is time to go.' Standing in the doorway, Aliah was dressed similarly to him in a loose linen shirt, fitting trousers, and a woollen coat, all in various shades of green. They both wore travelling boots with thick soles that laced up well over their ankles to support the long walk they anticipated.

'Yes it is,' he said slowly, turning back to face the room, holding out the small package he held in his hand.

'I have something for you.' He handed her the gift. She opened it to find it contained a necklace with a charm of the ancient sign for good luck, an open hand.

'Oh, Seamus, it is lovely. Is it the necklace you bought in the market in Bannock?'

'It is. It brought good luck to us then, and I hope it will bring luck to you now. I have a feeling we will need all the good fortune we can find on this journey.

'I have to say I am not happy at having to leave home again so soon. Lately I feel like a great wind is pushing me down a path I am not sure I want to be travelling on. Maybe that is what being part of a prophecy feels like, but I cannot in any way believe I am the wizard they talk about. Every time I think I might actually be the wizard, I look around for someone to jump out and say *tricked you*. Funny thing is, I would feel more relieved that it is not me, rather than embarrassed someone had caught me thinking I might be.'

Aliah put on the necklace and adjusted it under her shirt as she answered him. 'I know what you mean. I keep saying to myself, if I am the warrior who is to save us all in battle, then the Goddess help Aria.'

'Remind me again why we are doing this then?' he asked.

'Because we need to know the truth, otherwise we will always have this hanging over us.' Aliah flung her plait over her shoulder as she picked up her travel pack. 'And because the Malorians will send warriors to help fight the Carstenites.'

'Well, if you put it that way, I guess we had best be off and see if we are destined to save the world.' Seamus sighed wearily as he picked up his own pack and slung it over his shoulder. He knew better than to offer to carry Aliah's. At best, that would earn him a cold stare from those icy blue eyes, at worst, a tongue lashing.

Shrugging her pack on more securely, Aliah followed him out the door. 'I have not even thought as far as saving anything. I am getting through this by taking it one step at a time. At the moment I am concentrating on just getting to meet this seer. Everything else can wait until after that.'

There was some comfort in knowing Aliah had her doubts as well. With her uncertainty mirroring his, he felt less alone on this unusual journey.

As they entered the hallway, they were joined by Dominic who had retrieved his own travel clothes and pack from the ship. Instinctively the older boy reached for Aliah's pack to carry it for her, and Seamus had to laugh at the look of outrage she threw.

'I am quite capable of carrying my own things, thank you,' she forced the words out through gritted teeth. Sticking her nose in the air, she stalked off down the corridor, long blonde plait swinging behind her as if to emphasise her words.

Seamus laughed again at Dominic's perplexed face. 'She travelled the length of Aria pulling her own weight. I can imagine she finds it insulting you think she needs help now,' Seamus explained to his travelling companion.

'Everything I do is wrong. I will never understand her.' Dominic sighed.

'Why do you need to?' Seamus asked as they followed the princess downstairs.

'I do not need to understand her,' said Dominic somewhat defensively, in a way that made Seamus realise for some reason it was very important to Dominic that he did. Smirking, he had to stop himself from chanting *Dominic likes Aliah* in the most childish of ways. He hoped the spy could win over the princess, but he would have to get her to see past the work he did for her father first. Well, it would make for an interesting journey.

They quickly followed Aliah through the courtyard to the stables, where saddled horses were waiting for them. Mounting quickly in the pre-dawn darkness, they rode through the city and out towards a fishing village not far from Port Hand.

On arriving at the village, they found Liam, Walter, and Amelia waiting for them. Standing alongside them was a smaller cloaked figure who barely came up to Liam's shoulder. As they rode closer, Seamus realised Liam was arguing strenuously with Walter.

'This pack weighs a ton? What have you filled it with? Books?'

'Well, yes, of course books.' Walter stared benignly back at the irate squire, who groaned in frustration.

'What part of "we are to be travelling light and fast on foot" did you not understand?' Liam lectured. 'No one else will be carrying these for you when they get too heavy, you know.'

'I would not expect them to,' Walter calmly informed him. 'These volumes have information we may need and I did not have time to read them before we left, so I brought them along with me. Anyway, I have a spell that will ensure they weigh little more than a feather, so I do not see the problem.' Walter smiled and Liam groaned again, unsure what to make of the first wizard he had ever met.

Amelia put a comforting hand on Liam's arm. 'It will be all right, you'll see.'

Before Liam could say anything else, there was a loud crash, and they all turned to see the small figure who had been standing behind the squire, wrestling someone to the ground, a knife held to the intruder's throat. In the process, the small person's hood slipped back, and Seamus was surprised to see a girl of about his own age with short, spiky brown hair and large dark eyes too big for her elfin face. At the moment, those eyes were focused on the person below her and, before Seamus could stop himself, laughter bubbled up inside and forced its way out.

'Fine bodyguard you turn out to be.' When he managed to control himself he spoke to a wide-eyed Daniel, who was clearly surprised to find himself with a knife at his throat. 'Whoever you are, you can let him up. He is one of us.'

TRIALS

There was more laughter all around as Daniel scrambled to his feet and dusted himself off. He turned to his captor. 'Captain Daniel of the Arian Guard at your service.' He bowed to the girl who moments ago had him pinned to the ground.

'You are lucky to be alive,' the girl responded tartly.

'What were you doing, Daniel?' Aliah ignored the girl's rude response and glared at her friend.

'Joining you on your trip,' Daniel answered, as he picked his travel pack up off the ground.

'That was not your assigned duty.' Aliah used her princess voice as she berated the royal guard.

Daniel lifted his chin. 'I was ordered by your father to see to your safety and, as my king, his order trumps yours. I have left military liaison in the capable hands of Captain Hanks who, incidentally, will be of more use than me over-seeing Hand's contributions to the battle ahead, as the initial attacks will be at sea. Besides, I cannot let you all go off on a great adventure without me. Life is too short to be left behind.' He stood there waiting to see what Aliah would do, a confident grin on his face, and determination in his eyes.

Seamus knew Aliah could never stay angry at her childhood friend for long, especially when he happened to be right. The king's order would always take priority over anything Aliah said.

'All right,' Aliah conceded, dismounting. Shrugging her shoulders as if it made no difference to her whether Daniel came or not. She told him, 'You may join us if you wish.' Stalking over to the fishing boat moored nearby, her posture showed how closely she was holding in her anger.

The others followed in her wake and, when they were all assembled ready to board, Liam introduced them to their guide.

'This is Emer. She has been sent by the seer who has called us to Maloria, and has been tasked with taking us to meet the Prophecy Council. Once we reach land, she will guide us to Sanctuary, which, by all accounts is quite well hidden.'

'Are we destined to be led by women on this journey?' Daniel cried dramatically, and Seamus was surprised to see their guide's eyes crinkle with laughter, which she quickly smothered.

'Maybe when you can beat a woman in a fight, you will get a chance to lead,' Emer told him, her face a study of seriousness. 'Come now, we must be away or we will miss the tide,' she commanded, before Daniel could think of a suitable comeback.

They boarded the small vessel and took a position near the bow, where a canvas shelter had been erected for them. The trip would take them well into the morning, so they settled out of the crew's way, and tried to get some sleep.

The crossing was uneventful and the gentle rocking had them all asleep in minutes. Before drifting off, Seamus mused this time yesterday morning he had been in full court attire attending a meeting of his father's council. Now he was more humbly dressed, travelling on a fishing boat on another adventure. How quickly things could change. How odd his life had become.

Just as dawn was breaking, Seamus awoke to shouting. The captain had caught sight of a ship heading directly towards them at full speed.

'I cannot make out the insignia,' he informed them. 'And in these times, I cannot take the risk it is friendly. I will not be able to set you down on the beach at Exodus Cove as planned. The coast is a short swim away. If you slip over the side, I can head back out to sea and lead them away from you.'

'That would be perfect if we could all swim,' Aliah muttered, and the rest of her group gasped in astonishment.

'What? Am I the only one?' Aliah frowned, annoyed to have her short-coming made so obvious.

'Daniel, you take Aliah's pack. I will make sure the princess gets to shore.' Dominic took charge. 'Just for this once, princess, could you please do exactly as I ask, when I ask, because if you do not, both our lives could be in danger.'

Seamus could see Aliah holding in her frustration. She did not like to be vulnerable at the best of times, but she was in no position to argue. Walter offered to spell their packs so they could use them as floats. This done, with an additional spell to keep the contents dry, they all slipped overboard and kicked off for shore. Seamus looked behind to see Aliah lying on her back, Dominic had her chin cupped in his hand and was hauling her side-stroke towards the beach.

The captain kept the fishing boat between the swimmers and the approaching ship to shield them for as long as it was safe for him to do so. Occasionally Seamus glanced back over his shoulder to see how much time they had before the other ship realised there were swimmers in the water. Each time he looked, he saw Dominic and Aliah falling further behind the others, and he worried that when the boat moved, the two of them would be vulnerable to attack.

When he was three-quarters of the way to the beach, the captain was finally forced to move the fishing boat to avoid an imminent collision. A yell from the deck of the other ship warned him the swimmers had been seen. Instead of following the fishing vessel as a pirate ship would have done, the ship lowered anchor and the crew began readying a row boat for launch.

'Faster,' he yelled to the others between breaths. 'They are coming for us.'

They sped up and, with lungs bursting, finally made it to the expanse of sandy beach they had been aiming for. Seamus waited impatiently for Dominic to bring Aliah to shore. When they reached the beach, Aliah primly thanked Dominic for his help before releasing his grasp and moving to pick up her pack.

'This way. There is no time to lose,' Emer called. 'We have no time to dry off. We have to get into the forest before they land.' She turned and started jogging towards the cliff face.

Seamus looked up at the steep cliff looming over them. *How are we going to climb that?* he wondered as he shouldered his pack and headed after her.

Running on the sand was hard going even for someone as young and fit as he was. Seamus worried about Amelia and Walter, and turned to help them.

'Do not worry,' Walter shooed him onwards. 'I have a few tricks to make things easier for us that will not tire me as they use little magical energy.'

At the base of the cliff, Emer stopped and waited for everyone to catch up.

'Walter, can you create illusions?' she asked. The wizard nodded, too breathless to answer.

'It will only seem real from a distance, the closer they get the easier they will be able to see through it.' Walter finally managed to get his words out.

'It is the same with our mages,' Emer said. 'Can you create an image of us climbing up a pathway?' She waited until Walter nodded before continuing. 'Good, I know a secret passage to the top. If we can avoid them finding it, they will be forced to take the longer path at the end of the cove. It will buy us quite a bit of time.'

'If you can create an illusion, why did you not do that to hide us from the ship? Then we could have been set ashore as planned.' Aliah angrily rounded on Walter.

'Well, um, no one asked, and I did not think of it. Now you mention it, that would have been a perfect situation for an illusion spell. You have to understand I am foremost a scholar. I have rarely had to use magic in stressful situations. I normally have more notice to think through potential danger and which spells might be useful, like when we escaped through the sewers in Duncameron,' the wizard admitted, and he turned towards the rock face, ready to cast his spell. His answer seemed to quench the flames of Aliah's anger.

Intrigued, Seamus watched intently as Walter wove his spell, wondering if he would ever be able to do magic as easily as his teacher. At the end of his spell, Walter moved his hands as if he were pushing something up the cliff.

'I cannot see anything.' Seamus said.

'We are too close to the spell,' Emer told him. 'Come on now.'

She walked down the beach about ten paces, and they all followed. Emer seemed to disappear into a rock before their very eyes. As he drew closer, Seamus saw there was a gap between two rocks that was just wide enough for a person to slip between. Once they were inside, Emer led them to the top of the cliff via a subterranean tunnel. They were not in complete darkness as enough light diffused from the opening at the top for them to see, but there were a few stumbles from tired feet as they climbed.

At the top, Emer walked to the edge and looked over. Seamus joined her, seeing about twenty men searching the bottom of the cliff. Fooled by the illusion, they were looking for the path that would supposedly take them to the top. Dominic joined the two of them, staring out to sea.

'That is an Arian ship,' he said almost as if to himself.

'What do you mean?' Seamus frowned. 'Are those not pirates? We have been chased by one of our own ships?'

'Yes, I mean exactly that. You would find a merchant ship like that in any Arian harbour.'

'Which means someone is specifically chasing us?' Emer asked, frowning.

At a shout, the men below looked up as one. Seeing their quarry looking down at them, bows raised and the group at the edge of the cliff were forced to move back to avoid the arrows sent their way.

'We really must not delay, if that is the case. They will not likely give up pursuit while we are easy to find,' Emer warned them. 'Look, they have found the path at the end of the cove. It will not take them long to climb up here, and I would like to be well into the woods when they arrive so they will not know exactly which path we are travelling.'

Weary, wet, and cold from their swim, they picked up their belongings and trudged after Emer, over the scrubby grass towards the woods they could make out in the distance.

<h1 style="text-align:center">7</h1>

FULL MOON

Before following her companions, Aliah turned and could just make out the Isle of Hand on the horizon. If she turned the other way, she could see a strip of coastal scrub that changed to woodland some way in the distance. After her humiliating swimming experience, she wished herself back in the comfort of the palace on Hand. Sighing, she trudged towards the relative safety of the forest.

As they entered the shade of the woodland, Emer

asked, 'I know we are all tired, but we have no time to stop for refreshments as I have just seen the first of our pursuers come over the top of the cliff. We must hurry.' She led them off on a fast walk through the woods, on what could not even be described as an animal trail.

Dominic told them all to use some of their travel rations to keep their energy up as they walked, and he passed some to their guide. They kept up a brisk pace until well into the afternoon. A couple of times Emer had them pause, and she asked Walter to use magic to sense if there were pursuers close by. Both times he confirmed they were definitely near, but he could not tell exactly where. When they camped for the night, Emer instructed only cold food and no fire. Tired, cold, and hungry, they huddled together for warmth.

While they ate, Emer said she was going to scout around to see if she could find out exactly which course their pursuers were taking. Daniel and Seamus both offered to go with her, but she said she knew these woods like the back of her hand and she would be better off alone.

Aliah was tired to the bone, but she could not relax. Every noise had her jumping, wondering if the people pursuing had finally found them. Finally, her eyelids began to flutter closed, but they opened wide to when she spied a grey wolf looking through the bushes at them. Shaking herself awake, she went to reach out for Daniel, but before she could wake him the wolf disappeared. Her hand dropped and she gazed around the group to see if anyone else saw the intruder.

Dominic was on sentry duty, but his back was to her and he did not seem alarmed. Just as Aliah went to speak out, Emer emerged from the darkness. She spoke briefly to Dominic, then sat beside him. If they were not worried, then she may as well go back to sleep.

Stretching the kinks out of her body the next morning reminded her of why she did not like travelling rough. Before she could voice her complaints Emer beckoned them all over.

'We need to be quiet today. There is a group of about five military looking men about half a candle-mark to our left. As best I could tell, they have been tracking in the same direction as us, sometimes ranging out to see if they can find us. Fortunately if we veer to the right, we will distance ourselves from them, and will still be able to reach our destination. It will take a little longer so we will have to make better time than we did yesterday. I suggest we start off at a slow jog.'

Aliah bit back a groan. She was already tired and sore, but she was young and relatively fit. She glanced towards Walter and Amelia to see how they were taking the news and was surprised they did not look worried at all.

They broke camp quickly and followed after Emer, who had asked Walter to use his magic to cover their path through the forest. Aliah had seen Walter do this after their escape from Duncameron, and so was not surprised to see him drop to the back of the group where he could erase any sign they had been travelling through the trees.

Emer spoke little during their journey, except to give directions. When they took a break, she would politely answer direct questions about the land around them, the trail they were following, or about Maloria. She would tell them nothing about the Prophecy Council, or of what might happen when they reached their destination. They did find out that at this pace, it would take them almost two days to reach the Sanctuary, and even then she suggested they would be cutting it close.

'Close to what?' Aliah asked, but Emer acted as if she had not spoken.

All of their party were quite fit, but they dropped exhausted when Emer allowed them to rest that evening well after the sun had gone down. After checking the general area, she asked Walter if he could sense those following them. He told her they were now at the very edge of his range, so she allowed them to build a small fire and cook some rabbits Seamus and Liam caught while walking, so long as they kept the smoke from rising too high. After a warm dinner, they curled up to sleep.

Daniel took the first watch and, not long after he took his position by the fire, Emer went and spoke to him before slipping into the forest; no doubt to check they were safe.

Aliah could not settle that night again, fitfully dozing off and on. Not sure whether she was dreaming or not, a grey wolf wandered in and out of her vision. Finally she drifted off, and next thing she knew Emer was shaking her shoulder, telling her she needed to be up and on the move when the sun rose.

Their pace was brisk, but a little slower that day. As they walked, Walter took the time to train Seamus, explaining to him the steps he went through when erasing their path. He had Seamus practice by moving branches and debris on the forest floor. Aliah could see the concentration it took for her friend to move a branch out of someone's way and hold it there. When the strain got too much, the magic disappeared. At one stage, the branch swung back and hit Liam squarely in the face. He swore Seamus did it on purpose, in a good natured way that showed he was trying to make light of the whole thing.

Seamus dropped to the back behind the group, clearly upset Liam would suggest he had done such a thing on purpose. Apparently lessons were over for the day. It seemed Seamus did not have much of a sense of humour when it came to his magic.

While they were walking, Walter occasionally left Amelia's side and dropped a little behind to try and sense how close the people following them were. On one of these occasions, Daniel took his place beside Amelia. They were deep in conversation for a short while. It appeared to be something serious, but when Daniel rejoined her, he would not tell her anything. Frowning, Aliah decided to ask Amelia when she had a chance.

All was quiet until part-way through the afternoon when they were walking through a clearing in the woods and were suddenly surrounded by a group of men armed with spears and dressed in the colours of the forest. They had blended in so well, no one had known they were there until they suddenly appeared.

Stomach clenched in fear, Aliah joined her friends in a defensive circle, adrenaline pumping through her as she prepared to fight the pursuers who had finally caught them up. Looking around, she noticed Emer had remained where she stopped, clearly amused.

'Stand down,' she said in her lilting accent. 'They are our guides, not our enemies.'

'If they are friendly why did they appear like that? Why not announce their presence in a non-threatening way?' From the looks on her friends' faces, Aliah surmised she was not the only one annoyed by the way their guides had behaved.

Emer turned to a man who stood back a little from the main circle of warriors. 'I thought we planned for you to meet us at the boundary Eon. If you had stuck to the plan you would not have frightened our guests and nearly caused bloodshed.'

The elder man stepped forward. If Aliah had to describe him, she would have said he reminded her of a rat who had sucked a lemon. He was thin and balding, with wispy grey hair and grey eyes, and he had the air of a man who had been constantly disappointed in life.

'You are late. We came to see what happened to you,' he said in a petulant voice, indicating he did not like being challenged by Emer.

'We were followed so we could not take the main path. We have been avoiding pursuit for the last two days, which has put everyone on edge,' Emer responded. 'We still would have made it to the meeting place in good time. You had no need to change the plan.'

'There is not as much time as you think. The full moon is tomorrow and we must have time to vet and prepare the initiates. Your delay means we must rush.' Eon dismissed Emer's words and motioned for them all to leave.

Before she left, Emer turned to two of the men accompanying Eon. 'There are strangers in our forests. Make sure they do not find our home,' she ordered them, before following after Eon.

Aliah moved so she could join Amelia on this stretch of the journey, fully intending to ask her about Daniel. Forced into a jog to keep up with their guides, she did not get a chance, however. Finding it difficult to maintain the pace, she worried about Amelia.

When asked how she was doing, Amelia responded, 'I know how to feed my body additional energy to ease the aches and pains. Besides, I do not think we will be travelling much longer. Someone in the group we met has the ability to fold the trail.'

'Fold the trail?' Aliah was confused.

'Yes,' Amelia responded. 'It is a specific form of earth magic that shortens the distance you are travelling. The path we follow is flat, but if I use my magic I can see in between each step I take, the ground is raised a little, so the distance each step covers is almost doubled. They must be strong in magic to be able to fold the trail for this many people for this length of time.'

No matter how hard Aliah concentrated, she could not see the ground folding under her feet. She could tell landmarks they passed became distant more quickly than their slow jog would suggest, but if she tried too hard to see how it was done, she became dizzy.

Finally their guides halted and while they were all taking some refreshments, Aliah remembered she meant to talk to Amelia about Daniel.

'Amelia, what were you and Daniel talking about earlier?' she asked discreetly.

Amelia fixed her with a hard stare, then frowned.

'That is something for Daniel to tell, or not, as he chooses.' The older woman abruptly left to refill her water cup, leaving Aliah feeling she had just been told off.

When rest time was over, Emer approached them with some strips of cloth. 'From here, we need you to be blind-folded,' Emer explained. 'None but the initiated may see the pathway into the Sanctuary.'

When no one moved she said, 'Do not fear. You are under the protection of the Great Seer. No harm will come to you. These men will lead you and protect you with their lives.' She signalled to the men, and each of them stood in front of one of the group of Arians, ready with blindfolds.

Although she did not entirely trust these men, especially the one called Eon, and she was concerned about what needed to happen with the full moon, Aliah nodded her head and allowed them all to have their eyes covered.

It was truly disorienting not being able to see where she was going. Her guide did a good job of stopping her from stumbling while allowing them to keep their fast pace. After what seemed like an age, but was probably less than a candle-mark, the group stopped and were told they could take off their blindfolds.

Aliah stood at the edge of the forest, in a clearing in front of a rock face. Carved into the cliff were magnificent dwellings, some of which had openings two or more stories high. The rock face curved to either side of them, meeting with the edges of the forest. The number of entrances to dwellings made her head spin. The carvings around the entrances were even more astonishing, and she realised the work could only have been carried out by magic. The Sanctuary was an amazing city carved into a mountain.

Standing open-mouthed, Aliah slowly pulled her gaze from the marvel in front of her. When she did, she was relieved to find the rest of her group were in much the same state of awe. It seemed none of them had ever seen anything like this rock city before either. It was a magnificent sight in the light of the setting sun.

Directly in front of them stood a large opening with ornate pillars on either side. A group of men dressed in the same manner as the men who had led them through the forest were exiting from the opening, their leader an elderly man leaning on a staff. He had the most piercing blue eyes Aliah had ever seen—or perhaps they only appeared that way because his beard and shoulder length hair were snow white. He seemed to be looking right at her except, she thought for a moment, he could not be as he was walking like someone who had lost their sight. When he was right in front of them, he stopped and inclined his head to one side. As he did, she was able to confirm the man was in fact blind.

'Welcome to the Sanctuary.' He smiled with a warmth that softened his eyes. 'I am Caraig, sometimes called the Great Seer, but you may call me Caraig. I know who you all are, but for the sake of formalities, would you like to introduce your group?'

Aliah called each of them forward one by one, and Caraig formally welcomed them all.

'You must be tired after your journey. Emer will take you to the guest quarters so you may refresh yourselves, and I will visit with you soon.'

Aliah looked at the others, and they all seemed as bewildered as her. They had rushed here because of some supposed deadline and now were being sent to rest. It was all very odd.

'This way.' Emer turned.

They were so used to following their guide's directions they immediately fell in behind her, walking towards an opening on the left side of the cliff. They entered a doorway into what initially appeared to be a natural cave with a high roof, except the roof was smooth. There were no marks of the rock being formed naturally, or even chiseled out. Clearly a communal area with doors leading off it, the room contained tables and chairs arranged around a blazing fire, which made the room glow with a welcoming light.

'Each guest room will sleep three people, and in there is an ablution pool.' Emer pointed to the door on the far right. 'Someone is bringing refreshments, and Caraig will be here soon.' Her mission completed, she slipped out the door without another word.

'I get the feeling she does not like us much,' Amelia said.

Secretly thinking Emer's face was usually unreadable so it was actually hard to tell what she was thinking, Aliah said nothing, instead she diverted Amelia by asking, 'Shall we take the room on the end? If we hurry, we should have time for a quick clean before Caraig arrives.'

She could not wait to get out of her salt-laden clothes and wash her hair. At least then she might feel up to dealing with this rather strange place and its even stranger people.

Not waiting to see what arrangements the boys made, they opened the door to their room. There were brightly woven woollen rugs on the floor and walls, which helped soften the fact they were essentially in a cave. Gas lamps on a table between the beds had been lit to provide a warm light.

Aliah sank onto one of the beds, surprised to find it was lovely and soft. Covered in a warm, snug, brightly woven woollen blanket, it was almost irresistible. Fighting the temptation to curl up and sleep, she decided after two days in the same clothes and a dip in salt water, the need to be clean outweighed the need for sleep.

After unpacking a change of clothes, she and Amelia went next door to see what the bathing arrangements were like. They were pleasantly surprised to find a deep natural pool in the room beside them. Aliah put a hand in the water, sighing as its warmth spread up her arm. There were toiletries and towels in a basket by the door. She and Amelia wasted no time in shedding their clothes and submerging themselves in the water. Both of them could have stayed there all evening, soaking away their aches and pains, but they were aware others needed the room. Quickly they dried and dressed, then searched around to see how they emptied the pool. It was Amelia who eventually found two trap doors. One emptied the pool, and the other refilled it.

'I really want this system installed in the palace,' Aliah told Amelia.

'I am afraid this all relies on a natural spring.' Amelia smiled. 'Quite a smart design really, but it cannot be transported elsewhere.'

The main cave was empty when they left the bathing room, so they returned to their bedroom and stowed their belongings in the trunks provided. After plaiting each other's hair to keep it out of the way while it dried, they returned to the communal area to await Caraig. Walter, freshly washed and dressed, sat in the chair closest to the fire. In front of him stood a tray with a steaming pot full of some strange liquid. Aliah smelled it. It was not like any tea she had ever had, but it did smell a little like the coffee drink favoured by people around Duncameron.

'They call it caffe,' Walter said. 'It is like our coffee, only stronger. The woman who brought it suggested we might like to put a stick of sugar cane in it. If you do that, it is quite refreshing, if a little strong.'

Aliah fixed herself and Amelia a cup, smiling at the noise coming from the bathing area. Clearly someone was enjoying themselves in there. She was sipping her caffe and enjoying the unusual flavour when Liam and Seamus emerged from the room on the far right. So Dominic and Daniel were the ones making the ruckus in the bathing area. The five of them were happily drinking their cups of caffe when Caraig entered a few moments later, followed by Eon and Emer.

'I am sorry to barge in so quickly,' Caraig apologised. 'It is our custom to let guests bathe and have refreshments before any formal meetings occur. In this instance though, we have met the spirit of the tradition, if not the substance, and for that I apologise.'

Aliah found it disconcerting the way the seer stared

directly at the people he spoke to, even when they had not spoken first, as if the sightless man could somehow see them. As she watched Caraig speak, she attempted to determine his age. His white hair made him appear ancient, as did his reliance on his staff to move around, but on closer inspection she decided he must only be in his sixth decade. Realising she was staring, Aliah averted her eyes as the seer finished speaking.

'It is getting late in the day and we have so very little time to get everything done.'

'Everyone keeps saying we have very little time, but no one has explained why timing is so important.' Seamus frowned. 'In fact, no one has explained anything much at all.' Aliah could not have said it better herself.

'Please accept my apologies again.' Caraig took the seat Eon had dragged over for him, before taking his place with Emer behind the seer. 'I forget you have not grown up with the prophecy and its traditions as we have, but we must wait a moment before continuing as you are not all here.'

At that very moment, the door to the bathing room opened and Dominic led Daniel out. Seeing they had company, they dropped their dirty clothes back on the floor, shut the door, and went to stand guard behind Aliah's seat.

'I shall begin. Please enjoy your caffe while I speak. It has great ability to keep a person awake.' Caraig spoke their language in the same sing-song tones as Emer, and Aliah found it quite pleasant to sit back and listen to the elderly man.

'You know we believe that The Heir of Hand is the

wizard of a great prophecy, and that the Heir of Aria is the warrior. How did we arrive at that conclusion? Where do I start?' He paused, and it was hard to tell whether it was to think or for dramatic effect. 'All seers are able to see the future. Sometimes it is minor things such as a queen will have a daughter. These minor prophecies occur frequently, and are quite specific. Many people have the gift of this type of seeing.

'Every now and then, gifted seers will be able to see into the distant future and get a sense of crucial turning points in history. They see possible futures and the events that might affect the outcome. These prophecies are called Great Prophecies, and they are of such great importance they are recorded, studied, and passed down through history. Sometimes others seers add to them. Sometimes, even after many generations, they still remain unclear.

'Hundreds and hundreds of years ago, seers banded together to codify the Great Prophecies and to monitor their progress. The prophecy of the Wizard and the Warrior is one of the Great Prophecies. In fact, it may be the most important prophecy as we believe the futures of not just Aria and Maloria hinge on its outcome, but the future of all the known lands in our part of the world.'

'Because of this, we have done a lot of research and know a considerable amount about this particular prophecy. Our studies have led us to believe certain ceremonies must be completed before we are able to confirm the prophecy is active.'

'This all sounds a little airy-fairy to me,' Daniel interrupted. 'A group of people have seen into the future and have prepared themselves for something to happen sometime, yet there is a ceremony that must be followed exactly?' He raised an eyebrow.

'I agree completely.' Caraig smiled. 'It sounds like something someone would make up for a bit of a joke. But I can assure you, this is most serious. I have been watching events unfold, and I am sure we are now in the time of that Great Prophecy. There is more I could tell you about why things must be done in a particular order, however, until the Wizard and the Warrior have met the Prophecy Council and been approved, I have promised I will say no more than I have here.'

'All right,' Seamus pondered. 'Let us assume we believe all of this, what would happen now?'

Caraig turned to Seamus. Although he clearly could not see, it was as though he looked Seamus directly in the eye. 'You and Princess Aliahanna will meet the council this evening. You will answer some questions, and they will decide if we proceed.'

'Sounds simple enough.' Seamus checked with Aliah, who bowed her head in agreement.

'They go alone?' Dominic stiffened. 'You want us to let the heirs of two of Aria's most important families go somewhere and meet with unknown people without protection?'

Caraig laughed, and Dominic stiffened even more. 'They have nothing to fear from us. We have been waiting to welcome them for many hundreds of years.'

'We only have your word for that,' Daniel said. 'And nice though you may seem, we have only just met you.'

Walter pulled his attention away from the book on his lap. 'If we have not come here for this, what have we come for? And if this is our reason for being here, we need to trust these people to see us through something they clearly understand more than we do.'

'That does not mean we should just blindly do everything that is asked of us,' Daniel persisted.

'I agree with Walter,' said Aliah, and Daniel scowled at her. 'If these people had meant us harm they have had opportunities aplenty to so. Goddess, they could even have left us behind for those men from the ship.'

'Let me cut this debate short,' Caraig said. 'We must go to the chamber now as timing is everything. How about if I leave you Emer and Eon as surety? If Seamus and Aliahanna do not return, their lives are forfeit to you. I do not do this lightly as Emer is my daughter and Eon is my oldest apprentice.'

Hiding her shock at finding their guide was the daughter of the seer, Aliah glanced from under lowered lids at the two people standing behind Caraig. Emer's face was as impassive as always, but Eon screwed his face up in disgust, turning red with anger.

'I should be there with you, master. After all, I have been working with you towards this moment for decades, and I am your second on the council,' he complained in his whiny, nasally voice.

'I am sure you agree after all our hard work the most important thing is to get these two in front of the Prophecy Council. And I am sure you would want to do everything in your power to see that happen.' Caraig did not look at Eon as he spoke, and he definitely could not see the man's scowl showing he still strongly disagreed, even though he had been outmanoeuvred.

'You have your hostages. They will stay here until Seamus and Aliahanna return safely.' Caraig took a breath to continue, but Daniel cut him short.

'I will be making sure of that.' Daniel glared at the two who would be in his charge for the foreseeable future.

'As it should be.' Caraig smiled benignly. 'The rest of you, please feel free to make yourself at home here. If you need anything, or want to go anywhere, just ask. Our people are friendly.'

'I will certainly be making use of that.' Aliah just caught the words Dominic said under his breath before she looked at Seamus. He nodded his agreement to leave, and they both stood. She dared not look behind her at Dominic and Daniel as they left the Sanctuary with Caraig leading the way, lest she see how truly annoyed they were.

8
THE PROPHECY COUNCIL

Following Caraig from the guest rooms through to the main cave was almost like being in a dream. The entrance on the inside was just as ornate as the one outside, framing a picture of the setting sun. There was a walkway running around each of the three stories, enabling access to the numerous doorways they could see.

Caraig explained each opening took you to an area called a commune, which usually housed an extended family from a number of generations. They would look similar to their guest commune, but the larger, main room would have also cooking facilities and a lounging area. Most families cooked and ate together, but had separate areas for sleeping and privacy. The rooms branching from the main area would often contain a single family and were large enough to be broken into smaller room using curtains.

Each door on the walkways led to a family commune that would extend back into the mountain. Caraig proudly informed them the Sanctuary was fully self-contained. With a surprising amount of natural light from the openings into the main courtyard area and the skylights, a person need never go outside.

Although they were called communes, to Seamus they were still caves. Very large caves, but still caves. He wondered if he might be claustrophobic, even though he had not been here for very long, he already found it difficult to breathe normally. His brain could not comprehend there was air enough for all who lived in this closed off cavern.

At last they came to a communal area very similar to the guest one. There was a seating area and behind the seats were five doors. Caraig motioned for them to sit. He walked over to one of the doors, then turned.

'I think I can tell you this much before you enter. The Prophecy Council is a subgroup of our main ruling council. It is made up of people who have a specific interest in prophecy. They are not as sure as I am about who you are, but I am sure we can convince them.' Turning back, he knocked firmly on the middle door. The door was opened from the inside and Caraig entered.

'Funny,' Aliah said. 'But I feel like I am about to sit

one of the tests my tutors used to set for me so they could report progress to my father. My tummy is fluttery, and my palms are sweaty.'

'I do not think that is funny at all. I feel a little the same way, although I do not know why.' Seamus fidgeted in his seat, unable to get comfortable. 'Either we are the Wizard and Warrior, or we are not. There is little we can do to change that. Mind you, this does have all the elements of some sort of test.'

They sat in silence until the door opened and Caraig invited them to enter. Seamus took Aliah's hand, and for once she did not pull away from him and insist she could walk perfectly well by herself. It was as though she was agreeing with him that they would face this together.

The room they entered was twice the size of the area outside, but seemed smaller because most of the space was taken up by a large, round table, which was drenched in a flickering light from candles set into alcoves around the room, each about a hand span from its neighbour. Seated around the curve of the table facing them were two men who made Caraig look young, and a third, much younger man. Behind the two older men, stood two other men, around about the age of Seamus' parents.

Caraig walked around to take a vacant seat. When he was seated comfortably, the space behind his chair was conspicuously bare. Seamus wondered briefly if Eon was supposed to take that empty spot—if so, why Caraig had been so quick to leave his assistant behind? Before he had time to mull that question over, the man beside Caraig spoke.

'I welcome you to Maloria, and to the Sanctuary. Let

me introduce you to our Prophecy Council. You know Caraig.' He gestured to his left, then turned to his right. 'Mikel is our representative from the Writer's Guild.' He indicated the man to his right who had no one standing behind his chair. 'He sits for Brianna. She is ill and unable to attend today. Beside him is Angus, Head of our Guild of Scholars.' The last man smiled mischievously as he was introduced. Seamus liked him immediately. 'I am Vira, and I sit as the peoples' elected representative. The others are seconds, and will only be a part of the proceedings should something happen to one of us. And you are Lord Seamus and Princess Aliahanna.'

'We are happy to be called Seamus and Aliah,' Aliah informed them.

Acknowledging this concession, Vira continued, 'I believe it is your wish to be tested as the Wizard and the Warrior from the End of Days prophecy.' He gazed expectantly at them.

Seamus glanced at Aliah, hoping she would take the reins and answer. Aliah merely shrugged her shoulders and his stomach sank as he realised she was leaving it up to him.

'We were asked to come here as potential candidates. It would be a stretch to say we believe ourselves to be the Wizard and the Warrior. In fact, I would say it was quite the opposite.' Out of the corner of his eye he glimpsed Aliah nodding her head in agreement as she gently squeezed his hand.

Angus grinned at Seamus. 'The prophecy states the true Wizard and Warrior will not believe they are the ones until after they pass the test.'

'Well, that is just stupid,' Aliah spluttered. 'Who would actually believe themselves to be a part of a prophecy? Certainly not someone you would want to be your hero in a crisis. So anyone and everyone coming here to be considered for the roles would feel the same way.'

'I like her,' Angus told the group, and he actually winked at Caraig. 'She is feisty.'

Aliah squeezed Seamus' hand even harder, he assumed in an effort to control any further outbursts at the councillor's comments.

'So,' the council leader continued. 'You do not ask for this, but it is asked of you. Why did you come?'

Aliah nodded for Seamus to continue. *She probably did not want to risk saying what is on her mind after that outburst*, he thought briefly, before responding. 'Firstly, to be honest, for the warriors you promised to Hand in the war against Carsten.

'Secondly, because from what we understand of the prophecy, these two will save Aria from disaster, and if there is even the slightest chance it may be true, we owe it to our people to do what we can to identify them and help win this war.'

Seamus could tell nothing from the faces in front of him. Caraig dropped his head to one side as if in thought, but the other three men were looking intently at them and not saying anything. It was unsettling.

Finally, the man who had so far been silent, Mikel, turned to Caraig. 'It could be a deep sense of duty, or it could be seen as self-interest.' Was all he said.

'Or it could be both,' Aliah's fan Angus interjected.

'I fail to see how you could think it was in *our* interests to traipse through forests to the middle of nowhere on a slim chance we could help our people in the upcoming war.' Aliah forced out through gritted teeth. Angus seemed to be needling her in a way that made her lose her self-control. Wondering if this was deliberate, Seamus tried not to get lost in his thoughts as he needed to concentrate on what was happening in the room.

'At the very least you show your knowledge of the prophecy to be limited,' the council leader said to Aliah. 'The End of Days Prophecy is not about Aria, it is about the known world and the future of all who live here. If the conditions of the prophecy are not met, then all that we know will be destroyed, and humankind will be sunk into misery and despair'

'Well, that all sounds very dramatic,' Aliah said scathingly. 'How exactly is that supposed to happen?'

'If I may?' Caraig asked the leader, who nodded. 'The prophecy recounted in Arian histories is part of a larger prophecy that has built up over a number of years. The first part tells of the fall of the Talagran nation due to the unrestricted use of battle magic. They call that the decimation. This already came to pass when the Malorian nation formed. The second part tells of the loss of battle magic, and the spread of the Northerners. We believe that refers to the Natari invasion of what is now Aria.

'The final phase of the prophecy, and the least clear section, tells of the rise of a great evil and what will be required to stop it.'

'May we see the full prophecy?' Seamus asked, interested to see how it differed from what they had read.

'You may, but not until you have been confirmed as

the wizard. One of the requirements I spoke of is the Wizard and Warrior cannot know the full prophecy until they have undergone their testing,' Caraig informed them.

'Does it actually say that in the prophecy?' Aliah queried.

'No,' Caraig admitted. 'But in my younger years I had a true seeing from the gods. It told me the Wizard and Warrior will arrive not knowing who they are, but will have a deep sense of duty. The seeing said the council will know them for who they are and will send them to the cave of trials where the gods will test them. I had this seeing because the time of the Great Prophecy was drawing close, and we needed to know how to identify those who could save the world.'

'I am not so sure about the saving the world bit,' Aliah said. 'In fact, I am not sure I believe in the prophecy at all. But why not just take us to the cave of trials and get this over and done with?'

Seamus could not have agreed more.

'She truly is feisty, but my dear you should err on the side of caution a little more.' Aliah's fan smiled at the other council members. 'We are not just old men trying to feel important by deciding whether or not you should go to trial, we are looking out for you. For Caraig's true seeing told him anyone who attempted these particular trials and failed, would not likely return from the caves.'

Again, Aliah's grip on Seamus' arm tightened, almost unbearably. Wanting to calm the situation down a little he asked, 'Why was there such a rush to get us here?'

'Before entering the trial caves, all candidates must spend the night before in prayer and contemplation to rid the mind of all but the coming ordeal. As all but special trials are traditionally held on the day of a full moon, which is tomorrow, the reflection period needs to occur tonight. If we miss this, we would have to wait another moon turn before we could test you. By then, the Carsten invasion would be well and truly over and we may have missed the opportunity to fight off a great evil.'

'But you said this is about more than the Carsten invasion.' By the tone of her voice, Seamus could sense Aliah becoming more frustrated.

'It is, and it is not,' Caraig said.

'Let me guess, you cannot tell us until we have passed the trial?' Seamus asked dryly.

'No, we can tell you this now.' Clearly the council had no sense of humour as they did not even smile at Seamus' attempt at a joke. 'The Carsten invasion is not the great evil, but from what our seers tell us, the great evil is driving it. The people of Carsten have already been infected, and they will spread that evil should they succeed in invading Aria.'

'What do you mean "infected"? And what is the great evil?' Now it was Seamus' turn to be annoyed. He did not want to be a part of a prophecy if it meant everything was so vague.

'I do not mean infected like an illness,' the council leader told them. 'I mean the people of Carsten have changed over recent years. The country has become focused on war, and has conquered all the neighbouring lands. Then instead of concentrating on building a more prosperous, united country by repairing the damage after years of war, it is as though war has become an end in itself.

TRIALS

The people live in poverty, barely able to feed themselves. The weak and the sick are left at home, and everyone else is conscripted into the army. There is no one to till the fields, or tend the orchards, or to take out the fishing boats. This is what we fear will happen to Aria and Maloria should their invasion be successful.'

'So it is merely that the leaders want to continue with war.' Relief washed through Seamus. He had imagined they would have to face something far more scary than a king bent on conquering. Human leaders could be defeated in battle. Destroy the leaders, the war goes away.

'You could say that,' Caraig responded. 'Except, as best we can tell, one of the minor gods somehow has control of one or many of the leaders of Carsten.'

'So we merely kill those leaders?' Seamus asked hopefully.

'If only it were that easy.' Angus grinned wickedly. 'The god would merely seek to control the next leader in line.'

'And to make it worse, we also believe the god may be working in concert with, or have control of, some people high up in Aria. Maybe even magic users,' Vira, the council leader added.

'The Wizard Council,' Seamus and Aliah said together. Pieces fell into place to make some sort of confusing sense. Although Seamus had no idea how they would fight a god, he could glimpse the bigger picture, and this gave him some reassurance.

'So, in your opinion, are we the Wizard and Warrior?' How like Aliah cut straight to the heart of the matter.

'The fact is,' the leader said, after looking around the table. 'We really cannot be sure. We think there is a good chance you might be, we even *hope* you might be, but we could not say that definitely you are.'

'So where does that leave us?' Seamus asked them, confused again.

'If I may?' Caraig asked for permission to speak. 'It may be that this is exactly what is supposed to happen. You are ideal candidates, and you are the most likely we can find. But maybe you do not need to believe you are likely to be those spoken of in the prophecy before you enter the trials. Maybe the test will reveal to you personally, whether or not you are the Wizard and the Warrior.'

Seamus turned to look directly at Aliah. 'What do you think?' he asked. 'This is no longer the simple test we thought it would be when we left Hand. Now we are told we might not actually leave the trial if we are found not to be the Wizard and Warrior.'

'I do not know...' she started to say more, then paused. 'You?'

'I find all this prophecy stuff a bit like air. It seems to be all around us, but I cannot really see it clearly.'

Aliah closed her eyes as she considered what he had said.

'In saying that,' he continued. 'You could look back over the last few moon-turns and see a lot of things have conspired to get us to this particular point together. Two people, who otherwise would not have met. It is just as likely I am the wizard as I am not.'

'But would you bet your life on it?' Aliah asked him, frowning as she tucked a stray strand of hair back behind her ear.

Seamus chewed his lip and frowned. 'If I think rationally, no. But something in my gut is telling me I have to do this, even though I am scared,' he admitted, surprised at how openly he shared his thoughts in front of total strangers.

'Funny. Me too.' Aliah frowned. 'I need to know one way or another.'

They turned back to the four men around the table. 'We will take the test,' they said together.

'Tests,' Caraig corrected them. 'You will both be tested individually.'

Seamus shook his head, of course it would not be that easy.

'Are you sure you want to do this?' the council leader asked them again.

No, not really, and especially not alone, he thought. Out loud, Seamus found himself saying, 'Yes.'

Aliah twirled her plait thoughtfully, and had not yet answered. *Oh no, please do not pull out now.*, Seamus worried.

'We will do these tests you talk of once you confirm your warriors are on their way to Hand.'

Confusion spread over the faces of the men in front of them. They had not expected this. 'I believe they are mustering already?' Caraig asked them.

'We will send someone to the guest commune tonight to liaise with your guards.' Vira confirmed.

'We will go ahead then.' Aliah let go of Seamus' hand, ready to leave.

Once the decision had been made, a strange calm washed over Seamus. Which was odd for someone preparing for their potential demise, he admitted to himself. He could not really get his head around being the wizard, yet he did not really believe in his heart of hearts that he and Aliah would not come out of their individual trials alive either.

As he followed Caraig back to the guest commune so they could eat dinner with their companions, he likened his journey to the time he had been washed out of a boat caught in some rapids. While in the rapids, he could not control where he was pushed, he could only control how he reacted, and how he kept his head above water. He had to let go of his worries, and wait and see where their journey took him next.

Emer and a relieved Eon followed Caraig out, and soon after their departure, a sumptuous evening meal arrive. Seamus had never eaten anything as spicy as the meal they were presented with, and concentrated on the rich and varied taste of the food, rather than the various attempts to talk Aliah and him out of their decision.

Everyone seemed so worried about what would happen if they failed. How would they ever be able to tell Aliah's and Seamus' parents they had let them go to their deaths? But no one thought of what they might be able to achieve if they actually passed, Seamus mused as he tried a dish topped with some kind of nut he had never tasted before.

All the while Seamus felt as if he were enclosed in a bubble; a part of, but separate to everything happening around him. He was calm and centred in the midst of all their noise. He did not even bother defending his position, and he noticed Aliah did not speak either.

When the time came to leave for the contemplation rooms they were both hugged and cried over. Seamus did not know what to say, so said nothing at all. Caraig led them back to the commune outside the Council Chamber. After informing them all they needed for the night would be in their rooms, he bid them goodnight.

Seamus let go of Aliah's hand and she walked to her door, entering without turning around.

'Good night, see you in the morning,' Seamus said as she closed the door without looking back. Shrugging his shoulders, Seamus was saddened Aliah was so caught up in her own thoughts she had not even wished him a good night.

Taking one last look around the room, he thought he saw a flickering outside in the corridor. Shaking his head, he walked over to look out. Nothing there. *I must be dreaming.* He reached for the door to his room, entered, and closed it firmly behind.

The contemplation room was the most cave-like area he had been in so far. There had been nothing done to make it less like a cave at all. A single candle smelling of jasmine sent a flickering light around the walls. That, and a comfortable bed, completed the furnishing. Seamus lay down on the bed, and found his hand going to the chain he wore round his neck. His fingers worried the sign of the lady his sister had given him. It was hard to believe he might not ever see his family again after tomorrow. It was even harder to believe he was a person someone hundreds of years ago had written a prophecy about. He fully expected to spend a wakeful night worrying, but was asleep not long after his head touched the pillow.

9
ALIAH'S QUEST

'Wake up.'

Aliah grunted. She had only just gone to sleep, why would she want to wake up now?

More shaking and a more insistent, 'Wake up, Aliah.'

Slowly she opened her eyes and Emer's face came into view. Sitting up, Aliah's gaze focused on the cup of steaming caffe the other girl had in her hand, and the change of clothes she laid out on the end of the bed.

'You may not eat before the trial, but many prefer to

have some caffe before they enter the cave. Also, I brought you some leather trousers and waistcoat. In the caves you will need something a bit more sturdy than the fabric your clothes are made of. I will wait outside while you change.'

When she had gone to bed last night, Aliah had been strangely calm. She expected the nerves to come this morning though, especially with the possibility she might actually die during the trial. But the strange sense of peace and rightness from the previous night was still with her.

Slowly she changed her trousers and did the waistcoat up over her shirt, having first made sure the necklace Seamus had given her was safely tucked away. She plaited her hair and tied her boots securely. Finally, she placed her sword belt around her waist. After a few quick gulps of caffe, she had prepared as best she could for anything they might throw at her.

She emerged and Emer checked her over, shaking her head. 'I am sorry, but you cannot take any weapons of your own into the trial.'

Aliah did not move. 'You expect me to go into potential danger unarmed?'

Emer shrugged. 'Everything you need will be provided for you. It is the way. I am not sure why, but I believe it is some sign of trust. No matter the reason, you cannot take that in with you.'

Those few words were the most the other girl had ever said to Aliah outside of a command, making Aliah more inclined to listen, just this once. After placing her sword back in the contemplation room, she followed Emer out through the door.

TRIALS

'Where is Seamus?' She looked around quizzically.

'This is your trial,' Emer said as she led them from the commune.

'Oh,' she replied out loud. *But I did not even say goodnight to him, or wish him good luck for today,* she thought to herself, worried Seamus may think she did not care.

Although Emer led them through the main part of this strange city, hardly anyone was about so Aliah guessed it must have been early in the morning. Their route took them deeper into the mountain, through many large caverns with walkways running around them. Just when she thought they could not possibly go any further, Aliah glimpsed a pinprick of light in the distance. Growing larger as they walked, she saw the source was sunlight shining through another entrance to the Malorian Sanctuary.

'Why is this place called the Sanctuary?' Aliah asked Emer as they emerged into the sunlight.

'Because when the magic wars were being fought, many Talagrians came here to get away from the carnage. After the fighting finished, we made contact with the Malorians, joining to become one nation. This place became a centre of learning and retreat for the new Malorian nation. However, we still call it *Sanctuary* in recognition of its past role as a shelter from the war.' Aliah marvelled how in Emer's natural habitat, she did not seem nearly as forbidding as she had on the journey there.

The doorway they had come through opened into a natural amphitheatre. *This place is easy to defend as it would be hard to enter from the back. I can see why people escaping the war chose to stay here,* Aliah thought as she looked around.

Caraig waited for her in the shade nearby. He carried a knife, and a water bag slung over his back, both of which he handed to her as soon as she came alongside him. She settled them on her person as Caraig gave her instructions for her trial.

'The rules are strict and have been passed down over hundreds of years. This is all you may take in with you.'

'How long will it take?' Aliah asked him.

'Each trial is different. It depends on the person, what they are questing for, and how the gods decide to test them. However, each quest must be completed within twelve candle-marks. A bell will sound at six candle-marks, then at nine candle-marks and then at every candle-mark after that. At the last bell of the twelfth candle-mark the cave will be closed off and will not open again until the full moon, when we can hold other trials. That is all I am allowed to tell you. There are three caves. You choose one and enter. I will wait here for your return.'

'Why did Seamus not start his trial with me?' Aliah asked Caraig.

'This is your quest. He has his own. Which cave?'

'Has his quest started?'

Caraig shook his head. 'You have been told all I am permitted to tell you. Each person is to have their own quest. Concentrate on yours.'

Realising she would get no more information from Caraig, she turned her attention to the three cave entrances directly opposite where they stood. How to choose? Did it matter? She brushed a strand of hair behind her ear and stilled her mind. This was a quest of the heart for her and so the heart side it must be. 'The cave on the left,' she told Caraig.

He led her to the cave entrance. She checked the knife was securely tucked into the belt at her side, and that the water bag would not slip from her back. With a deep breath, she entered the cave.

'Goddess be with you.' The blessing came from behind as the darkness engulfed her.

After the brightness outside, it took a moment for her eyes to adjust to the lack of light. The narrow entrance way meant she had no option but to go straight ahead. Her path started sloping upwards, and very soon came to an abrupt end. In front of her was a sheer rock-face. Her only choices were to go back or climb.

Fortunately some natural light came from somewhere above, helping her make out hand and foot holds in the rock face. The climb did not look too difficult. Although there were plenty of places for her hands, nerves caused them to shake. She was physically fit, but climbing was not something she had ever been good at.

Beginning her assent, it seemed only moments later her arms and legs started cramping. As she climbed, she glanced up, then down. *Not even half way up,* she thought wearily. At that stage, she was high enough that a fall to the ground would badly injure her. A little higher, and it could result in death. She searched and found a ledge where she could sit and drink some water, allowing her weary limbs to rest.

After too short a time, she started off again. The actual

climb was no harder this high up, but her arms and legs were already tired, so she moved much more slowly. The cramps in her arms started again, and a strand of hair kept falling in her eyes, no matter how often she shook it out. As the sweat slithered down her back, her legs began to shake. As she wiped the sweat of her brow with her arm, she searched for another ledge to rest upon.

There was nothing close, so she forced her protesting limbs to carry on until she found a small crevice where she could wedge herself and look for the best place to rest. There, just to the right, was a a small ridge jutting out from the rock face. One last push and she reached the small shelf. As Aliah flopped down her arms and legs were shaking, relief flooded through her as she thought how close she had been to falling to the ground.

Taking a sip of water, she glanced down. The ledge where she sat was higher than the highest tower in her father's castle. If she fell from there, she would not survive. Exhausted, she could not believe she still had a quarter of the climb to go. Closing her eyes, she contemplated the enormity of what she had left to do. Her ears picked up a rustling sound and her eyes flew open as the sound grew louder.

As her eyes adjusted, she spied a colony of bats heading straight for her. Angry at having their territory invaded they swooped, trying to knock her off her perch. While swinging her knife in front, she slowly stood up, and shuffled until the rock face pressed into her back. There was less chance of falling from this position, but the knife was not very effective against so many bats determined to see her out of their cave. They left her covered in cuts and scratches. She could not go on like this. Something had to change, and soon.

Quickly, she grabbed the water skin off her back and, holding it by the strap, she swung it around. The water bag cut through the swarm of bats, knocking many of their number to the ground. Another sweep and more bats fell to their doom. At first this made the bats attack harder, but they were quickly becoming fewer in number, so she kept it up. Suddenly, as one, they realised the cost of this battle was too high and flew away in a squawking flurry.

Aliah's body shook with exhaustion, but if she sat now, she would not have the energy to get back up. Taking a quick drink of water, she cleaned her wounds as best she could, slung her water skin over her back, and started on the final ascent. Using the adrenaline produced during the fight, and before her body could protest that it could go no further, she started climbing, determined to reach the top before the bats regrouped.

That last quarter of the climb took her twice as long as the rest put together. Tiredness caused her to loose her footing a couple of times, but fortunately she managed to keep a hold, and quickly found new places for her feet.

At long last, she pulled her weary body over the edge and flopped flat on the cold ground. For a moment, she stayed on her back, panting and staring up at the light coming through the roof of the cavern, enjoying the feel of the cool earth on her tired muscles. A bell tolled six. It had taken her half her allotted time just to climb up here. Forcing herself to sit up as her stomach clenched in worry, as this was unlikely to be the sum total of her quest.

Aliah looked around. At the far end of the cave stood

an altar, and on that alter sat a sword. Something in her gut told her to complete the quest she needed to take possession of that sword. Taking a deep breath, she tensed to stand. Before Aliah could move though, a low growl rumbled from the shadows, close enough for it to vibrate through her body. Moments later a mountain lion stalked into view. Crouching low, the lion slunk towards her.

Great, I only have a knife. If only the sword was not over the other side of the room.

As the lion approached, she slowly shuffled backwards on her bottom. Her hand knocked against something... something wooden. She did not know how big the object was, but it was all she had. She stopped moving and so did the lion. It tensed, ready to pounce.

The lion's muscles released and it flew through the air towards her. Aliah rolled to the left, away from the edge of the cliff face and, picking up the wooden object with her right hand, rolled onto her knees. With all her might, she swung whatever was in her hand at the lion's head. It fell to the ground, stunned, and shook its head groggily. It started to rise, but before it could recover and attack again, Aliah stood on shaky legs and ran at the lion, took a swing with her leg, and kicked it over the cliff. A twang shot through her thigh and Aliah dropped to her knees, heart racing. That was all she needed, a pulled muscle. Still, she was alive, and that was all that mattered.

Slowly standing, she bent over, hands on knees, and gulped in lungs-full of air, trying to calm her nerves. Her body trembled with fatigue, but her mind was alert to what might advance from the shadows to stop her from achieving her goal.

Surveying the altar, she searched for any obvious traps to prevent her from taking the sword. It sat on a wooden pedestal with nothing apparently securing it there. That meant the threat would come from somewhere else.

Warily, she crept forward. As she did, the darkness at the back of the altar began to shimmer, and a serpent larger than any she had seen before slithered out from behind.

'Nooo...' She groaned. 'It is not fair. I have nothing left. I cannot fight you.'

To her surprise, the serpent responded. 'Life is not fair. It sometimes asks more of us than we think we can give. But if something is worthwhile, the truly worthy will find they have a little more inside, if they just dig deep.'

The serpent reared up, standing a head taller than Aliah. 'You can end your quest here and the world will face its threat without the Wizard and the Warrior. Or you can find a way to defeat me.'

Once again, Aliah gulped in great lungs-full of air, while searching around for any way to evade or defeat the serpent. Whatever she did, it needed to be done quickly. Not only because time was running out, but also because she did not have the energy for a prolonged fight. She stared the serpent in the eyes and then, without giving anything away, she formulated a plan.

Drawing her knife, she moved to the left of the serpent, away from the altar. Slithering, with its head raised, the serpent followed her, slowly closing the distance between them. Aliah kept moving steadily to the left. As it moved, the serpent lowered its head due to the slope of the cavern ceiling. When Aliah finally reached the wall on the left hand side, about half-way between the altar and the ledge, her adversary's head was level with hers and she could almost see it smile, believing it had her trapped.

Now. Aliah moved as if she was rushing forward and the serpent rose to strike, hitting its head on the ceiling. At that exact moment, Aliah hit the ground in a roll to the left, landing on her feet. Still, the serpent only missed her by a hair's breadth. As the serpent rose ready to strike again, Aliah ran to the altar, grabbed the sword, and swung as her enemy struck. Ducking back just in time, the serpent surveyed her with dark eyes.

Although backing away, the serpent blocked her exit down the cliff. However, Aliah had gained a surprising new advantage. As she gripped the sword in both hands her fatigue disappeared. In addition, she could clearly see the serpent's moves, anticipating them, almost as though she read its mind. No, it was more like she was seeing moments into the future, which allowed her to assess what the serpent would do.

While she got used to this new insight, she practiced moving the serpent around, all the while looking for another exit. The serpent and the lion must have come from somewhere. Moving behind the back of the altar, she could not find where they had entered the cave. She checked the whole cavern and found the only way out for her was the way she had come in.

Sighing with fatigue, a plan began forming in her head, to kill the serpent so she could begin her descent. As she moved into position to strike, her newfound skill showed her that to complete this trial she did not need to kill her enemy, just get away without getting hurt. Changing her tactics, she began moving towards a place where she could easily start her descent.

Almost as soon as she made her decision, the serpent changed its form. The scales melted away, revealing a rather tall, see-through woman. Aliah would not have described her as beautiful, her face and bearing were too haughty for that. But she was certainly striking, and it hurt to look too closely at her. Tensing, Aliah began to reassess the situation. Would she now have to fight this woman?

'Stand down, princess, you are in no danger from me.'

Unable to fully believe that, Aliah stayed tense, ready to strike if need be.

'It takes a special kind of warrior to choose not to kill, even when it may be the easiest course to take. You have shown you have the courage, the ingenuity, and the pure heart required of the warrior. You have passed your trial.'

Aliah let out a sigh of relief, but the woman held up her hand. 'This trial will seem as nothing when you face the truly great evil that walks the world. Though you have little time, you need to learn to master your sword and to work hand in hand with the wizard. You also need to understand that although the wizard may strike the final blow, he cannot defeat your enemy without the warrior.'

'How do I master the sword? What can it do?' Aliah asked.

'That is for you to learn yourself. Go now! Your quest is nearly over, but you must hurry or you will be trapped by the closing door and all your good work will have been for nothing.' With that, she disappeared as the ninth bell chimed.

Aliah put the sword down the back of her shirt, muttering under her breath some words no royal child should know. As she lost direct contact with the sword, her renewed energy left her. She cursed again. There was no way she could climb down while holding the sword, she would just have to do the best she could without its help.

Knowing she only had three candle-marks to get back to the cave entrance, she quickly lowered herself over the ledge and reached for footholds. Descending as fast as she could, she did not even stop for water, though her mouth was dry and her lips cracked. The tenth bell tolled and she still could not clearly see the bottom. The eleventh bell chimed, just as she lost her footing again in her exhaustion.

About three body lengths from the bottom, the first of the twelfth bells filled the cave. Turning around, she slid all the way to the end and started running to the opening. Ten paces. Five. Two paces from the opening the twelfth bell finished tolling and the door began to slide shut. Launching herself towards the door, her hands grasped at the edge of the rock as it slid shut to no effect.

Pounding the rock in frustration, Aliah collapsed on the floor. Lying on her back panting, she stared into the blackness. Her head spun as her hand reached to the neck of her shirt to grab the necklace Seamus had given her. *I am sorry, Seamus, I let you down.* A tear slipped from her eye, and she imagined she saw Dominic's face just before she lost consciousness.

10
SEAMUS' QUEST

Seamus was riding through the woods in Hand, heading towards the high plateau. He could hear nothing but the sound of his horse crashing through the undergrowth. This was his favourite place in the world, and he was more relaxed than he had been in a long time.

'Seamus. Seamus!'

Who would be calling him this far from the palace? He ignored the voice and carried on riding.

'SEAMUS.'

He was roughly shaken and his perfect morning slipped away. Back in the cave he had fallen asleep in, Emer stood over him with a cup of caffe in her hand.

'Glad you decided to join us.' She looked down at him. 'Here, drink this and dress in the clothes I brought you.' She indicated some clothes she had draped over the end of the bed. 'I will meet you outside when you are done.'

He dressed quickly in the leather trousers and vest Emer had provided, all the while taking sips of his caffe. He was a little hungry, but his stomach churned so much he could not eat a bite, which turned out to be a good thing as when he emerged from his room, Emer informed him he was not allowed to eat anything before the trial.

'Are you ready then?' she asked. He shrugged his shoulders, nodding. She turned and led the way out of the council commune.

'What about Aliah? Is she not coming with us?'

'This is your quest,' was Emer's response, and Seamus looked closely at the girl who had been their guide. Although her face was normally inscrutable, he imagined a touch of sadness there.

Seamus' stomach shrunk even more. For some reason, he had thought although they had separate trials, he and Aliah would at least set out together. Alone, without Aliah, his confidence was deserting him. As if sensing his sadness, Emer touched his arm, gently leading him through the door.

Following Emer through the tunnels further into the Sanctuary he took note of the people moving about. Most ignored them as they went about their daily business, some greeted Emer, and a few stood and watched as they passed. It was strange to see people doing the ordinary things people did in any town, but underground. It was not dark and cavelike exactly, as natural light was flooding in from some where, it was just that it seemed so... well... confined.

'Does living inside a mountain not bother you?' Seamus asked Emer.

'I was born and grew up here, this is my home so I know no different,' she answered. 'But, truth be told, I do prefer to be outside. I am fortunate that as a protector I spend most of my days roaming through the forests.'

'A protector?' Seamus asked, intently watching Emer's face. If you looked closely enough you could see small changes of expression, tell tale signs of what Emer was feeling, like the way her eyes softened when she spoke of Sanctuary.

'One sworn to protect the Sanctuary from harm and ensure all live in peace,' Emer explained.

'Ah.' Seamus understood. 'We would call you a guard. Daniel is a guard in Aria.'

Emer actually chuckled as she remembered when she met Daniel. 'That explains his eagerness to join you all on your journey. A true protector never deserts their post.'

They left the Sanctuary by a back entrance. As they exited the cavern into a natural amphitheatre, they stepped into mid-morning sun. Seamus was surprised he had been allowed to sleep for so long. Waiting for him by the back entrance was the High Seer.

'It is time for your trial,' Caraig said formally. He handed Seamus a knife and a water skin he could sling over his shoulder.

'You must choose one of the three caves to enter, you then have twelve candle-marks to complete your quest. A bell will toll at the sixth candle-mark, and the ninth candle-mark, then every candle-mark after that until the twelfth. At the twelfth bell of the twelfth candle-mark, the cave will be closed off, and you will remain inside until the gods open the cave for the next trial.'

Great. Shut in a cave for goodness knows how long. What more could I wish for? He studied the openings in front of him, chewing thoughtfully on his lip. *The left cave looks as good as any.* To Caraig he said, 'I choose the cave on the left.'

'You may proceed.'

'Is that it? No ceremony or wise words?' Seamus raised an eyebrow in surprise. He thought he detected a little bit of a smile from Caraig as he voiced his thoughts.

'If it helps, I hope the grace of the gods is with you.'

Seamus shrugged his shoulders, not sure if it was any help at all. He could put the moment off no longer. Walking towards the cave on the left, he entered its cool interior. He found himself in an enormous cavern. It was so tall he could not see the ceiling. It was so round he could not see the far side. It was bathed in natural light and in front of him were seven figures, three male and four female.

The figures were taller than most people he knew and, it may have been a trick of the light, it seemed as though he was looking right through them. He could not be certain as he could not look directly at any one long enough to really see them. For some reason, his gaze shifted away just as the one he looked at came into focus. It was much more comfortable looking at all seven as a group.

'Come forward,' one—or was it all of them?—commanded.

Reluctant to move, Seamus turned around to find the cave mouth he had entered through was longer there. His only options were to step forward, or stay still. He took a tentative step forward.

'You wish to be tried as the Wizard of Prophecy?'

Maybe it was not the time to go into the fact he was not sure he wanted the position and all it might entail. After all, he had made the decision to come here. 'I do,' he found himself responding.

'You do this knowing the threat facing the world is bigger than anything faced by humankind before?'

What do they mean by "humankind"? Are they not human? He wondered. *Are these... Gods?*

'So I have been told,' Seamus answered, a little more wary now he thought he had guessed who these seven were.

'You know that one of our own has decided to conquer your world?' they asked him.

'I do. I also do not understand why the other gods cannot stop him.' Seamus responded, taking a chance he had guessed their identities correctly.

'If only it were that simple,' they answered. 'If a god were to interfere directly with the working of another god, there would be all out war. A war of the gods would destroy more than your land, it would destroy all the known worlds and time itself.'

'So you can do nothing?' Seamus was flabbergasted, but also quite pleased with himself that he had realised he faced the gods before they had told him.

'We did not say that. We have been helping your kind

for millennia to prepare for this moment. We have warned you and we have made it possible for the Wizard and the Warrior to be born to combat this evil.'

'So you tell me how to defeat this god, and Aliah and I go forth and fight him?'

'No, that is beyond what we are able to do.'

'Can you even tell me which god we are facing?' They must surely be able to give him this simple piece of information, Seamus decided.

Silence fell as the gods looked at each other. Then one stepped forward, a woman, who was vaguely familiar. She had the same face as the statues of the goddess he had grown up with.

'I am sorry we cannot tell you even this. We will give it some thought and see if there is any way we are able to help you find out using resources you already have. If we have any ideas, we will find a way to get them through to you.

'The time for questioning is now over. Do you confirm that you take this test willingly, knowing you could die during it, and also knowing should you pass the trial, you will have committed to doing all you can to fight the evil plaguing your land?' The goddess spoke in a strong, compelling voice.

He took a deep breath and decided to say exactly what was on his mind. 'I do this willingly, but I think you have chosen the wrong person. I am no mage. I can light fires, and I can sometimes move things. Any attempts to do more have ended in disaster.'

The goddess smiled benignly at him. 'We have been watching your progress, and we believe it is as we expected.

TRIALS

You are perhaps the most gifted mage of your time, but your gift is not something often seen in your lands, so no one has the experience to help you master it.'

'Well, that is useful,' Seamus said sarcastically. 'I have a great gift but will never be able to use it.'

'You are perhaps too quick to judge, young mage. Your gift has come from all of us. From me, you have been given the ability to nurture and heal, from the others, you have been given foresight, control of the air, water, fire, and land, and the ability to kill with a thought. Although you have been given these gifts you have only a small amount of magic in each. You can use each gift individually, which is how you have been approaching your training to date, but your true power comes from combining your magic and using them together.'

'That goes against everything Walter has been teaching me. He said many people have two, maybe three, forms of magic, but all mages are usually strongest in one. We have been trying to find my one.'

'That is the usual way gods bestow gifts. However, your gifts are special, forged in response to specific circumstances. Because of this, should you pass your trials, we have taken it on ourselves to train you in how to best use your magic. You will earn a wand made from the elder tree at the heart of the known worlds. This is the only tool that will allow you to channel such diverse, melded magic. We will not leave you to face your foe without being as prepared as we can make you.'

'It sounds like you have chosen me to be the Wizard from birth, ensuring I had the right mix of magic. If that is so, why do I need to go through a trial?'

The goddess moved back in line with her fellow gods, and Seamus found once again he could no longer look directly at her. The gods answered his question together.

'It is a great power you have potential to wield, but you do not have the key to unlock its full potential, only we can help with that. However, while you have been born with the power, we need to assess whether or not you are the right type of person to use it. We need to test your resolve, and test you personally to see whether or not you are capable of using the power wisely. So, we ask once again, do you agree to this trial knowing it may end in your death, and knowing you will then be committing your life to defending your world against great evil?'

Again, Seamus took a deep breath, but did not answer immediately. He did not really want to die, but he did not want to see his world overrun by war, and see the people ground into the ground by uncaring rulers. In the end, he did not really have a choice. 'I agree.'

'Then let the trial commence.'

As Seamus was thinking that this was more like the introduction to the trial he had expected, the seven gods melted away, and he found himself in the palace on Hand.

Seamus stood in the doorway of the family quarters in the palace on Hand. The noises of battle surrounded him. Two guards were fighting what looked to be outlanders. Behind them stood his sister, clutching the hand of her nanny, fear written on her face. The guards were tiring, there were too many attackers. Behind him, there was a full blown battle as more barbarians fought to get past the guards at the top of the stairs. For the moment, the guards managed to keep them at bay.

Fear and anger rushed through him. How dare these people threaten his family and his people? He could help them, but first he needed to get Cara to safety. Closing his eyes, he reached out for his magic. Grasping hold of it, he pushed out a small flame. Instead, a rush of fire leapt from his hands, burning all in its path. Trying to call it back, Seamus cried out as the magical flames burned uncontrolled, killing those from Hand and Carsten indiscriminately. Through the flames, he could just see Cara's nanny pulling her up the stairs, away from the fire.

Dropping to his knees in despair, Seamus cried uncontrollably as he was whisked back to the cavern of the gods.

'I cannot do it,' he cried as he relived the destruction he had caused in his mind. 'I am not strong enough.'

A figure stepped to his side, and he peered up to see the goddess. 'What you did was unforgivable, using magic to kill. You need to take a deep breath and calm yourself.'

Slowly getting his emotions under control, Seamus thought his was probably the shortest trial ever.

'We had not understood how much not being trained how to use your magic would affect your ability to wield it under pressure,' the goddess said once he stopped crying. 'It is especially susceptible to influence by emotions, more so than the usual gifts, but we had not fully understood how much. What were you thinking when you released you magic?'

Seamus thought for a moment. 'I was scared, and angry, but I was thinking to call fire to try and help my family. I have never been able to call forth that much fire before, and I panicked. I could not control it.'

'Think back,' the goddess commanded. 'Has anything like this happened before?'

'On the ship,' Seamus answered. 'Walter was teaching me to move things and I could not make anything move. I got frustrated and blew up a barrel of tar.'

The goddess leaned her head to the side as if examining him. 'What have you learnt from this?'

I am a bad wizard, he thought to himself.

'I am a god, I can hear your thoughts. You are an untrained wizard. Think again.'

This time when Seamus thought hard about the two incidents, understanding finally hit him. 'If I act without a plan, with emotion and no thought, then my magic flares out of control.'

The goddess disappeared, then reappeared with the other gods. They seemed to be conversing. While he head learnt something today, he wondered why they had not ended his trial and sent him home.

'We have been unwise.' Seamus' attention was jolted back to the cavern. 'We thought you could learn to control your magic without help. We have set you up to fail.'

Shaking his head disbelievingly, Seamus stood up. 'I have failed then?' The silence that followed his question was total.

'You did something wrong for the right reason, but you did it because you did not know any better. Had we trained you, you may have acted differently. We need to confirm this before we decide.'

There was more silence as the gods looked to each other, then the goddess moved closer to him again.

'Your magic is different to others. You do not need spells, hand gestures, or chants for it to work. You need to clearly envision in your mind what you want to happen, then your magic will follow. Do you understand?'

Seamus turned this over in his mind, thinking what he might have done differently had he known this, then answered, 'I think so.'

'We will try you again. The battle in the family quarters is lost, but there are others who need your help.'

Sick to the stomach with worry, Seamus found himself at the back of a very crowded formal reception room on Hand. His water skin had disappeared, replaced by a sword, and he had a thin black wand in his hand. There was a battle raging around him. The guards of the castle were fighting what appeared to be more barbarians. At the other end of the hall, by the throne, his father was fighting off one very large and determined attacker, Seamus' mother and brother behind him. His father was slowly being pushed backwards towards the wall. Very soon, he would have nowhere else to go, and Seamus could tell the man he faced was a much better and stronger swordsman.

There were too many men fighting between them for him to get to his father to help. He had a sword for sure, but he was about as much use with that as a newborn baby. He had magic also, but fire was the only thing he could really use, and his control of that was not very reliable. If he used it he could kill a lot of innocent people, and if he only saved his family, what about the others? The men in his father's guard? The people crammed up against the walls, trying to keep away from the weapons being swung in battle? Should he use magic to save them and confirm their fears about him? If he did, what would his father think?

The loud thuds of barbarian soldiers trying to get through the double doors came from behind him. For the moment, the Hand guards were still managing to keep them out. However, Seamus could see the doors bulging as the soldiers outside attempted to force entry. It was only a matter of time until the enemy burst through, and they would be overrun by foreign soldiers. When that happened, the battle would be lost.

Think, he told his brain. *There must be something you can do.* Fire was the only tool he felt confident using. Slowly a plan began to form in his mind. If he concentrated, it was almost like he could see things happening before they did. He could use that.

He ordered the guards away from the door behind him. They paused, but seeing who he was, soon responded. As they moved away from the door, he sealed it off with a wall of fire. Now knowing he could produce a lot of fire, he found it as easy as making a small flame, he just had to concentrate to keep it under control.

Next, he took a knife from the belt of one of the guards, and surrounded himself in a wall of flames. He easily moved to the centre of the room, as everyone moved away from the heat of the fire to let him through. Keeping in mind what had happened in the family rooms, he focused on keeping control of the flames, making doubly sure they did not expand to touch anyone.

Stopping when he had a clear aim, he took a deep breath and threw the knife at the sword arm of the man fighting his father, letting out his breath with relief as the man's sword clattered to the ground. Seamus' father moved quickly to hold his sword to the man's throat as the barbarian clutched at his injured arm, attempting to remove the knife.

'Who is next?' Seamus boomed in his loudest voice, and the fighting around him stopped as all in the room took in his presence. Glimpsing a movement to his right he felt, rather than saw, a knife coming towards him. A sweep of his hand, and the knife fell uselessly to the floor before it reached the ring of defensive fire.

Scanning the room, he located the knife thrower. Seamus' eyes bored through the crowd, and caught sight of a barbarian trembling in fear. As Seamus raised his hand, he thought of pulling the air from his attacker's body, not stopping until the last moment, when the man slumped to the ground, not dead, merely winded.

'Anyone else?' No one moved. 'Those who do not belong here, drop your weapons and move to the middle of the room.' There were loud crashes as swords and other weapons hit the floor. The barbarians moved to the centre of the room and were soon encircled by Hand guards. Some of the court men busied themselves gathering the discarded weapons.

Behind him, Seamus heard guards from the town

arriving outside to deal with the barbarians still trying to get into the Throne Room. Then, before he could decide what to do next, he found himself back in the cave, facing the seven gods.

The goddess moved forward from the group of seven. 'You have done well, young wizard. You showed you could use your minor gifts to manage a situation without having to resort to killing as your only option. Even though you had the wand to amplify your power, you showed restraint. You have earned the wand you now hold.' She stepped back.

Seamus glanced down to see that a plain, wooden wand had replaced the shiny black one he had held in the Throne Room. This one may not have been as impressive looking, but he could feel the energy throbbing through it.

'Although you have won the day today, you should not forget you still need much training in how to use your powers before you will be ready to face the god, young wizard. Also know this, although you have demonstrated restraint and shown you have a good heart, if you ever misuse what has been gifted you, you will find that what has been given, can also be taken.'

Surprised by that last comment Seamus wondered, *am I not really the wizard then?* But that thought was quickly lost as another filled his head.

'What about my family? Is Cara all right? Or did I burn her with the others?' He needed to know.

'Seamus, did you really not realise? This was a trial of our making, none of it was real.'

Seamus' shoulders sank in relief, then tensed in anger. 'You made me live through that just to test me?'

'We had to be sure you could make good decisions

under extreme pressure.' The goddess did not apologise, merely explained.

Lost for words, Seamus did not know what to think.

'Remember, you are the Hand that will deal the blow in battle, but you cannot do that without the arm to support you. It is the combined power of the Wizard and the Warrior that will win the day. You will also need others for the coming fight. The man who is not what he seems will be needed, but it is the wolf who will be especially important to you.'

Shaking his head slowly from side to side, Seamus was even more confused than ever. But before he could form the questions he wished to ask, the gods faded. Left alone in the cave—which suddenly seemed much smaller in their absence—Seamus decided there would be time to ask those questions later.

As he walked out into the late afternoon sun, he thought, *that took longer than it felt*. Maybe time moved more slowly when you were in the presence of gods. His second thought was, *that was almost too easy*. Although he believed he had killed some men and lost his sister, it had only been for a short time until the gods had explained it was all an illusion. He had not been in any real danger. All he had done was show he could learn and be himself.

It made him wonder if the gods knew he was the only one stupid enough to take up the mantle of the wizard and face the danger ahead.

Outside the cave, he found Caraig waiting. He had been joined by Dominic, Daniel, and Emer. To say they looked worried would have been an understatement.

'Ah, Seamus.' Caraig smiled. 'Congratulations on the success of your quest.'

Seamus looked at Dominic, who refused to meet his eyes. Daniel on the other hand, stepped forward and took him by the shoulders.

'Did you see Aliah in there?' he asked impatiently.

'Aliah?' Seamus was bemused. 'No. I thought you knew, our trials were to be separate.' Suddenly his mind focused. 'Daniel, what is happening here?'

Caraig stepped forward. 'Aliah began her quest at the fifth candle-mark this morning. We are now heading towards the sixth candle-mark in the afternoon.'

Looking at the worried faces, Seamus finally realised what had caused them 'Did she only have twelve candle-marks to complete her quest as well?'

Caraig nodded.

Seamus' stomach clenched with concern. 'What cave did she choose?' He looked around to see which one had the closed door. Their mouths all stood wide open.

He dashed into the middle cave, and then the one to the right. They appeared to be normal caves and they were empty. Turning to Caraig he asked again. 'Which cave did she choose?'

'The same cave as you,' Caraig answered 'But there is nothing we can do. The gods have closed the door back to this plane.'

'The hell they have,' Seamus said angrily, and pushed past the others to head back to the left hand cave.

When he entered, it looked just like the other two. Seamus sensed rather than saw Dominic join him, but he may as well not have been there at all, because it was not him Seamus wanted to speak with. Angrily he threw his wand on the ground.

'I will not do it,' he yelled. 'Without Aliah, I will not go forward.'

'You are the wizard,' came the words in his head.

'I might be the wizard, but I will do nothing without her, unless you tell me how I fulfil the prophecy without my warrior.'

The cave disappeared and he was once again standing alone facing the gods. This time he forced himself to look at all of them, even though it hurt his eyes and his head throbbed unbearably to do so.

'You cannot refuse to move forward. You made a promise. You have been chosen and tried, and you are the only one who can deal the fatal blow to the god.'

'I will not.' Seamus stood defiant. If they took his warrior, and they could take his powers if he misused them, then he really did not want to be the wizard.

'What do you want from us, mortal?'

'I want to know what happened to Aliah.' Seamus stood with his hands on his hips.

'Aliah passed her trial, but did not complete her quest within the time allotted. She was mere steps from the door when her time ran out.'

If anything, this answer made Seamus even more angry. 'You mean she is the warrior, but you are holding her because of some time limit you imposed?'

There was silence. The gods appeared to be deep in

thought. Seamus watched as they looked at each other. Some shook their heads, some nodded. Finally he had his answer.

'That is one way to look at it. The other, is that we open the portal for a given length of time for a quest to occur. When it closes, the quest is at an end.'

'I have never heard anything so stupid in my life.' Seamus spluttered in astonishment. 'Hold on. You allowed me to come back after I had completed my quest. How could you do that?'

'You are still within your allotted trial time.'

Seamus bit his lip, trying to piece what he knew together. 'So, is Aliah with me on this plane still?'

'Yes, she is.'

An idea began to form in Seamus' mind. 'Can I see her?'

As one, the gods turned and looked to the left. Seamus saw a form lying on the ground behind them, clutching a sword.

'After the time of the quest, mortals left behind fall into the dreamless sleep. They can stay like that for months before fading away.'

'So, Aliah is here and cannot leave. I am here and I can leave, but only if I leave within the time allotted to my quest?'

The gods nodded as one. Seamus sat on the floor, his mind made up

'What are you doing?' Although the faces of the gods did not change, they sounded astonished.

'If she stays here, then I stay with her.' Seamus folded his arms to emphasise his point.

'What about the fact you agreed to save the world as

the wizard?'

'I agreed to save the world as the Wizard along with the Warrior. You told me I could not deal the fatal blow to the god without the warrior. You have confirmed Aliah is the warrior. Or do you know of another warrior who can help me?'

There was more silence.

'If there is no other, then I cannot leave here without her because I will not be able to do what I need to without her.'

Seamus waited, the gods waited. A bell tolled.

'The time for your trial is running out. You must leave.'

'Not without Aliah,' Seamus responded.

'The world can not get through this crisis without you.'

'Without me and my warrior,' Seamus answered stubbornly.

The silence lasted longer, and another bell tolled. The changing expressions on the gods' faces were the only signs they were communicating.

'One more bell and the doors will close. You will be left here with the warrior and the world will have to weather this crisis without you.'

Seamus' resolve wavered a little. Did he really want to be stuck here? Then he thought about what he would be facing, and what would happen to his people if he lost this battle. They would only have half a chance of ending the threat they faced without Aliah. Although fear squirmed in his stomach, he really had no choice. He said nothing.

Finally the goddess stepped forward.

'Are you certain you can work as a team with the princess? After all, it was not so long ago you were angry with her for leaving you in Sunnydale without a word and abusing your trust.'

Seamus went to answer *of course,* but stopped himself. The goddess was right. Not that long ago he had sworn to himself he would never trust Aliah again. When had that changed? He was not sure when it had happened, just that it had. He could not, and would not, face the renegade god alone.

'I will not do it without her,' he answered determinedly.

Everything went black and suddenly he was in the cave entrance, sitting on the floor, wand in hand, with Aliah asleep in front of him. Before he could stand, Dominic had Aliah in his arms, hastily exiting the cave. Seamus moved quickly to follow him, before the gods changed their minds.

11
A RIGHT BUN FIGHT

As she awoke, all Aliah could think about was how much she ached all over. There was not a single part of her that did not feel like she had been in the most horrendous fight. Her hands ached worst of all, almost like they were continuously cramping. She opened the fingers of one hand, and it closed back onto something cold and hard, clutching it as if her life depended on it. She half opened her eyes, surprised her hands were grasping a sword.

'Pleased you could join us again. I was actually starting to get worried.'

Slowly she turned her head. She was in the room she and Amelia had chosen in the guest quarter. Dominic lay back on one of the other beds attempting to appear relaxed. He might have pulled it off, had he not been tapping his foot and frowning.

The tapping stopped and he swung his legs over the edge of the bed. Leaning towards her, he frowned again. 'Are you ready to give up that sword now? No one has been able to get it out of your hands since you left the cave.'

Sheepishly, Aliah thought, *it is just a sword, why do I not want to let it go?* 'I have a feeling it does not like being touched by anyone but me,' she told Dominic, feeling rather foolish. 'Although for the life of me I do not know how I know that.'

'Odd.' Dominic responded. 'Swords do not normally care who holds them, although I have always suspected they prefer to be wielded by someone with at least a little skill.'

'It is odd,' Aliah admitted. 'Then again, it is a god given artefact, so I am not sure whether this is normal or not. What I am sure of is that I cannot carry it with me always. It will not be allowed at state functions.'

Dominic's frown deepened. 'Perhaps it is a touch thing. I want to try something.' He took the rug folded at the end of the bed he sat on, then opened it up, and placed it over the sword. Now able to pick it up, he lay the sword on the end of his bed.

'Mmm, interesting. Maybe it is a built-in defence against someone else using it,' he mused. 'We should see if the people here have a sheath we can purchase for it.'

TRIALS

Aliah smiled wanly. 'You are a very useful person to have around.' She tried to sit up and could not. Collapsing back on the pillows she groaned in frustration.

'You need to rest. You were unconscious and pretty beat up when Seamus brought you back.' Dominic sat on the edge of the bed.

'Seamus brought me back?' Aliah puzzled. 'Brought me back from where?'

Dominic's face showed more worry, if that were even possible. 'What is the last thing you remember?'

Aliah screwed up her face, trying to concentrate. Then it all came back to her. 'I failed the test. I remember getting to the door just as it closed.' She frowned. 'But if I failed, how do I still have the sword? How am I here, and not stuck in the cave?'

Dominic shrugged. 'I am not sure of the details, but Seamus would not accept that you had not come out. I followed him back into the cave. We were standing there, and he disappeared for the blink of an eye, then reappeared with you in his arms. He mumbled something about damn gods and extra tests as we were walking out. That is all I know, although I suspect he went and had a strong word with someone about their rules. Was it tough?'

'Harrowing, and one day I may tell you all about it. But not today.' She closed her eyes, even talking tired her.

'So? We all want to know. Are you the warrior? Caraig said the sword was proof you were.' Dominic's voice came from a great distance, and she opened her eyes.

'Yes, I am the warrior. Well, I think I still am, even though I got caught behind the door.' Aliah closed her eyes again. 'What I would not give for a nice hot bath to soak my aching muscles.'

'That has been arranged. There is a girl outside who can help you.'

Grateful Dominic had anticipated her needs, she was about to thank him when, *wait, a girl is outside?* 'I would prefer Amelia helped me. If she would not mind, and some food would be good. I am sure I will feel better soon.'

'Ah, Amelia is not here.' Dominic would not meet her eyes. Something was up.

'Who is here?' Aliah demanded.

'You and me.' Dominic seemed to find some spot on the blanket very interesting.

She raised an eyebrow. 'And the others are...?'

'In a Council Chamber,' Dominic said the words very quickly, almost as if he thought she would not hear them if he spoke fast.

Questions swirled through her mind. She chose one. 'Daniel went and left you here? That sounds unlikely.'

'Daniel was here until a candle-mark ago, when he was called away to help Liam organise meeting up with the muster of Malorian warriors.'

'Oh. And the others did not think to wait for me before they began their discussions?' Aliah's voice hardened.

'Yes, they did. Well, at least Seamus did. He kept saying something about the hand and the arm. Sounded bizarre to me, but it seemed important to him.

'He insisted on staying here with you, but you were sleeping so soundly, he decided it was better to go and make sure they did not set any plans in stone until you were awake.'

Dominic repeating the words the serpent had used

was comforting in an odd sort of way. 'Right,' she said, forcing her body upright. 'I need a bath, a change of clothes, and some food. Oh, and some of that caffe.' And with that, she shuffled out of the room with as much dignity as her aching body would allow.

Stopping at the door, she looked down at her arms. The scratches from the bats were gone. And, although her body ached, her leg muscle did not seem to be strained. She was in much better shape than she should have been after her trial. Maybe it was not a case of the sword not wanting to be touched by others, maybe it needed to touch her so it could heal her wounds. Thinking of ways she might be able to test her theory, she went to bathe.

A candle-mark later Aliah entered the Council Chamber on Dominic's arm. The warm soak and food helped, but she had pushed her body to the limit. There was no doubt she would have been better off staying in bed. When the ruckus from the Council Chamber reached her ears, she wished she had done just that.

It was more like a bun fight in a bakery than a council meeting. The table had somehow been removed, and the room was packed full of people, some of whom Aliah had never seen before. Not much planning could be done when everyone was talking at once. She spotted Seamus sitting in the corner to the left, arms resting on his legs and looking at an odd shaped piece of wood. *Not wood, a wand.* She and Dominic sidled over to him and took two other chairs leaning against the wall.

'We did it,' she whispered to Seamus, a grin plastered all over her face. He smiled wearily.

'I know. I cannot believe it. They gave me this.' He showed her the wand. 'It might not look like much, but I can feel the power in it.'

'I have a sword. But of course you have seen it. It also has some strange powers. I am not sure how to use it yet, but I think I am supposed to learn.' She frowned as voices rose in the chamber. 'What is going on here? I take it this is not a celebration of our being the ones to fulfil a great prophecy?'

'No, it is nothing like that. In fact, that seems to have been forgotten. They have been yelling and arguing for two full candle-marks.' Seamus grimaced as someone else shouted.

'About anything important?'

'Well… it seems Amelia has had what they call a "true seeing" to do with our great prophecy.'

'When did this happen?' Aliah frowned.

'From what I can tell, while we were returning to our rooms after our trials.'

'Why has it caused such a furore? I mean, we knew she could sense things. We knew there was a prophecy. Another seeing about the prophecy should not have been such a big deal.' Aliah yawned and shifted in her seat. She really would rather be back in bed.

'Do you want everything from start to finish?' Seamus sighed. Aliah raised a questioning eyebrow, and Dominic nodded.

'Just the summary version please,' Aliah spoke for them both, stifling yet another yawn.

TRIALS

'Thank goodness. It started with Daniel calling everyone together to let them know how unhappy he was your life had been placed in jeopardy. As you can imagine, that was not well received. The meeting was interrupted by Eon, who is Caraig's trainee or something, blabbering about Amelia. Apparently she had fainted and they could not rouse her, and Caraig needed to come and hear what she was saying.

'We had a bit of a break while Caraig went to see Amelia. Amelia and Walter came back with Caraig, who promptly declared to all that Amelia had a true seeing, and they have been arguing and debating like this ever since.'

'Do you know what they are actually yelling about?' Dominic asked.

Shrugging, Seamus answered, 'No one thing, from what I can make out. Eon is apparently trying to gather support for his point of view that Amelia did *not* have a true seeing at all. Caraig wants Amelia to stay here as he says he finally has a successor. He insists they need to restudy the prophecy in light of Amelia's seeing. Daniel wants us to leave as soon as possible so we can get back to the fighting that will now be happening. That military looking man over there wants Daniel to stay so he can help organise the fighting men from Maloria. I do not know what Liam is doing. He has had his head down, talking to that man dressed like a protector the whole time, and they have not been loud enough for me to hear. I think that is about all of it.'

'Wow,' was all Aliah could think to say. 'So you have not been a part of any of this?'

'I am pretty sure none of this has anything to do with

what we are supposed to do next, although much of it is important in the grand scheme of things.'

Aliah nodded. 'I feel the same. I am sure you and I are meant to head back to the coast and take part in defending against the invasion.'

It was Seamus' turn to nod. 'There is nothing further we can do here, and they might need what little help we can give them against Carsten.'

'And I will be accompanying you,' Dominic inserted.

'I think that is right too,' Seamus confirmed.

'Not that I need your permission, wizard boy.' Dominic smiled but his voice was serious, making a point to Seamus.

'No, I did not mean it like that.' Seamus frowned, and he paused, as if trying to find the right words. 'In the cave, I sort of came into my powers, or more like... I now understand what they are and how they work a little better. As part of that, I realised the feelings I get—the notion something is right or wrong—is a form of foresight. It has been stronger this afternoon since my trial, but maybe I am just paying more attention to it.

'As I have been sitting here, I have come to the realisation we are not all meant to go on to battle the Carstenites together. I believe it may be because the battle we need to face is still a way off.

'I think to fight that battle, we all have to prepare in different ways. But you and I must stick together no matter what. We are the hand...'

'...and the arm,' Aliah finished for him, not really feeling much like a unit as her stomach sank in recognition of the changes that had occurred between them. With Seamus having foresight, he would be best to take the lead. If he could foretell the right thing to do all the time, she was really only the hired muscle. She needed to concentrate on her role as warrior, even if only to prove to herself she really was the warrior in spite of Seamus having to save her.

Seamus smiled. 'Some of our individual trials must have had cross-overs, we should compare notes. In the meantime, I feel Dominic must come with us. I think he is the man who is not what he seems. I also have to find a wolf to come with us too.'

'A wolf? Are you sure?'

As she spoke, Aliah saw Emer stiffen on the other side of Seamus. She hesitated, frowned, then leaned down.

'Apologies, I could not help but overhear your conversation.'

Laughing, Aliah said, 'This is not the place for private discussions and we were not talking quietly. If you know something that might help us, we would be happy to hear it.'

Emer inclined her head. 'I have an idea about how to find your wolf. Here is not the place, but if you come with me after this meeting is over I will show you.'

Seamus was clearly relieved. 'Great, I really had no idea where to start looking, and I did not want to delay our departure trying to find a needle in a haystack.'

'So are we ready to contribute then? I think this one is yours to take the lead. I do not have the strength or the will to take part in this today,' Aliah spoke to Seamus.

'I guess so, although I am not sure what to say. I will have to trust this new foresight I have, I guess. Well, here goes.' He stood and offered Aliah his arm so they could make a united front. Pleased by the gesture, not just because they would appear as a team, but also because she could barely stand by herself, Aliah took her position beside Seamus. Dominic stood behind her, and Emer fell in behind Seamus. Something about this group had Aliah feeling she could face anything.

As all eyes turned to them, Aliah swore she witnessed the very moment Seamus got his foresight. He stood taller and radiated confidence.

'Aliah and I have had a long day and we need to get some sleep. Before we leave, we wanted to let you know what we will be doing next.'

Aliah could see the others stood poised mid-debate. Walter held out his hand and stepped forward. 'But we have not agreed to a course of action yet, so how can you know what you will be doing next?'

Seamus glanced around the room, ensuring he had everyone's attention before he spoke. 'Aliah, Dominic, and I are leaving tomorrow. That is not up for debate. The only thing that might delay us is the fact we need to find the wolf we are to travel with. Emer thinks we can sort that out tonight and, if that is the case, we will be heading back to the coast.'

Caraig's face froze and he looked towards Emer. Emer was staring back, almost like they were communicating, and Caraig frowned. Emer turned away and Caraig's attention returned to the meeting. *I wonder what that was about?* She had no time to think it through because Walter spoke, and she turned her attention back to the discussion taking place. Walter seemed to be telling Seamus they would need to wait because there were other things that needed to be agreed before they could all leave.

'No, Walter. If any of you had asked, we would have told you that Aliah and I know what we must do, and standing here, I came to realise what you all must do. Amelia, you need to stay here with Caraig for however long it takes to interpret your seeing. You are not needed to fight the invasion, but what you find out now will help us with resolving a bigger problem.'

Before anyone could argue this, Seamus plowed on. 'Walter, of course you must stay with her because it will require your combined knowledge, along with Caraig, to interpret the seeing in a timely manner.'

Aliah could see Caraig nodding, but Eon stood behind him, scowling and looking daggers at Amelia. *He is not happy about something. I must remember to warn Amelia and Walter to watch out for him.*

'Daniel, Dominic is well able to escort us back, your job is to ride out with the Sanctuary forces tonight. You are needed in battle.'

Liam stepped forward. 'Yes, Liam you are to go with him. You know the coast better than anyone else here and that knowledge will be invaluable in the battle we face.'

'Thank you, Seamus. I have been training in a new form of fighting with Dirk here, and I would like the opportunity to continue, and learn what he has to teach.'

'I am sure it has nothing at all to do with Dirk's daughter,' Emer whispered under her breath.

Seamus did not falter, in spite of his smile at Emer's observation. 'Liam, I sense your lot in life is about to change. I have a feeling you will be representing Hand's interests in the Sanctuary for many years to come, should we be successful in repelling the threat that heads towards us.' Liam's grin nearly split his face.

'Now, if you will excuse us.' Seamus made to leave, but Walter's voice stopped him.

'Seamus, how am I to train you for the coming battle if I am to remain with Amelia? I cannot just abandon you, no matter how much I personally want to stay.'

'Walter, we have not had much success with training to date, and a couple more days would not make much difference.' Seamus smiled. 'During my trial I found out why I have had such a problem learning to manage my powers with traditional methods. My gifts are unique, and I think we are safe to say if the best teacher in the human realm could not teach me, then no human could. I will be taught to control and channel my powers by new tutors, who understand how I must use them.'

Walter went to say something else, but Amelia placed her hand on his arm. 'It is as he said, Walter. His powers are god given, and he must be trained by the gods to use them.'

'You are not abandoning us, Walter, you will merely be helping in a different way,' Aliah reassured him. He relaxed a little, but the frown between his brow told Aliah his duty of care towards Seamus had him warring internally.

'Walter, we are the Wizard and Warrior. No one else can carry our burdens, no one else can do what we can do—or what we will be needed to do—to save Aria. You have got us this far, but now you need to let us go and concentrate on what your role is to be in the final battle. You will know when it is time to follow us.' Seamus softened his words with a smile.

As they made to leave, Daniel grasped Dominic's arm.

'We need to talk.' Aliah inclined her head in agreement and the two men left the room to find somewhere quiet. Seamus watched Emer, who had been detained by her father, as she looked regretfully back at him. Aliah guessed that whatever she had to show him would have to wait until tomorrow.

As they slowly walked through the corridors, Aliah kept her arm through Seamus', partially because she was tired, but also because after the day's events she needed to know he was still there with her.

'Thank you for coming back for me,' she said as she leaned her head on his arm.

'There was not any chance I was going to do this alone.' Seamus laughed.

'Was it another test?' she asked. 'I nearly had my foot through the door as the last bell rang. I could not believe they were going to fail me for the sake of a footstep.'

Seamus stopped walking and turned to her. 'You had passed. I was still being tested. They wanted to test my resolve to work with you.'

'And you passed?' she asked, suddenly worried that he still did not trust her fully after she had deserted him in Sunnydale.

'We are both here, are we not?' Seamus turned and they carried on walking. As she leaned into Seamus for support, Aliah suddenly had a new spring in her step. They were here together, and that was what mattered most.

By the time they arrived back at the guest commune, Aliah was leaning more heavily on Seamus for support. Even so, she had insisted they share the details of their trials with each other to see if they could learn anything new by comparing their experiences.

Sitting down, they poured some caffe from the pot that had been left for them. Dominic arrived soon after. Seeing them deep in discussion, he yawned and retired to bed, tactfully giving them some privacy. After having shared their stories, Seamus thought Aliah's experience had been much tougher than his, and his guilt at the ease with which he had obtained his wand rose. The concerns nagging at the back of his mind all evening surfaced.

He had not yet told Aliah his power could be removed at any time if the gods judged he was not using them correctly. He had to force out the confession. The uncertainty of not knowing what would cause this to happen, made him feel the gods had not really endorsed him as the wizard, and he was going to be continuously on trial. Aliah was quiet for a moment after he spoke, so quiet he wondered if she had actually fallen asleep. Continuing to look into her cup of caffe, she finally responded.

'I believe you are looking at this the wrong way. Firstly, let me say, you must be the wizard. I do not believe they would have given you your wand if they had not thought you were, or that you were capable of fulfilling your destiny. In the same way, I believe I am the warrior even though I did not make it through the door before it closed. They would not have given me the sword if they did not believe in me. It is now up to us to live up to their faith in us.

TRIALS

'As far as your test being easier, well it is easy to design a test for strength, endurance, and ability to fight in unusual situations. It is probably not very easy to design a test to show how someone will deal with abilities beyond those any human before them has had. They showed you had a good heart, and you would not kill just because your family were threatened. Maybe all they needed to know was you could, and would, limit the power you use.'

Feeling a little more confident, he decided to risk telling Aliah about his first test, when the fire got out of control, and his concerns about being able to access something that could so easily kill others. He suspected this was the reason the gods decided to continue his trial. Aliah was silent for a moment, twirling her plait as she often did when she was thinking.

'I really do not know any more than you Seamus. They gave you the wand so they must trust you. Perhaps it is a warning for you to be careful with your magic, and to take care in your lessons.'

Seamus sighed inwardly. It was not that he had not already said that to himself, but more that it was good to hear it come from someone else. Aliah looked up from her caffe and her tired blue eyes captured his gaze.

'You *are* the wizard, and I believe in your ability to control your powers and fight the rogue god with me.'

'Thank you,' was all Seamus could think to say in response, but it seemed inadequate recompense for the comfort her words brought to him. Briefly, he wondered if the gods saying Aliah was the arm to his hand described their mental bond, rather than something physical. Unable to think of any words to explain his gratitude to

Aliah, he changed the subject and asked about the battle focus she got when she held her sword.

Aliah attempted to describe it for him, and he concluded it worked in a very similar way to his foresight. Together, these tools would give them an immense advantage in the upcoming, if only they could learn to use them effectively in time.

As he mused, he noticed Aliah's head dropping, although she strongly denied needing sleep when he suggested they go to bed. So he helped her out by admitting he was quite weary himself, and if they wanted to start their return journey tomorrow, he would need a good night's sleep.

Once in his room, he found he was exhausted. Not long after lying down, he fell into a deep sleep. He half-woke at a light touch on his shoulder. Thinking it was Liam annoying him before going to bed, he shoved the hand off and told him grumpily to leave him alone.

'Will you sleep through the upcoming battle?' A voice vibrated through his entire body. He sat bolt upright to see one of the seven gods in his room. The female god stood before him, dressed as a Malorian protector.

'Come, we need to train.' She turned, expecting him to follow her. Liam was asleep in the bed beside him, but he did not even stir. 'None will see us except those who know how to look.'

What does that mean? Seamus mused as he followed the goddess out to the amphitheatre at the back of Sanctuary, which was now bathed in moonlight.

'We have seen that you already know how to use fire. I am here to begin your education on the other elements; how to control each one, and how to use them together to greater effect. In each area, you will never make a great wizard, but your ability to use all elements together will make you strong in a way no other wizard has been before you. We will start slowly, beginning with air.'

Seamus found the word "slowly" to be an understatement. The goddess would explain once, then expected him to follow exactly what she said without any mistakes. Every time he could not do what she said, he worried the goddess would strip his powers from him. She did nothing of the kind, however, and he spent the rest of the night learning how to master air and land, and then how to mix these elements along with fire defensively. He learnt to use the elements with a light touch, and with full force. Then, when he could barely stand, the goddess led him back to his room.

Before she left him, he found the courage to ask her the question that had been on his mind the entire lesson.

'Wait, please. I would like to know, if you can remove my power if I displease you, does that mean you do not trust me to be your Warrior?'

If a goddess could be said to smile, this one did just that. 'Seamus, you are our wizard. You have our wand and our support, but you need to understand no mortal has ever held the power you will when you are fully trained. We do not know how that power will affect someone even as pure hearted as you, so we need to have the ability to remove that power if it corrupts you, or it places the world in danger.

'You will make mistakes while you are learning, that is only to be expected, but it is the thoughts behind your decisions that will tell us whether or not the power is too much for you. Sleep now, you will need all your strength in the coming days.'

The goddess led him to his bed, touched his forehead, and Seamus was asleep before he even lay down.

12
SURPRISES

Seamus awoke when Liam began moving about their room. 'Sorry Seamus, it is early, go back to sleep.'

'Where are you going?' Seamus asked, feeling strangely awake and invigorated in spite of his nocturnal activities.

'I am going to early training,' Liam said into his shirt as he pulled it over his head.

'They start training this early? Wow, the soldiers here are really dedicated.' A blush crept up his cousin's neck. 'Oh, special lessons. Perhaps with a girl?' He laughed, and received the pillow from Liam's bed in his face as payment.

Liam left, and he had no sooner shut the door than it opened again admitting Walter, his face a picture of worry and concern.

'It is funny, Walter, but I do not need my newly discovered foresight to know what you have come to say. It is written all over your face.' Seamus sat forward, hugging his knees.

'And just what is it I am going to say?' Walter asked dourly.

'That you cannot stay here with Amelia because your duty is to teach me all you know.'

Walter's eyes widened in surprise. 'Well, yes, I was going to say something along those lines.'

It took all of Seamus' control not to sigh, instead he said, 'Even if I did not know that Amelia will need you here with her more than we will need you with us, I still would not ask you to come along just to train me.'

As he spoke, Seamus picked up his wand from beside his pillow, pointed it at the chair, moving it from the wall to behind Walter. Then he concentrated really hard, envisioning Walter seated in the chair. Walter eventually sat down, a stunned look on his face. It would have been funny if Seamus had not been making an important point. For a wizard to make a person do something even as small as sitting, took a lot of power, and a lot of training. Yesterday Seamus had barely been able to move an object, let alone a person.

'I spent last night training with a goddess. She began teaching me how to use my powers,' Seamus explained. Then he continued to tell Walter what he had learnt during his training and how his powers worked by using thoughts alone, rather than the traditional way where wizards manipulated the elements using spells and gestures. By the time he was dressed and they were sitting down to breakfast, Seamus had managed to convince Walter his training was best left to those who had given him his gifts.

Walter was thoughtful as they served themselves food, then he shook his head. 'When I first met you, you were leaking magic all over the place. You were just like every other untrained wizard. Then, when I taught you to control your powers and I could no longer feel them, I thought to myself you were going to be very strong. I did not question anything when one of the strongest wizards could not sense your power. Even then, it must have been changing, becoming something else.

'When you could not learn to control your magic, I assumed it was because you were starting a little later than others. It is all so obvious when I think back.' Walter finished musing and began eating his food.

It was good to see Walter was no longer worried about abandoning him, and was at ease with his role supporting Amelia. Now Seamus could leave the older man behind, without feeling any guilt. Turning his attention to his breakfast, Emer walked in though the door behind Walter before he could manage to drink a mouthful of his caffe. She inclined her head, indicating he should come outside with her. Reluctantly, he asked Walter to excuse him, and leaving his meal behind, followed the Malorain outside.

Emer kept walking until she came to the edge of the forest, where she turned to make sure Seamus was still behind her. She disappeared into the shade of the trees followed by Seamus, who suddenly stopped short. Not only had he lost sight of Emer, but sitting there in front of him was a grey she-wolf, calmly licking her paws. He did not know what he had expected Emer to show him, but it certainly was not this. Something was tugging at the back of his mind, but he could not grasp it.

'Emer,' he called. 'This is not funny. Where are you?' The wolf appeared to shimmer and there, standing in its place, was Emer.

With everything that had gone on in the last couple of days, Seamus had thought himself beyond the ability to be surprised, but he was wrong. Emer shimmered again, and there was an eagle flying back towards the dwellings. Seamus could do nothing but trail after her, all the while wondering just how much more his poor, tired brain could take.

Although there was much he still had to do to save Aria, and potentially the world, a large part of him wished he could slink off somewhere quiet and have some time to himself. Some time to think about what he actually wanted to do with this life. Shrugging, he pushed those thoughts away, he had other things he needed to concentrate on now.

He found Emer alone in the guest commune, sitting in the seat Walter had vacated. Seamus sat back down with his breakfast in front of him. It had not even had time to get cold.

Emer helped herself to breakfast rolls and caffe. 'I have organised horses for you, Aliah, Dominic, and myself. We can leave after breakfast, if you think you can be ready.'

TRIALS

Seamus was still too stunned to speak, but the situation called for him to say something. 'You changed into a wolf.' It was the best he could manage.

Emer's deep brown eyes sparkled with laughter. 'Yes. And an eagle.'

Is it just coincidence I saw an eagle on Hand? Seamus wondered, but instead of voicing that thought, he came out with, 'How?' He was doing himself proud this morning.

'It is a unique form of magic,' Emer told him around mouthfuls of breakfast. 'Shape shifting is one of the oldest magics, but there is normally only one or two born each generation who have the gift. Most shape shifters can change to one other form, two is very rare.'

'I have so many questions. I want to know what it feels like? Do you think like the animal you turn into? How long can you stay changed for? What happens if you do not turn back?' He paused. 'But really what I want to know is... what makes you think you are the wolf that is supposed to come with us?'

'You mean apart from the obvious?' Emer raised an eyebrow in enquiry, and Seamus had the grace to blush.

'Yes. Apart from that.'

Emer put down her cup of caffe. 'Two things. One is the wolf was the first form I took, and still my preferred form. And two, my father had a true seeing when I was born. He told me the day would come when the wolf would be called to action in defence of Maloria. I have discussed this with him, and we both agree it must be that time.'

Seamus sat back, drinking his caffe and staring at Emer. Then it dawned on him. 'Emer, did you change into wolf form when you were on Hand?'

A smiled tugged at the edge of the girl's mouth. 'I may have.'

'And you came out riding with my brother and me?'

'Wolf form is the best way to move through a forest. I can cover great distances more easily.' She did not really answer his question, but Seamus was convinced she was the wolf he had seen.

He slowly shook his head. He still could not get over the fact this girl in front of him could become a wolf and a bird. There was little doubt she was the wolf he was told should travel with them, but how could he ask her to join their battle when her land was not yet under threat?

'Shall I break it to the others I am joining you, or would you like to do it?' she asked, and Seamus almost laughed out loud. She was so confident it was funny and maddening at the same time.

'You could at least pretend I had a say in this,' he grumbled, and it was Emer's turn to laugh.

'I want to come so much I do not want you to even consider the possibility I might not be your wolf,' she admitted, staring down into her caffe so she would not have to meet Seamus' eyes.

'But why do you want to come so much? You will be leaving your home and your family. Sanctuary is not even threatened, and we may not survive the upcoming battle, let alone the fight with the god.' Seamus could not understand her eagerness to leave her loved ones behind.

'It is hard to explain.' Emer's brow knitted together a little, nearly, but not quite, frowning. 'And it does not sound very noble. Since my father found I was destined for great things, I have not been allowed to do anything apart from training, least I not be ready when I am needed. I was surprised my father even let me become a protector until I realised he thought I would need military training if I was to meet my destiny.

'Then he let me escort you all here. That was the first time in my life I had been allowed to leave the Sanctuary. I hoped he was finally giving me some freedom, then I found I was likely destined to be a part of your group, which was the only reason he let me go.

'If this is not my time, then I will have to remain here doing nothing. I want this to be what I was born for so much, I cannot bear to think you might all leave without me.'

Emer's face was earnest, and he realised he had known for some time that Emer must be a part of their group. She must be the other person in the prophecy who was not what they seemed. Another piece of the puzzle had been found. Part of him wanted to leave her hanging for a while, but he could not do it.

'I think you are meant to come with us,' he admitted to her. 'I will tell the others you are joining us, but I will leave it up to you how you tell them about your unique abilities.'

Emer beamed. 'I will make sure the horses and supplies are ready, and meet you out front in two candle-marks.'

After Emer disappeared, Seamus walked towards the door of Dominic and Daniels' room. He could hear arguing from within. Deciding to forego normal courtesies, he opened the door to find the two older boys arguing over who was meant to be Aliah's guard and had the right to return to Hand with her.

Seamus sighed. 'I thought we dealt with this yesterday, boys.' They turned as one to the sound of his voice. 'If it were not enough that I know it is meant to be Dominic who comes with us, he is also mentioned in the prophecy. *Old and new blood will combine, With the two who are not what they seem…* Dominic is a spy and is clearly one of those who is not what he seems. I do not think you can say the same about yourself, Daniel?'

It was too much to ask they take his word for it, they had to battle it out themselves. Dominic smirked, clearly happy to have Seamus on his side. Daniel launched into the argument that his orders had come from the king himself, and no mere duke's son could alter them. Aliah was his responsibility, and he had better fighting skills with which to protect her should anything happen. Clearly he was the better guard, because it was what he had trained for. Dominic countered Aliah was more than able to fight off any direct attack, she was the warrior after all, and what she really needed were skills to compliment her own, such as his.

'What good is being able to gather information going to be in a fight?' Daniel argued.

'I did not mean that skill, although gathering information is always useful,' Dominic answered. 'I meant *this* skill.'

Seamus thought he could no longer be shocked, but this day was intent on proving otherwise. Dominic moved over towards the wall and then seemed to simply melt into it until he disappeared. Both he and Daniel stood there, mouths hanging open. They remained open even when Dominic re-emerged.

TRIALS

'Umm... Er... Well... I guess that is a useful skill...' Daniel started, then seemed to simply run out of words.

'What... How...' Seamus added to the conversation, wondering to himself what use foresight was if he was going to continue being surprised like this. It struck him that his foresight would not be able to tell him everything.

'I do not know exactly what, except that it is some form of magic. How? I concentrate on not wanting you to see me and blend into the background.' Dominic smiled sheepishly. 'I discovered it one day when I was in a certain duke's library and he entered with another man. I did not want to be found so I started thinking, "please do not see me, please let me blend into the background". I was sure I would be caught, but they came in, had their meeting, and left without even knowing I was there. Later, I used a mirror and trained myself to blend in with my surroundings at will. It has come in most useful in my line of work.'

'So does that make you a wizard?' Daniel asked.

'I am not sure,' Dominic admitted. 'No wizard has ever suggested they could sense magic in me, and none has ever noticed when I have been hiding in a room. Yet this is not something everyone can do.'

A thought occurred to Seamus. 'The other night when I left you all to meet my father in the library, I thought I heard someone on the stairs behind me—was that you?'

Dominic had the grace to look embarrassed. 'Umm... er... yes. Aliah asked me to follow you to see where you were heading...'

'...and that was how she knew where the library was.' Seamus finished for him. 'And when I nearly sat on you in the armchair by the fire...'

Dominic laughed. 'Sometimes blending in is useful to play jokes on people.'

'Well, I am sure it comes in more useful when you are spying, although it is kind of creepy to watch.'

'It is useful when looking after your friends as well,' Dominic interrupted. 'I followed you and Aliah to the Council Chambers the other night. I spent the night outside your rooms, and I escorted each of you to your trial.'

Seamus' eyes widened in amazement. 'I thought there was someone there, but I could not see anything.'

'It was a close thing,' Dominic admitted. 'When you came through the doorway to check, you nearly stood on my foot.'

'Really?' Seamus shook his head in wonderment, but then focused on the issue at hand. 'All this is irrelevant. Dominic comes because he is part of the prophecy, Daniel stays with Liam to marshal the Malorain forces. If you need more reason than that, Dominic is perfectly able to do as good a job as you protecting Aliah, Daniel, but I would not feel safe with him running a battle strategy for the Marlorians.'

The two looked at him with a new respect. 'Have you been taking lessons in statesmanship from Aliah?' Daniel asked smiling. 'I concede. I cannot fight your logic, and I certainly would not let Dominic loose on the battlefield.'

Pleased to have settled that long running argument, a sudden thought stopped Seamus from leaving. 'Daniel, I thought you were to ride out with the Sanctuary forces last night?'

'Do not panic. The main force left as planned. A few

of the protectors who are coming did not get back to Sanctuary until last night. They rested and will head out today to catch the others up. I can leave with them.'

'Oh, all right then. We leave in two candle-marks,' Seamus informed Dominic.

'What about the wolf?' Dominic asked before Seamus could leave the room.

'I have found her, and she is the other who is not what she seems,' Seamus told him. 'Emer will be leaving with us.'

'She is quite fierce, but I would hardly describe her as a wolf,' Dominic joked.

'I am betting you will change your mind on that,' Seamus said as he left the room.

Seamus, Aliah, and Dominic walked out of the guest commune and into the clearing in front of the Sanctuary to find Walter, Amelia, and Caraig waiting to send them off. Standing nearby, Emer had four horses saddled and ready with supply bags. When she saw them emerge from the doorway, she walked over and asked Dominic and Aliah to please come with her. They looked at Seamus, who smiled and confirmed they had time. The others followed Emer into the woods, and Seamus turned to Amelia and Walter, who were deep in discussion with Caraig.

'I am happy to stay for a while,' Amelia said to Caraig. 'To look into my seeing and what it means. I believe I am meant to do that, but I cannot see how you think all of this means I am your successor.'

'You are the first seer in your generation to have a true seeing. I have had many apprentices, but none have done what you did,' Caraig responded. 'You are my best and last hope for someone to follow me.'

'It might be unusual to have a true seeing, but that does not make me a great seer.' Amelia stood her ground, looking to Walter for support.

Walter seemed reluctant to say anything until Amelia forced his hand and asked directly for his opinion.

'Well, I do not see that what Caraig suggests will hurt. If you underwent a trial, you would at least know one way or another.'

'I thought trials took place on a full moon?' Seamus interrupted. 'Does that mean Amelia would have to stay here until then?'

'I am not staying here a full moon turn.' Amelia was adamant.

Caraig held up his hand to forestall any further protests. 'In special cases we can petition the gods to hold a trial before the next full moon. If they agree then they will open a doorway to their realm.'

Amelia did not look pleased. 'And what if I did undertake this trial? What if it turned out I was a great seer. Would I then be able to go and help fight the god?'

Caraig answered. 'Of course you could, if that is what you are called by the gods to do.'

'Called by the gods? I am afraid I do not have much time for all that rubbish,' Amelia answered. 'Though, if a great seer does not need to remain in Sanctuary, I might consider undertaking the trial.' She frowned as she pondered this new information.

TRIALS

Seamus chuckled at an image of Amelia facing the gods; he was not sure who would come off worse.

Aliah and Dominic emerged from the edge of the forest, stunned looks on their faces, bringing Seamus back to reality. Emer followed a few paces behind. Was she actually grinning? As they got closer, Dominic said to Seamus, 'Makes my trick look kind of small, does it not?'

'Your trick?' Aliah asked. 'You mean there is more? I am not sure I can take any more surprises.' Aliah appeared overwhelmed, and Seamus knew exactly how she felt.

'One for later, fair princess,' Dominic said annoyingly, and Aliah gave him her most cutting look.

They began stowing their travel packs on their horses when they heard a flurry behind them. Eon stormed out of the main entrance, his face beetroot red and screwed up in anger. He had barely left the doorway when he began yelling,

'How could you? A stranger to be the new Great Seer. After all the work I have put in. After all I have done for you.' He rushed at Caraig and Seamus notice a knife in his hand. Before he could raise it to strike, Seamus used air to bind the apprentice in place, arms pinned firmly at his sides.

Eon's face turned an even darker red and he opened his mouth to speak again. Tired of his tirade, Seamus used air to fill his mouth as a sort of gag. Satisfied with his work, he went back to packing his horse, missing the look of shock that passed between Aliah and Dominic.

'Eon, I am sorry you had to hear this from someone else. I did try to find you so we could talk about it, but you were not in any of your usual haunts, and no one had seen you. I have always been honest with you, many have the minor gift of foresight as you do, but only those with the potential to be a great seer have a true seeing. You have not had such a vision, and you may never have one. Amelia has had a true seeing and has agreed to undergo the trial to find out if she is indeed worthy to become my successor.'

'I agreed to think about it,' Amelia interjected.

Caraig carried on as if Amelia had not spoken. 'It is time you thought about what you want your future to be.'

'Argh. Ahhh.' Eon struggled to speak.

'Seamus, if you would please let him speak?' Caraig asked, and Seamus released the air-gag.

'But she is an *outlander!* And she is a *woman*. She is not worthy,' Eon spluttered.

Caraig sighed. 'There is nothing to say the Great Seer must be Malorian, Eon, or that it cannot be a woman. And you know as well as I do the trial will decide whether or not she is worthy.'

'I will never accept her as Seer,' Eon spat out. 'I would kill her before I would see her take my place.' He struggled against the bonds that held him.

By this time two protectors emerged to take Eon back inside. Seamus loosened the bonds enough so the apprentice could walk, and he warned the protectors the magic constraining Eon would be totally gone by the time they were inside the Sanctuary. Caraig followed after them, turning to wish them a safe journey and good luck, assuring them Eon would be managed by the elders and Amelia would be safe.

TRIALS

'I wish we could come with you.' Amelia hugged both Seamus and Aliah. 'Do not let any harm come to them,' she warned Dominic. 'Or you will have me to deal with, young man.'

'Amelia, we are the Wizard and Warrior, we can take care of ourselves.' Aliah laughed.

'Have you changed that much since you tried to set off up the length of the country in no more than the clothes you stood in?'

Aliah blushed, remembering how Amelia had to provide provisions for her journey from Port Marden to Bannock.

'Come, Amelia, we have done what we can to prepare them. It is time to let them follow their own path.' Walter put his arm around Amelia's shoulders. 'I wish you luck, and will pray to the goddess we will see you again soon.'

Realising Amelia and Walters' relationship may be more than friendship, Seamus was pleased for his aunt. He hoped he and Aliah could ensure Amelia and Walter had time to find out what it was they felt for each other.

'Thank you, Walter, for all you have done. You have prepared me well for what I must face.' Tears stung Seamus' eyes at the thought of leaving his mentor. He shook them away and grasped the older man's hand. 'I could not have done this without you.'

'Oh my, what a thing to say.' Walter shook his head as if shaking off the compliment. 'You were already a fine young man, I only showed you a few things to keep your magic in check.'

'You did more than that,' Seamus said. 'You taught me to live with my magic. For someone from Hand, that is a great gift.'

Walter shuffled his feet in embarrassment, and Amelia saved his dignity by pulling Seamus into another hug. 'Look after yourself, and we will soon see you in Port Marden.'

Holding her tightly, he whispered in her ear, 'Do not let them force you into anything you do not want to do.'

'As if they could.' Amelia laughed, letting him go.

Farewells done, they turned their horses and headed for the coast, but were stopped in their tracks by a shout. They turned to see Liam and Daniel running out towards them.

'Did you think you were leaving without saying goodbye to us?' Liam panted as he caught up with them at the edge of the forest.

'With you having to catch up with the Sanctuary forces who left last night, we did not think you would still be here,' Aliah answered for them all.

Liam handed Seamus a letter. 'Please give this to the duke. It explains what I am doing here and why I am not following his orders.'

'You know I would have explained it to him, and he would understand,' Seamus said.

'I do, but things must be done properly.' Liam tapped Seamus on the leg. 'See you soon, cousin. We will have your back, never fear.'

Seamus clutched Liam's arm. 'I know you will. Be careful.'

'And these are for you,' Daniel said to Aliah as he handed her some documents. 'To take for your father or whoever is in charge when you reach Port Marden. They contain details of how the Sanctuary forces will offer support in the upcoming battle. Well, what we have managed to agree to so far. We have based them on details we were discussing in Hand. Safe travels, and try to keep out of trouble. *And* try not to give Dominic too hard a time. He really is only doing his job, you know.'

Aliah hugged Daniel. Seamus could see it was as hard for her to leave him behind as it was for him to stay, even though both agreed it was the right thing to do.

Aliah let go, and Daniel stood back. 'Caraig assures us all you need to do is make sure the battle is not lost before they identify the god we are to fight, and how to defeat him.'

'Well, if that is all, I am not sure what we are all so worried about.' Dominic laughed as Aliah remounted, and he turned his horse around.

'Hold on,' Seamus stopped them. 'Daniel and Liam are going with the others to catch up with your warriors. How will they make it to the battle in time if they are skirting around the forest?' he asked Emer.

'Some of those travelling with them have a special trick to help get there quicker. We will be taking a game track along the base of what you call the Ariel Mountains to save some time, and we should come out about a day's ride from Port Marden.'

'What trick?' Seamus was intrigued.

'Did you not notice we travelled to Sanctuary more quickly after meeting with Eon?' Emer asked, and Seamus shook his head.

'I will explain it to you as we ride, for we really must be leaving.' The four entered the forest and started their journey back towards the coast.

For two days the four from the prophecy travelled through the forest towards Port Marden. Occasionally Emer took to the air, or ranged forward in wolf form, to ensure their path was safe. Each night, unbeknown to the others, a different god woke Seamus to teach him more about what he could do with his abilities. Before the god left him on the second night, he informed Seamus that soon the hand and the arm would need to train as one, as they would need to work closely together to defeat their enemy. When he turned to ask the god when he would start training with Aliah, Seamus was alone in the clearing.

Each morning when he awoke, Seamus felt as refreshed as if he had a full night's sleep—certainly more refreshed than his travelling companions. However, on the third morning, Seamus was as irritable as if he had not had any sleep at all. He was worried about training with Aliah. Did their training together mean they would have to physically fight the god? He was not sure how they would do that, especially as his skills were not that practical in close combat. It was so frustrating to have this gift of foresight and still know so little.

Emer made them some caffe for breakfast, and that helped calm him a little as they prepared for the last day of their journey. Because they were now close to the coast, Emer in wolf form, and Dominic on his horse, went ahead to make sure they were not going to fall into any traps.

The scenery was so monotonous, Seamus found his mind wandering, but he was jolted awake by a screech in his head. *Run. Danger.* He looked at Aliah, but she carried on riding, leading Emer's horse as if nothing was amiss.

He heard something crash through the undergrowth, and Dominic's horse bolted towards them, stopping abruptly just before he would have bowled Seamus over. Aliah was off her horse within seconds, sword drawn. Seamus followed her lead, and was soon by her side, knife in one hand, and wand in the other, their horses as protection behind them.

Seconds later, soldiers wearing uniforms unknown to them entered the clearing and surrounded the two fighters. Two men on horseback followed the soldiers. Aliah gasped as she recognised them; Millard, and his protégé Gaius.

Seamus' stomach sank. Millard had been King Terion's advisor, but Walter had found he was plotting the downfall of the royal family, believing wizards should rule Aria. Gaius plagued Seamus and Aliah in Duncameron, and if there was anyone who could make him nervous, it was this particular wizard. Gaius was a people sensor, he could track people by smell.

Inspire by the unease the wizards brought out, they were not the immediate threat. Seamus counted six soldiers between the wizards and them and their relaxed stance told him they believed they had Aliah and himself at a disadvantage. That would give him the opening he needed.

We need.

What?

I said the opening we need...

Aliah?

This is weird, but it seems we can mind link when we

hold the wand and sword.

Distracting.

Shhh.

'Little Princess.' Millard sneered as he edged his horse through the soldiers in front of him. 'I finally have you where I want you.'

Gaius stayed behind the soldiers, the smirk on his face showing he was clearly pleased to have Aliah at his mercy.

'I am sure you believe that.' Aliah sounded strangely calm. 'You need to be careful though, Millard. You have really shown your true colours, turning up with foreign soldiers.'

'I no longer need to hide my allegiance. My true master lies off the coast, and soon he will ensure I rule in Aria.' Millard stayed on his horse, towering over Seamus and Aliah. 'Now you will come with me. He has been looking forward to meeting you both.'

'I do not think so,' Seamus interrupted.

'You, boy, you think to say no to me, the most powerful wizard in all of Aria?' Millard straightened in his saddle, as if to make himself more imposing.

'I think you may need to rethink your definition of power,' was all Seamus said in response, in a voice that sounded much calmer than he felt. As he took a deep breath in preparation for the coming fight, Millard's power gathered.

Aliah, he is going to strike with magic.

Can you stop it?

Seamus had no time to answer as a bolt of pure power was released from Millard's hand. Without even thinking, Seamus used air to divert the attack upwards. He mentally thanked the gods for his training as he deflected another attack the same way, and then decided to conserve energy by erecting a wall of air.

Another volley of attacks were repelled by his blockade, and Millard's face contorted into a snarl. Gaius looked around, clearly trying to identify where the magical defence was coming from.

'What... what is happening? Gaius, can you feel where that magic is coming from?'

'I can feel no magic. I do not know what is happening.' Gaius frantically looked around. 'There is no wizard.'

'Arrrh,' Millard groaned as he tried another volley to break the shield.

'We are not so easy to beat,' Aliah told Millard as Gaius motioned for the soldiers to move in closer.

'Who is doing that?' Gaius asked, still trying to identify where the magic was coming from.

'My friend Seamus has powers you could never understand,' Aliah told him.

'He has no magic,' Millard snarled. 'I can not feel any around him.'

'Or I am stronger than you could possibly imagine,' Seamus said as he struggled to maintain his air shield against another attack.

Out of the corner of his eye, a soldier charged at Aliah, who moved to parry his blow and cut his horse's saddle strap. Her movements almost a blur as Aliah's skills were boosted by her god-gifted sword. The soldier fell to the ground, dazed.

'That cannot be. My power comes from a god,' Millard shouted. 'You cannot be more powerful, unless...' The realisation of who he faced was reflected in his eyes. 'The wizard...' he whispered.

At that moment, a wolf rushed from the cover of the trees, snarling and snapping at the hooves of the horses who, unsettled, broke formation. Dominic appeared out of nowhere behind Gaius. Jerking the wizard from his saddle, he pressed a knife to Gaius' throat before the wizard knew what was happening. The wolf turned and stalked the two men, then sat down in front of Gaius and snarled.

Seamus used the distraction to drop the wall and wrap the two wizards in air, preventing them from using all but minor magic that would not be strong enough to harm anyone. By the time the soldiers had their horses under control, the two wizards were out of commission. Aliah stepped forward, sword at the ready.

'You have a choice. You can continue with your attempt to capture us and risk getting yourselves and the wizards hurt, or you can let us leave peacefully.' Aliah spoke to the soldiers.

'We have our orders. We are to bring you back alive. We will do that with or without the help of the wizards.' The leader of the group urged his men forward to once again surround Seamus and Aliah.

'Dominic, I can handle the wizards. Aliah might need your help though.' Seamus moved back towards their horses, still maintaining the web of air around his charges.

Dominic disappeared from view and reappeared beside Aliah, sword in hand. One of the soldiers jabbed at Seamus, thinking him unarmed, and Emer growled and snapped at his horses hooves. As Emer forced the horse and rider away, she moved in to set herself between Seamus and the soldiers.

Somewhat protected, Seamus watched as Aliah and Dominic fought side by side, their swords moving so fast he could barely keep track of them. He had not realised the spy was such an accomplished swordsman. Soon they had soldiers moving back towards the trees. As their sword-work slowed, it appeared they were tiring more quickly than their attackers. In addition, Seamus could feel one of the magicians working to undo his air weave. He knew he could not hold it for much longer. Slowly he put all the pieces together, realising they could not win this battle. They had moments before the tide would turn against them. They needed another plan, and quickly.

Aliah, we need to run. When I say go, we need to head into the woods taking separate paths.

All right.

We can double back and meet up by the coast at sundown.

Dominic and I can stay behind and harry anyone who follows.

… Emer?

I can mind speak with people close to me when I am in animal form. How else would I be able to communicate?

I do not know? In fact, I did not really think about it.

I can tell Dominic the plan.

There was a pause. *We are ready. Can you double the air around the wizards so they are held for a time?*

I think so. It is sort of like weaving a basket. If I pull together a few more strands, I can tie off the end. Seamus concentrated for a moment. He had only succeeded doing this once before in training, and doing it while already holding a weave in place was even harder.

Seamus, can you hurry please?

This is not easy, Aliah. Ah, there. Done.

'Go.'

Aliah and Seamus took off in opposite directions, Emer ran directly at the soldier's horses, causing them to bolt and add to the confusion. Dominic moved to the tree-line and simply disappeared.

It only took a couple of heartbeats before the commander was directing his soldiers to split up; half to follow Aliah, the others to track Seamus. They deserted the two wizards, leaving them to concentrate on removing their invisible bonds.

13
THE BATTLE FINDS THEM

Seamus crashed through the forest, following the path Emer's wolf form set for him. Branches whipped around his face and roots grabbed for his ankles. Just when he thought he could go no further, Emer told him to hide—their pursuers were close.

Looking around, Seamus spied a fallen tree and managed to wriggle under it, pulling some forest debris in front of his face just as the thud of horses' hooves came up behind him. He glimpsed Emer moving to eagle form as he squeezed back as far as possible into his hiding place.

'I am sure I saw him through here.' The voice was not far away.

'Well, you can get off your horse and go and look,' another voice ordered.

Saddle leather creaked, followed by the crackling of someone walking through the dead leaves littering the forest floor. The tree above Seamus shifted as it took the weight of a man, and he held his breath.

'What do you see?' The question came from behind.

'Trees and more trees. No wolf. No boy. But I do see something not often seen this far into the forest. There is an eagle here.' The voice was so close to Seamus it was as if it were coming from right beside him.

'It is probably injured. Unless you are planning to catch it for dinner, we had best get moving.'

Seamus readied himself to attack in Emer's defence, until the tree shifted again and the sound of retreating footsteps were accompanied by a grumbling, 'Not enough meat on it for one, let alone three.'

Slowly letting out his breath, Seamus waited until he could no longer hear hoof beats before wriggling himself back out from under the tree. He brushed debris off his clothes as Emer walked up beside him. It was comforting to see her in human form.

'I followed them for a little bit, then went high to see a way forward. If we go in that direction.' She pointed almost at a right angle to the path the soldiers had taken. 'We should reach the edge of the forest near the road to Port Marden without encountering any further danger.'

TRIALS

Seamus looked where she pointed. 'You could not choose a way that included an actual path?' He sighed, resigning himself to fighting the forest. To his dismay, Emer burst out laughing.

'Seamus, you are a wizard with the power to command the elements. Do you not think you could make a path should you wish one.'

'But then everyone would know where we have gone,' Seamus said, and immediately regretted it as Emer laughed even louder. He realised how silly he sounded as he thought about it. Of course he could move the forest around them, then let it fall back into place as they passed. He could remove any sign of their passage the way Walter had taught him.

He concentrated and took a couple of steps, willing the forest to move. His first attempt was clumsy. He created a clearing around them, and he could actually feel the forest groaning with the effort. He stopped and thought again. What was the minimum they needed for comfortable travel, and how could they get it without disturbing the forest? An idea came to him. He imagined hard disks of air under his feet, and an air tunnel in front of him. He took a few steps and found himself forest-free, and no longer harried by the forest's disapproval.

'I am ready, but you will need to walk close to me.' Seamus turned to Emer. No longer laughing, she watched him thoughtfully.

'Inventive,' she responded. 'But you need to keep your use of magic small lest you tire yourself. I will fly for the moment and keep a look out.' Before Seamus could say anything, Emer changed form and flew up through the trees.

The rest of the day passed without incident, but by evening, Seamus was tiring. When he stopped for a break, Emer dropped down beside him and hopped over to a bush.

These are good to eat, and there is a stream twenty paces behind it. Eat til you can eat no more. Drink. Then we will rest until the moon is high enough to travel safely.

The berries were good, and Seamus had stripped the bush nearly bare before his stomach stopped groaning. After quenching his thirst, he waited for Emer to join him.

'Left you some berries,' he told her.

Emer smiled. 'I just had a rabbit. Eagles do not mind their meat raw.' Seamus shuddered at the thought and Emer laughed.

'It is a useful ability when you need to travel without a fire,' she lectured him.

'That is all very well Emer, but as you pointed out before, I am a wizard who can control the elements. I could cook you meat without needing a fire.'

'Really?'

'Well, I am pretty sure I can.'

In a flash, Emer again turned into an eagle and disappeared into the trees. A few moments later, she dropped a dead rabbit beside Seamus and changed back to human form, the challenge clearly written on her face.

Seamus studied the rabbit and thought about all the skills he had learnt. At last, an idea came to him. He warmed the air around the rabbit, increasing it slowly so as not to burn the flesh, then willed the hot air through the rabbit's body. He counted to one hundred, then used the knife in his belt to test the meat. Not quite ready.

TRIALS

Trying again for a further count of fifty, he tested again. Perfect. He looked triumphantly at Emer.

'Well, I have never seen that done before.' She sat down beside him, and he apportioned the rabbit between them.

After eating a more satisfying meal, they settled down to rest and wait for the moon to rise.

Seamus awoke to the touch of Emer's hand on his arm. She had her finger to her lips, and beckoned for him to follow her. As he rose, hushed voices sounded close.

'There they are.'

In the bright moonlight, they had been easy to spot. Emer pulled him by the arm. 'Run.'

They took off into the trees at a sprint as Seamus wondered why foresight could not have warned him their pursuers were close. Learning what it could and could not tell him was frustrating.

At first they managed to keep ahead of their pursuers, and were even keeping to the course that would take them to the meeting place on the coast. As if the soldier knew where they were heading, they suddenly changed direction, cutting off the route to their destination. Each time they managed to make headway towards their destination, the soldiers changed their tactics. It was as if they were herding them back towards Sanctuary.

Lungs burning, Seamus could run no more. Looking around, he found a thicket of prickly bushes and started for them. 'We can hide in there.'

'Are you mad? We will be cut to shreds,' Emer whispered.

'That is exactly what the soldiers will think. That is why it is the perfect place to hide.' Seamus concentrated and used his magic to pull some of the branches apart.

'We cannot both fit in there.' Emer was unconvinced his idea would work.

'If you were in wolf form we would.' Seamus told her.

Sighing, Emer changed. *All right, we can give it a try.*

In spite of Seamus' magic parting the branches, they both received quite a few scratches as they crawled into the hiding space, and even more when Seamus closed the branches behind them. Then every time they tried to move thorns clutched at their clothes and tore at their skin.

Cold and sore, with limited ability to move, they stayed cramped in the bushes while the soldiers searched for them, then searched again. Every now and then, a soldier entered the clearing in front of their hiding place. Occasionally they would stand a hand's breadth away from where Seamus and Emer hid, but none even considered their thorny hiding place as somewhere to look.

Candle-marks passed, but still the soldiers did not give up their chase. Seamus's muscles began to cramp, but still he could not move for fear of giving their position away. At one stage, he half dozed, leaning his face on Emer's warm back.

Just before the sun began to rise, the soldiers called off their search, agreeing it would be easier to catch their quarry on the coast. When the forest was free of the sound of men and horses, Seamus let out his breath and had the bush release them from its midst. Seamus stretched out his muscles, and actually sighed with pleasure.

Those leaves over there—no, those ones, can be used on our scratches.

'Do I just rub them on?' Seamus asked.

Yes.

He dealt with Emer's cuts first, then was amazed at the relief the leaves brought to his own wounds.

'Do you know where we are?' Seamus asked looking around, not certain which way they needed to go to meet up with Aliah and Dominic.

Yes. We have a lot of time to make up. Have you been taught how to feed yourself energy so you can keep going for long periods of time?

'No.' Seamus knew it could be done, just not how.

Let us start at a slow jog then, and we will see how we go.

As they headed towards the coast, Seamus reviewed everything he had learnt about magic and how to use it, trying to devise a way to give himself energy.

Seamus' plan had worked better than Aliah expected. Used to being the one taking the lead, it had been strangely liberating concentrating on responding to orders, rather than giving them. Still, she had been surprised at how sound Seamus' decisions had been. *His foresight must give him great advantage,* she marvelled as she ran.

As she tired and started to think of her next move, she took control of the chase. The horses were not as mobile through the woods as a person. With her sword still in hand, she was also extremely sensitive to her surroundings.

Dominic was running behind her, using branches, stones, and knives to dissuade any pursuers who came too close. Eventually she found a dry riverbed and began following it towards the coast, stopping every now and then to hide as a pursuer came too close. Late into the afternoon, the woods began to quieten down and she could no longer hear anyone following her.

She stopped by a stream to get a drink, and was startled by Dominic appearing right in front of her. With her sword on the ground she had not sensed he was nearby.

'We seem to have outrun them.' Aliah smiled.

'Sorry, princess, but no. I overheard them when you started following the stream. They know where we are headed and have planned to ambush us when we reach the coast.' He bent down to scoop a drink of water. Aliah scowled and picked up her sword.

Seamus, they are waiting for us on the coast.

That is not good.

Do we risk a coastal trip?

I feel like we should avoid the coast and head straight for Port Marden. Stay separate. Come out at the edge of the mountains as Emer planned.

As Seamus' words entered her head, he transmitted his belief this was the right way to move. For that moment, she understood Seamus' foresight. Taking a straighter path to the coast now would result in certain capture, and she and Seamus were not yet ready to face a god.

We need to stop communicating this way. Because it uses magic I worry the wizards can use it to track us. No more mind-speak until we are near Port Marden.

All right.

Aliah turned to update Dominic, who was still drinking. He told her the plan sounded fine.

'Just how long have you been able move from one place

to another like that?' Aliah asked out of the blue, hoping to shock Dominic into an answer.

But Dominic was better trained than that. He carried on as if nothing were amiss.

'I think if we go that way, we should be able to reach the base of the mountains again, and follow them to the coast.'

'Dominic, if we are to work together I need to know how you move like that,' Aliah said patiently.

Sighing, Dominic kept his gaze on the woods as he answered. 'It is not that I move, as such. I sort of blend in with the surroundings, which allows me to watch and move around without being seen.'

'Oh, that is a little creepy.' Aliah shivered.

Dominic continued looking away, not able to meet Aliah's eyes. 'That is what most people think. That is why I do not tell them.'

'Still, it must come in very handy in your kind of work,' Aliah joked. Realising this was quite a sensitive issue for Dominic she did not want to make him any more uncomfortable than he already was.

'I try not to use it too often, but it has saved my neck on more than one occasion.' Dominic still would not meet her eyes. Concerned, she was sure he thought she did not want him travelling with her because of her dislike of spies, and now the discussion of his gift had made the situation even more uncomfortable. This saddened her, because lately, she had begun to rely on his advice and the different perspective he had, and she really liked the way he always supported her.

'Well, I guess it is no less strange than getting strength

and speed from a sword that only allows you to touch it. And at least you do not have to carry anything around to actually access your gift,' Aliah said, attempting to repair the damage. She leaned over to try and see Dominic's face, but he turned even further away.

'We need to get moving. It will take the rest of today, and almost all of tomorrow, to reach Port Marden, and we will still have to walk most of tonight.' Dominic turned and started walking. Aliah sheathed her sword and followed.

The silence hung between them as they walked through the forest. Any of Aliah's attempts at conversation were met with either silence or curt answers. Eventually she gave up trying. She did not understand why Dominic was so stand-offish after having talked about his gift, but if he did not want to talk to her, then she was fine with that.

As dusk fell, they continued walking through the forest. When it grew dark they stopped and rested for a while, drinking some water from a stream. They found a sheltered space and curled to catch some sleep. Aliah awoke some time later to find herself snuggled close to Dominic, drawn to the warmth of his body. Stretching the stiffness from her limbs, she allowed her eyes to become accustomed to the moonlight.

Disturbed by her movement, Dominic began to rise. 'Come on, sleepyhead.'

'No. Wait a moment.' Aliah grabbed his arm and pulled him back down. 'What is the problem with your gift? You seem embarrassed by it, when you should be pleased to have such a useful ability.'

Dominic turned away, before raising his eyes to look

at her. 'I saw your reaction when we talked about my special skill. Everyone who knows I have it finds it difficult to deal with. No one likes to think someone can spy on their most private moments without being discovered. My father is so disgusted he will no longer speak to me. In fact, he will not let me back in the family home.' He turned away, as if he did not want her to see the hurt written on his face.

'Oh, Dominic. I did not know. I mean Daniel told me you were estranged from your family, but I thought it was because your father is, well... you know... he is quite a brute.'

'We never really got on. My brother and I are nothing like him, but I used to visit home occasionally to see my twin brother and his wife. My father wanted nothing more to do with me when he found out I used my gift to uncover one of his plots to bring a vassal in line. He was disgusted by me, although I am not sure whether my gift made him feel that way, or the fact I refused to use it to further his petty schemes. I do sometimes get letters from my brother, when he can sneak them out. That is all the contact I have with my family.'

Aliah stood and looked down at Dominic. 'Well, that is his loss, not yours. If he cannot see past something that makes him feel uncomfortable to the person you are inside, then he is not worth worrying about.'

Dominic laughed as he rose to his feet. 'That is one of your dukes there, princess, perhaps you should speak a little more respectfully of him.'

'Perhaps he should do something to actually earn my respect. As for your brother, will he not stand up to your father and be his own man?' Aliah retorted.

'Please, do not judge him harshly. Our father is not an easy man to live with, and it was hard enough to stand up to him when we were both there. Now he has no one on his side, and if my brother does not speak out against my father's excesses, then it is not because he supports him. He bides his time, knowing soon he will be able to do things differently.'

'You are more charitable than I. I believe if someone stands by and watches something bad happen and does nothing, then they are equally guilty.' Aliah tossed her plait over her shoulder and adjusted her sword.

'On that, we can agree to differ. Where you see black and white, I see shades of grey. Shall we get moving?'

'Lead on.' *And that is why your council is so valuable,* Aliah thought as she followed him. *Your views help me see things in a different light.*

'You know you came to my home when you were younger,' Dominic told her as they walked. 'Your father needed to sort out something between my father and a vassal.'

Aliah sorted back through her memories and came across one of a dark eyed boy who had left his home and travelled with them back to Bannock. Surely that boy could not have been Dominic—his eyes were blue. 'Did you leave home with us?' she asked.

'Yes,' Dominic answered in surprise. 'I cannot believe you remember me. It was an important day in my life, it was the day your father took me into his service, I did not think it would be something another child would remember.'

'I almost did not for a moment. How is it you have blue eyes now?'

Dominic stopped and stared at her. 'You really do remember? It happened slowly. At first, I barely noticed it. My eyes lightened and I thought it just my body changing as I grew up. Then I noticed the more often I used my gift, the quicker my eye colour changed, until they ended up the blue you see now. The colour has not altered for a while, so I am thinking they will either stay this colour, or the changes will be minimal.'

'Mmm, that is interesting. It is almost as if your magic is taking a toll from you. I wonder if that is the same for all magic users?'

'Much as I would love to stay here and discuss the impact of magic on individuals, we need to keep moving. We should keep quiet from here on in as we do not want to alert anyone to our presence.'

They walked in silence through the rest of the night, using the moon to light their way. Not long after sunrise, the forest started to thin. As they were about to emerge into the open, Dominic stopped them both. 'Let me go ahead to see what I can see.'

He disappeared, and Aliah strained her eyes, trying to track him. Frustrated with not knowing what he was doing, she put her hand on the sword hilt, closed her eyes, and tried to use her other senses to find Dominic. She opened her eyes with a start as she sensed something, then closed them again and concentrated.

With her eyes closed, she could see an image of the vista in front of her, and moving along that vista was a shimmer. Focusing, the shimmer turned to the clear form of a man. She gasped as he transformed into a brilliant light behind her closed eyes. His gift was as beautiful and god given as hers.

Aliah followed Dominic's progress as he crested the hill. Her gaze followed him as he lay down flat on the ground and looked around. For a moment, he released his gift and waved for her to come forward As she moved, he turned his hand palm down and patted it towards the ground, indicating she should keep low.

She joined him on the crest of the hill, overlooking the bay where Port Marden sat. There were no soldiers anywhere in sight, but the scene before her caused her to utter a strangled cry. A full blown sea battle waged in the strait between Hand and Port Marden, and the Arian ships were outnumbered by three to one. As they watched, an Arian ship listed and floundered, allowing an enemy ship to head for the beach to off-load soldiers.

'Oh no, we are two late.' Aliah collapsed on the ground. 'We can do nothing from here, and once they have a foothold, they will be almost impossible to remove with the numbers they have.'

'Is there nothing your gift can do?' Dominic asked equally dismayed, rolling over, and watching her as she surveyed the battle ahead.

'Not that I know of. Seamus had mentioned the two of us training for battle, but we have not yet had a chance. I am almost sure in this instance I would need his magic to have an effect on this.'

Dominic burst out laughing, and she hit him on the arm. 'This is not funny.'

'Well it is when you say you need Seamus to fight this battle, and as you speak he emerges from the trees.'

Aliah turned to see Dominic was telling the truth.

Seamus jogged up the hill, followed by Emer in wolf form. She resisted the urge to call out to them in case there were foreign soldiers anywhere about.

'Were you followed?' Dominic asked as the two came within earshot.

'No,' Seamus gasped as he slowed to a fast walk. 'We are all safe now, the Sanctuary forces have already reached the coastal road, less than half a days march from here. Our wizard friend is about half a candle-mark in front of them. With any luck, the Malorians will catch him up and deal with him for us.' He grinned at them.

'I would not say we were all right,' Aliah interrupted. 'Come and see.'

Amelia stared in wonder at the sight before her. In the scene that had appeared on the sheet of ice covering the rock wall, she saw hundreds of ships fighting a battle. Amazed at the number of ships the Carstenites had brought to Aria's shores, she was still unconcerned about the outcome of the battle.

'You are not worried Aria might lose this battle and all you know will be lost?'

'No,' Amelia answered. 'I sense this is not the day our forces are overrun, this is the day we show the invaders what we are made of.'

'You are confident that Aria will win the war?'

Amelia turned from the scene in the ice in front of her and faced the assembled gods. She touched her lips with her forefinger and thought for a moment before answering. 'The outcome of this war is still in flux. I sense something will happen today that will change the balance a little in favour of Aria, but it will not be enough for a decisive outcome.'

'Good,' the gods answered in unison. 'You understand the limits of your gift. We have one more scene to show you. This is not from your present, but from the past.'

Turning to the cavern wall, it shimmered and Amelia was transported into another cave. There were priests of some order she could not identify, placing a casket on a stone altar. She sensed the words they chanted were powerful ones, perhaps a spell of protection? The vision wavered, then disappeared.

'Well?' the gods pressed her. Not to be rushed, Amelia thought through what she had been shown for a moment. She had no feeling for why it was important, so she used her common sense to interpret it instead.

'I believe you showed me this because it has something to do with the outcome of this war. It is unlikely to impact the battle between Aria and Carsten, so it must have something to do with the god to be defeated. Maybe we will need to find that casket if we are to be successful?'

The gods did not smile, but Amelia could sense their approval. 'Good, you do not just rely on your sight, you also have strong powers of reasoning.'

Amelia blushed like a young child being praised, then mentally shook herself. She had no need of praise from the gods, she had lived her life until now without their help. Besides, this trial may not be over yet, and she needed to concentrate if she wanted to come out in one piece. She waited for the next challenge, but the gods seemed to be having some sort of internal conversation. Finally they broke away and spoke to her.

'For the last step in this trial we will need to look into your very essence. If you are a true seer, you will be able to accommodate a godly consciousness entering your mind; if you are not, it can send you insane. You need to be warned there are only one of two outcomes if you proceed from here. Firstly, you are not the seer, and you leave here as if you were a child, never again to be an adult. Or, secondly, you leave here as a chosen seer, never to see the world through your own eyes again. You still have the choice to end this trial and leave as you are now.'

Amelia froze. What a choice to have to make. While she wanted to leave because she did not need to be anything more than she was now, something niggled in the back of her mind and stopped her. For a seer, everything that happened had a meaning. Why, after all of these years of waiting, had the successor to the seer finally been found when the Wizard and the Warrior had also been identified?

'If I choose not to go forward with this trial, will Caraig still be able to advise Seamus and Aliah on their quest to beat the god?'

There was a pause while the gods debated their answer. 'We are not sure if telling you this will upset the balance of forces, but we all agree you need to know only the seer chosen in the time of the Wizard and Warrior can be of direct help to them.'

Her stomach sunk. She really had no other option. 'I will proceed.'

Another short pause, and then a blinding light entered her head.

14
THE BATTLE

Emer shimmered and changed back into human form. Aliah briefly wondered what happened to her clothes when she turned into a wolf or eagle, before following the two new arrivals to the top of the hill.

'Oh no.' Seamus' face dropped. 'They have nearly landed their first boat, and after that...'

'Is there anything you are able to do?' this time Dominic directed his question to Seamus.

Seamus quietly followed the scene below. 'Would you

say the battle is being directed from that large ship at the back?' he eventually asked.

They all watched the battle unfold for a moment longer. 'It is hard to tell,' Dominic said. 'We would need to be closer to find out for sure.'

'I can help out with that,' Emer answered.

'No.' Seamus' tone was emphatic. 'It is too dangerous.'

'How can you help?' Aliah asked.

'When Emer is in her animal form she not only mind-speaks, she can also link with specific people and share what she sees. She showed me how when we were trying to find exactly where you were.'

'That is great. You can get a better view of the battle and we can see what we need to do,' Aliah said enthusiastically.

'No. It is too risky. A bird has no place in the middle of all that fighting. It would be too dangerous.' Seamus stared out at the sea, a determined look on his face. Emer put her hand on his arm.

'Seamus it is not your decision. I am a guard. It is my job to fight battles in whichever form is best suited. If I am able to do this, then I must help.' Emer stared at Seamus, waiting for his reaction.

Aliah stepped between the two of them. 'Seamus, we need her. She is here for a reason, and perhaps this is it. She is right, it is her decision.'

Seamus sighed. 'I cannot see any other way to stop the battle that does not kill most of the people out there. There is only one way forward, and that is to remove whoever is leading the battle. To do that, we need to know exactly where he is, and for that, we need Emer to fly above.'

'What exactly do you mean by "removing him"?' Aliah

asked frowning.

Seamus turned to look at her. 'We may need to kill one to save many, but it may suffice to knock him out if we can control our magic to that degree.' Seamus held her gaze.

'Have you ever killed anyone before?'

'No,' he answered, not counting the men he burned in his trial because that was not real. 'And I am not sure I want to after the experience I had during my trial.'

'Me neither. Can we control the magic enough not to kill him?'

'We can only try.' Seamus did not sound confident, and that surprised Aliah. Surely his foresight would tell him if their plan would work.

'Are you sure the gods will allow this?' She needed to check it would not be considered misusing his powers. It would be a shame if he lost them just when they needed them most. This was magic directed against a person, with a high risk the person would be injured, making it very close to being battle magic.

'I do not know, but I can see no other way to stop the Carstenites from gaining a foothold in Aria. I hope that, because we aim to incapacitate not kill, the gods will understand.' Seamus sounded confident, but he chewed worriedly on his lower lip. 'I do not know what will happen if we kill him by mistake though.'

'And you are sure there is no other way?'

'When Emer offered to fly over the battle, I had this feeling the way to defeat the attack today is for us to remove the battle commander. To do that we must risk killing him.'

'Then that is what we must do.' Aliah said firmly before Seamus could voice any more doubts. They had to trust his foresight. 'Do you know how?'

'I think so. I think it has something to do with me providing the magic and the intent, and you using your strength to send the magic that little bit further.' A furrow formed between Seamus' brow. 'I wish we had trained for this, but we will just have to do the best we can.'

'Whatever we are going to do, we had better do it fast, before this battle is lost,' Dominic interrupted.

Emer immediately changed into her eagle form. *I will start with a sweep, and share images with you all. This will give you a big picture. When you know exactly what you want to do, I will link mind to mind with Aliah so she can use my eyes to direct the attack.* With a sweep of wings, she caught the breeze and rose to the air.

Within seconds, Aliah was looking at a bird's eye view of the fight below. From above, it was obvious which boat directed the battle. It hung at the back, and on the foredeck stood a figure pointing and moving ships as if moving pieces on a game board.

I can feel the power coming from him, can you? Emer asked.

Yes. Seamus and Aliah sent back. *He is the one we need to stop.*

Oops. The picture blurred as Emer plummeted.

'What was that?' Seamus broke off, looking around them. 'Oh, no.' He pointed along the coast towards Port Marden. On the trail just below them were the soldiers they had evaded, rejoined by Millard and Gaius. One of the soldiers had a crossbow out. He had nocked another arrow and was again aiming at Emer, who had righted herself and flown out of range. Millard and Gaius were arguing and gesturing. The soldier ignored them, concentrating on Emer.

'How did Millard get around us?' Seamus asked.

'We cannot worry about that now,' Dominic advised. 'Let me take care of them. You focus on turning the tide of this battle.' Dominic disappeared.

'How do we do this?' Aliah asked, looking to Seamus for direction.

'Hold your sword, we need to mind speak from now on. It will help if we can share thoughts.'

I am not sure what the gods would have taught us, but I think we need to meld our powers in some way. If I think about what I want, the way I normally work magic, then when the thought is formed in my mind, you point your sword at the figure on the deck, like a wizard uses a wand. Imagine pushing all your power through that sword. Once we are working together, we can use Emer's sight to show us whether or not the attack is hitting the target, who I am pretty sure is the King of Carsten. Do you understand?

Aliah nodded, taking a deep breath.

Before we start, we should give Dominic a little time to get down to the soldiers so he can disrupt their activity.

He is nearly there. He has just dipped behind a rock and has pulled out some knives. I think we are good to try this.

How can you see him?

I will show you later, Seamus. Now focus.

Emer?

I am here.

Are you all right? His heart was in his mouth as he waited for her answer.

The arrow just grazed past me, throwing me off track. I am good now. When you are ready, let me know. I will link and swoop down so you can see where to send your bolt of magic.

Seamus took a deep breath and placed his hand on Aliah's shoulder. He closed his eyes and used his senses to find Aliah's life force, just as his teachers had shown him to find it within himself. Fortunately, he felt a strong pull as her force was boosted by the sword she carried. He could not believe this was working.

Then he lost the connection.

Aliah looked round at him with such belief in her eyes that the full force of her trust almost crushed him. *What have I done to earn that?* He took a deep breath, wondering when it was she had decided he was the one in charge. He was the one getting magical training, sure, but he knew no more about this than she did.

Then it dawned on him; because he could sometimes see which path they were to take, she expected him to also take the lead. Now was not the time to explain to her that even when he could see the best path, there were many ways it could be travelled, and it was too much to expect him to decide which way on his own.

Taking another deep breath, he connected with Aliah again. Once he was sure the connection was strong, he used the training Walter had given him in the basement in Duncameron. He thought of his magic as a life force flowing through his veins, and he sent it through his arm and out through his hand to mingle with Aliah's. As the two life forces met, Seamus felt something rather like a twang, then what he could only describe as an "Aliahness" infused his body. He waited a moment more allowing the life forces to entwine, like two strands of twine wrapped around each other, making a stronger rope.

That is so strange. I feel like you are a part of me.

We need to test this out before we actually use it on someone.

Are you sure that is wise Seamus? As soon as you use your power, the god's chosen will know you are here. Emer interrupted.

Aliah?

Emer is right. We have to trust ourselves. Go for the attack, and if we get the first one wrong, they will at least be on the back foot while we ready ourselves for a second attempt.

All right, we will go ahead then. Aliah, first we have to gather our strength. Imagine you are gathering your energy to deliver the hardest punch you can give, but hold it. At the same time, I will imagine pulling air from around our target—the man on the ship directing the battle, who is likely the king. When I say, put all your gathered strength into pulling backwards from where the sword is pointing.

So, I just point the sword like a wand at our target and imagine pulling backwards? That is it?

Yes and no. It is a little more complicated than that, but in its raw form, yes. Ready, Emer? You need to circle over the king so Aliah knows where to direct the attack.

Ready.

Aliah?

Ready.

Here we go.

Seamus felt Aliah's power building as he watched Emer fly towards the ship. She started circling, then slowly spiralled lower. As Emer connected with Aliah, sharing her vision of the deck of the ship, out of the corner of his eye he saw the soldier below raise his bow. Before he could release the arrow, the bow dropped to the ground and the soldier clutched at his arm as a red patch of blood spread under his hand. Aliah's body tensed and Seamus was drawn back to the task at hand, taking comfort in the fact Dominic had them well protected.

Once again looking through Emer's eyes, Seamus concentrated on pulling the air from around the king figure on the ship, in much the same way he had with the man in his father's court during his trial.

NOW, he commanded.

Aliah raised her arm and pointed. There was a rush of energy and Seamus threw his power through Aliah's sword, out towards the ship. When the distance was right, he commanded, *Pull!* Seamus imagined pulling back on a rope like in a tug-of-war and felt Aliah's strength join with his. Through Emer's eyes, he saw water surge up from the ocean near the command ship. They had missed their mark. He broke off the attack and the ship rocked as the water they drew up with their spell spilled back into the ocean.

Loud shouting penetrated his consciousness, and Seamus looked down to see Gaius and Millard had spotted them. Fortunately, the wizards were both pointing and gesticulating, obviously arguing over what to do next.

Quickly. We need to move before Gaius and Millard can coordinate a counter-attack. Seamus sent to the others.

In response to his thought, Aliah's power begin to build again. Without needing to be told, Emer began her downwards spiral. Unfortunately he could also feel Millard pulling energy into himself, preparing to attack.

Are you ready?

Just about.

Emer?

Yes.

Aliah tensed, preparing to release her power.

Emer?

At Aliah's query, the man who was his intended target came into focus. The picture was clearer this time. The man they believed to be King of Carsten was staring directly at him. His eyes bored through Seamus, like he was staring into his very soul.

Seamus? Aliah called him back to the task at hand.

He shook his head. *NOW!*

Aliah raised her arm and released her power, at the very last moment Seamus changed his intent. As Aliah's force stretched out towards their target, he sent his magic inside of her power-stream, imagining his force as something akin to an arrow inside a tunnel of air. Just as the point of his imaginary arrow touched the king, he pulled back with all his will, and Aliah pulled with him. Seamus kept pulling the air from the king's lungs, then, as the king struggled for breath and started to sway, Seamus cut off their attack.

Emer rose high above the Carsten command ship. Sailors gathered around a man who had fallen to the deck—the man they had attacked. With their commander out of commission for the moment, would it be enough to stop the attack for the day? They could only wait and see.

'Can you tell if they will stop now?' Aliah asked.

'Foresight does not work that way,' Seamus told her, his attention focused on the battle before them.

Suddenly his ears filled with the sound of screaming and his eyes burned with a bright explosion. Everything went blank, but before he could adjust to using his own eyes again, the ground moved beneath his feet and he sunk into darkness.

As she tried to disconnect her vision from Emer's, the ground crumbled beneath Aliah's feet, and everything went dark. Aliah struggled to breathe. Buried under a mound of dirt, Aliah struggled to stay calm and control her rising panic. She pushed with her arms and the earth overhead give way a little. Breathing became a little easier, but she would need fresh air soon or she would suffocate. Pressure built behind her eyes and her head throbbed, making it hard for her to think.

Do not think you have won. The battle may be over, but I will win the war!

'What is going on?' Seamus' voice came very close to her ear, and she realised she was lying on top of him in their dark prison.

'You have merely destroyed the body of my servant, I

am still very much alive. Soon I will find another servant to do my bidding and bring me through to your plane of existence. Then beware, I will be truly unstoppable.'

'Are you hearing this?' Seamus whispered.

'Yes. Do you think it is...'

'Yes, I think so. He said we killed the king, but I am pretty sure I saw him breathing.' Aliah could almost see Seamus frowning in the darkness as he wondered what actually happened.

You know I am a god, I can hear your every word and thought if I choose to. I know you think to fight me and win. You are but children, still unsteady on your feet. You cannot defeat a god. At best, you can delay my plans like you have done today. But I will join you on your plane, and I will rule the land as I see fit. There is nothing you can do to stop me.

The rantings of this pompous god made Aliah's blood boil. *If we are such unworthy opponents then why are you wasting your time scaring us off?* The thought jumped into Aliah's head before she could stop it, and as soon as it finished, the god presence abruptly left.

'Ahhh,' Aliah spluttered. Dirt filled her mouth as she was pulled back by her feet.

'Aliah? Seamus?' Dominic's voice seemed to come from far away. Then, suddenly, fresh air filled her lungs and she gazed up at blue sky. The pressure on her ankles ceased, and she sat up to see Dominic pulling Seamus from a pile of dirt.

'What happened?' she asked, turning to Emer who was back in human form.

'You were attacked by magic and the ground you were

standing on collapsed, burying you both.' Emer told her.

'No,' Aliah shook her head. 'I mean with the battle.'

'Oh. We knocked out the Carsten King with our last attack. Just after he fell to the deck, my head was filled with screams of rage, and the ship he was on exploded,' she replied and turned to look out to sea. 'It looks like their forces lost co-ordination when their command ship sunk. They have retreated back in line with the Isle of Hand, but they are still fighting.'

'Oh no,' Aliah cried in dismay as Seamus stumbled to his feet to take a look as the battle continued below.

'I may be able to help.' He tipped his head to the side as he considered his options.

'How?' Aliah asked. 'There is no other single target for us to fight at the moment.'

'I have an idea, and I think I can do this alone.' He closed his eyes and started moving his hands. Aliah placed a hand on Seamus' shoulder so he did not feel he was doing this alone. With the other hand resting on her sword hilt she found if she closed her eyes, she could follow what he was doing. He pulled air to him, then started to push it away, towards the sea. The water rose in between the two sets of ships as Seamus used the air to put pressure on the sea water to move the Carsten ships out a day's sail beyond Hand.

When the sails barely dotted the horizon, Seamus released the air. Turning back to them, he collapsed to the ground. Emer rushed to him and rolled him onto his back. 'He is all right. The magic has taken a bit out of him. We need to get him food soon or he will become very ill.'

'Food? Where are we going to find food out here?' Aliah

swept her hand, taking in the barren countryside.

Aliah turned to Dominic, surprised to find him grinning from ear to ear. 'Funny enough, we may just be in luck.' He pointed to the coastal path below, and Aliah turned to see two horsemen in strange livery heading up the track towards them.

'What?' she asked, confused, not understanding why Dominic was so pleased to see complete strangers in the midst of battle.

'While you and Seamus were doing your magic thing, our friend Millard caught wind of it and directed a blast at you both. I managed to get a knife in his arm which threw him off, hence this.' He gestured to the debris that were once the ledge she and Seamus had been standing on. 'He was about to strike again when we all heard the thundering of hooves.

'From what I can make out, the Sanctuary troops spied a ship about to land soldiers on the shore below, and sent a party on ahead to ensure they did not reach the beach. Realising they did not want to be caught alone by our troops, Millard and his off sider thought better of finishing you off, deciding their interests were best served making their escape with the retreating longboats. Last I saw of them, they were swimming out to sea.' Dominic laughed.

'So, if I am not mistaken, those two riders should be...' he continued.

'Daniel and Liam,' Aliah exclaimed excitedly as two riders crested the hill heading towards them.

15
PORT MARDEN

After a day of travelling through the forest on foot, it was a relief to once again be on the back of a horse, well fed and on her way to the relative safety of Port Marden. Although Aliah was more than capable of looking after herself, she really had not enjoyed being hunted. Seamus, looking wan but awake, shared a horse with Emer. Dominic and Daniel were riding on either side of her as the city walls came into sight.

Camped out along the base of the walls were guards,

each gathered around the banner of the lord who had brought them, another large group of fighters under no banner camped nearby. Aliah voiced her surprise at the number of citizens who had flocked to Port Marden to fight for the freedom of their country.

Their party stopped well before the walls at a road block staffed by a mixture of guards and free fighters. As they waited to pass through, Aliah's eye caught one of the free fighters watching her. She glanced away, then glanced back as the man sauntered towards her.

'Hello again,' the fighter said, grinning. 'I did not think to find you at this battle. And I see you found our friend.' He nodded towards Seamus. 'You are both a long way from Duncameron.'

Aliah frowned and tugged at her plait, then managed to see through the grime to his face. 'Able.' Surprised, Aliah beamed down at him, pleased to again see one of the group of people who managed to smuggle her through to Bannock a moon or so ago. 'I am where I should be, but what are you doing here?'

'Boss and some of the others in our group, Megan included, have joined the fight to save Aria from invasion. We have not seen much of the real fighting.' He shrugged. 'We get mostly sentry duty, or drills for the moment. But every man and woman is freeing up a guard from duty for the real fight.'

'And what about Pauley? Did he manage to get back home?' Aliah asked about the young boy who had guided them through the sewers to escape Duncameron. They were so closely pursued he had been forced to join them as far as Bannock.

Able laughed. 'He was only home for a short time. He decided to join us and come and fight for Aria. He is a brave one, that lad.'

Aliah glanced towards Daniel, who was taking care of the formalities. They had all agreed they did not want anyone to know the Heir to the Throne was with them until they were safely in behind the walls of the town. She frowned and turned back to Able.

'Ah, I see, you are still incognito,' Able said. 'Do not fret, I will not give your secret away. There are still those who say they are on our side, but I would not trust them with my back turned.'

'Thank you, Able. Please say hello to Megan and the Boss for me. I am pleased to see you supporting us, but would not wish harm to come to any of you.'

'I will do that. And do not worry about us, we look after each other.' Able turned to retake his post, giving her a brief wave as a small part of their group moved forward. The guard commander had been reluctant to let such a large armed force pass into the city area, despite Daniel's assurances they were allies. Finally they agreed a small party would enter the city, and the rest of the troops would stay at the guard post until they received new orders.

At long last, they entered the city walls and Aliah relaxed a little, although she was strangely nervous about once again becoming Princess Aliahanna, and taking on all that position entailed. She stayed that way until they entered the courtyard of the local garrison, and Tomas, the Captain of the Palace Guard and Daniel's father, came out of the main doorway. Again, she tensed, waiting to see who she needed to be wary of here.

Dominic came up beside her and placed a hand on her arm. 'Remember, it is best we wait a little and see who is with your father before we announce your presence.'

Aliah turned to argue, then stopped. Of course that was sensible, given the circumstances. Daniel dismounted, saluted his father as a senior officer, then hugged him hello. Relief that his son had arrived back safely flickered over Tomas' face, to be quickly replaced by a formal demeanour.

He gestured for stable hands to come and take their horses and their small party dismounted, following Tomas into the commander's quarters. There, much to her surprise, they were greeted by her father and The Duke of Hand.

Duke Damon took one look at his son and wrapped him in a bear hug, leading him to a chair to sit down, with Emer trailing close behind. Aliah turned to find her father, arms opened, ready to give her a similar welcome.

'Father,' she whispered. 'We thought it best if no one knew I was here.'

King Terion laughed. 'Good thinking, but as you will soon find out, there is no need for that any more,' he said as he drew his daughter into his arms.

The king led her to one of the chairs around the council table that dominated the room. Duke Damon, Liam, Tomas, and Daniel were already seated. Dominic took up a position behind her chair. As they settled down, a wizard entered the room. He was wearing the gold lightening bolt sigil that showed he was a strong magician, and had risen to the highest ranks in the Wizard Isle.

He was vaguely familiar, but Aliah could not immediately name him.

'Ah, Pieter, please join us.' King Terion gestured to a spare seat at the table, and the Gold Wizard took his place. 'You already know Tomas, and his son Daniel, and Duke Damon. This is Duke Damon's heir, Seamus and his squire, Liam. And this is obviously my Heir, Princess Aliahanna.'

Aliah noticed the look of surprise on the wizard's face, instantly telling her he could be trusted. Wizards from the rebellion had known where she was from the time she left Bannock on her mission to Hand, and this man clearly had no idea she would be likely to turn up in Port Marden.

'Aliah,' King Terion continued with the introductions. 'Tomas has been promoted as my new Chief Advisor after finding out Wizard Millard was a traitor. The Wizard Council has been in a bit of a flux as they try and weed out all the other traitors. In the meantime, they have sent Pieter to advise me on all matters magical. I asked him for a report on what happened today during the sea battle we appeared to be losing, then strangely won. In particular, I wanted to know if someone used battle magic to turn the tide in our favour.'

Aliah glanced at Seamus, who shook his head. Like her, he probably wanted to know what the wizard had to say before they apprised Terion of what really happened.

'As I have already told you, Your Highness, there was some strange magic in play. All wizards on your staff felt what can only be described as a draining of magic. Once before a spurt of water flew up, and once before our far-seer saw the King of Carsten collapse on the deck of his ship. As we sensed no loss of life, we believe the magic caused the king to fall, almost as if he had received a strong punch.

'Whether or not this is battle magic is not clear. It is a grey area as the attack did not appear to be aimed to injure or kill, but rather to disable the king. If there was no intent to injure, then this is something similar to how we hold people in bonds of air to prevent damage to themselves or others. Without knowing what the magic user intended, I would err on the side of this not being battle magic.

'Then there was a scream, and what we magic users can only describe as a building of pressure in our heads. The ship exploded. The explosion was definitely magic used with the intention to kill, and so would be against the Wizard's Law. The power seemed to come from on board the ship itself, unlike the other attacks which we know came from somewhere along the coast.'

Aliah placed her hand on the hilt of her sword. *That is exactly as Emer described it. Did the god really destroy the ship in a fit of anger?*

I think so. I know the worst we might have done was to kill the king as we tried to disable him, and I do not believe we did that—we only made him collapse. I also know the type of magic we used would not blow up a ship. Besides, we were tumbling into a dirt prison when that ship exploded.

Relieved Seamus' opinion was similar to her own, Alain still had doubts. *I hate to say it, I am a little relieved we did not actually kill anyone. However, I still feel responsible for what happened to the crew on that ship.*

TRIALS

I mean, we caused the god's fit of anger because we disabled the man he was using.

I understand what you are saying, but we can really only be responsible for our own actions; not what others do in response to them. Seamus' voice in her head was confident, but as she took her hand off her sword, she thought they would have to agree to disagree on this point. As her attention returned to the meeting, Aliah heard her father asking the wizard about the wave that pushed the ships out to sea.

'Creating the wave seemed to use the same type of magic as the initial attacks, and came from the same location. As far as we can tell, there were no ships or lives lost during that use of magic, which is a good thing. However, it is harder to determine whether this action was actually battle magic. Once again, much relies on the intent of the user. If they were sending ships away in a controlled manner with the intention of savings lives, it was not battle magic. If they were striking at the enemy without thought for what would happen, then that would indeed be against the law. Without being able to question the magic user, we will never know the answer to that question.

'However, whether or not battle magic was used is the least of our worries. What concerns us all is that if the intent in both of these attacks was to injure, and battle magic was used, we are in trouble. There is not a wizard here who would even know where to begin to counter magic such as this.'

'Sorry? I am unsure what you mean by that.' The king closed his eyes wearily as he tried to understand the implications of Pieter's words.

'We are concerned because this is a type of magic unlike our own, we have never seen anything like it before. This means we would not have anything prepared to counter the magic or disable the user.'

There was silence around the table as the elder members of the council took this in, and the younger members tried to look innocent of the knowledge of what went on. The king looked thoughtfully at them all, before turning his attention back to the wizard.

'Thank you, Pieter. We will need to consider all that you have told us, about the battle and the potential threat. I will call you if we need any further assistance, in the meantime, I suggest you all put your heads together and see if there is anything you can think of to counter such magic should it be directed against us.'

Dismissed, Pieter stood, bowed, and left the room. Pieter had barely shut the door when the king turned to his daughter with his eyebrows raised.

'All right, Aliahanna, what do you know about this?'

'I am not sure what you mean.' Aliah tried to stare her father down and failed. Her face flushed as she looked down at her hands.

Fortunately, Seamus came to her rescue. He placed his wand on the table in front of him. Aliah raised her head and glared at him. He shrugged his shoulders. Well, if Seamus believed this was the right course of action, she had best go along. She took out her sword to place it in front of her.

'Umm... it seems after some debates and trial by gods, we are the Wizard and the Warrior who were prophesied as the saviours of our people.' Seamus barely got the words out before they were inundated with questions, the disbelief of their elders apparent in every word.

The questioning continued as servants came in and lit the wall sconces. It continued as others came in to feed the large fire that warmed the room, and through the serving of the evening meal, and the clearing away of dishes. Some time later, it seemed all their questions had been asked and answered and the room was silent.

King Terion looked Seamus directly in the eye. 'All right. I can nearly believe you have been tested and you are the wizard and that my daughter is the warrior, but that still does not answer one question. Have you brought back battle magic?'

Seamus wanted to answer immediately, but he stopped himself and thought through what the king was actually asking.

'Well, Your Highness, I wish the answer was a simple yes or no, but the truth is more complex than that.'

The king stared at him, not letting him off the hook that easily. 'Young man, you had better come up with something better than that or I will be forced to have you stand trial before the Wizard Council.'

Seamus chewed on his lip, thinking carefully about his answer. Battle magic as he understood it was using magic to deliberately injure an enemy, and his problem was that he would very definitely have to try and hurt anyone the god attempted to use if he thought it would stop him. The question was, had he really used battle magic today?

'The wave I caused was no more than pushing the ships away to end the fighting, and was no different to a wizard binding a criminal in my mind. Although I have to be honest and say it was more a reaction to the continued fighting, rather than a well thought through plan.

'As for what I did to the King of Carsten? If you literally take battle magic to mean magic used against an enemy, then on the surface I guess the magic we used to stop him would fall into that category. Our intention was to wind him, but we knew what we were doing would not be very precise, and there was a chance we might kill him. We continued, even though we knew death was a potential outcome, because we felt it was the only way to prevent Carstonites from winning the sea battle and invading Aria.'

He stopped talking for a minute, not sure how best to say the next bit in a way the council would not automatically think he had lost his mind. He took a deep breath, feeling somewhat like he was jumping off a cliff.

'We took this dangerous action not just to save Aria, but also to prevent a god from achieving his aims of causing the devastation of our world.' Amidst gasps of surprise, Seamus pushed on. 'We believe Spearon was possessed by a god, and no ordinary attack from your guards would have affected him in any way. So, you could say we were not attacking a man but a god, and so we did not use battle magic as the law defines it.'

After the initial shock, there was silence in the room as the council digested his news. Seamus could not say exactly what he expected the reaction of the Arian War Council to be, but laughter was not exactly on the list—until he realised the laugher was because they did not believe him. When they stopped, the king directed his cold, calculating blue eyes at Seamus once again.

'You have imagination, I will say that. Unfortunately you will have to stand in front of the Wizard Council and answer one count of using battle magic.'

'Then I must stand trial with him.' Aliah rose and moved to stand beside Seamus. 'It was our combined magic that felled the god.'

'Aliah, you cannot be serious. You do not have magic.' King Terion set off laughing again as Duke Damon stood to command the council's attention.

'Your Highness, you seem to be taking this all too lightly. I know it is hard to believe our children have been chosen as the Wizard and Warrior, and have come to rid us of the evil that plagues us, but stop and think for a moment.

'I have commissioned research into the prophecy, and I am slowly gaining some understanding of its importance as it has been woven through our history for hundreds of years in various forms. You knew your daughter had travelled with my son to be tested as the Wizard and Warrior of prophecy. On some level, you must have considered whether or not Aliah may actually be the warrior, and thought about the impact of that. Even I realised my son might return the wizard of legend.

'Add to that the fact your own advisor described the attacks made from the shore today as being like no other magic. That strange magic could have come from our children, whose gifts they say come from the gods themselves, and if so, would account for them being so different.

'If we can admit the possibility all this might be true, is it really such a stretch to believe these gifts and powers have been bestowed on our children because they will actually have to face a god?' There was stunned silence as the duke finished speaking and sat down.

King Terion was no longer laughing—in fact a frown settled on his face, while deep in thought as he processed Duke Damon's words. Tomas also looked puzzled, and he was the first to respond.

'I have never been one for blind faith, Damon, and you are asking us to put aside one of our most sacred laws to trust these children had only good intent when they used magic against a man. You, who have abhorred any use of magic all the years I have known you.'

'It is hard to believe, but if you had read the documents I have over the past few moons, you would recognise there is more going on here than a simple invasion.

'If you cannot believe the hand of the gods is involved, then think on this. Why would the King of Carsten be driven to invade Aria? They are a warrior-like people, but they must have stripped their country bare to mount a force the size that arrived on our shores.

'We must also consider, would a warrior-like people take the time to subvert the Wizard Council and offer up Aria to our traitors? When they invade other lands, they raise their army by promising land and plunder to their troops. That runs counter to offering Aria to Arians. So why are they spending such large resources to conquer a land they do not intend to hold?

'You also know the Carsonite soldiers we have captured were very keen to surrender. When questioned, they told us they had been forced to leave farms and shops and fishing boats to join the army. This is all very unusual, as we have discussed before today. Is the reason Seamus and Princess Aliahanna gave us any more far fetched than those we have already come up with?'

King Terion sighed. 'You do have a point. And as I think on what you have said, if the fate of our land does lie in the hands of our children, I would be very foolish to have them locked up. On the other hand, this is quite a leap of faith.'

There was silence as the King tugged at his beard, thinking things through. Dominic stepped forward. 'If I may, Your Highness...'

'Yes, young Dominic.'

'I am obviously one of those who has already made the leap of faith Duke Damon is asking you to make, but I have had more evidence of the existence of the gods than you, which made it easier for me. I could not ask you to make that same jump without more information, so may I suggest a compromise?'

The king nodded for him to continue.

'How about you let us leave and go about what we have to do to stop the invasion, and stop the god. Once we have won the battle, then you will be able to judge whether Seamus and Aliah have told you the truth. If you believe they have not, then they will undertake a trial in front of the Wizard Council. If we lose, well, there will be no need to make the decision.'

There was silence as the king considered Dominic's proposal. 'Once again, Dominic, you have shown me why I wish you were your father's heir. What say you, Seamus and Aliah? If we so deem, will you stand trial after the war is over?'

Seamus looked at Aliah. For once he was not chewing his lip in thought, he was resolved as he reached for his wand. She reached for her sword to put back in its sheath, and as she did so, she heard his words. *I know you want to argue this through until the bitter end, but this may be the only way we get out of here to do what needs to be done.*

Pausing, she considered her options. Seeing this was for the best, she nodded and turned to her father. 'Yes, father, we agree.'

As if he had been holding out just for this, Aliah had no sooner agreed to her father's terms than Seamus collapsed, slipping from his chair to thump on the floor. Aliah was rooted to the spot with shock. Emer pushed her out of the way, and she and Duke Damon helped the boy to his feet.

'He has been drained by today, he needs rest before we decide our next steps,' Emer declared.

'I will show you to your rooms.' Tomas stood. 'I am sure all of you could do with baths, a change of clothes and a good night's sleep.'

'Tomas, by all means take the others to their quarters. They should be ready by now. I need to talk to Liam and Daniel about the additional soldiers they brought with them today. They need to be properly housed and deployed.'

Aliah followed Tomas out of the room and through some corridors to a section of the building she assumed usually housed officers. 'You and the other young lady are in here.' Tomas indicated a door. 'We are short on space so you will have to share. There should be a bath in there ready for you to use, and someone hopefully has found you each a change of clothes close to your size.'

'You go ahead,' Emer said to Aliah. 'I will see Seamus settled, then return to see to myself.'

The others continued down the corridor as Aliah opened the door. She had to bite back her squeal of joy when she saw a full sized tub in the room, steam from the water rising above it. It was all very well being a warrior and saving the world, but nothing could beat the pleasure of soaking in a hot tub. In very little time at all, she removed her clothes and sunk into the delicious bath. Luxury, she sighed, closing her eyes. All too soon, the water began to cool and she hurried to wash off the dirt and wash her hair before it was completely cold. After towelling herself dry, she was weary to the core. Quickly pulling on a sleep gown, she slipped in between the sheets of one of the beds and was soon oblivious to everything around her.

16
THE BEGINNING
OF THE END

Seamus could not remember a time when he had been so exhausted. As he attempted to roll over, his body would barely follow his commands. Shaking his head, he remembered how he had drawn energy from around him when travelling with Emer, and he reached into himself to find his magic. There was nothing there. He sat bolt upright in pain. Had he burned his magic out? *Oh no, the gods must have taken it. What did I do wrong?*

His thoughts were interrupted by a knock on the door.

He opened it to a servant with orders to fetch him for an urgent meeting. Wishing he had had time to bathe and change his clothes, Seamus followed the servant through the dark stone corridors to the Council Room, all the while worrying about the loss of his magic. How would they defeat a god without it?

All except for the king and his advisor Tomas were there when Seamus arrived, still a little groggy headed from overuse of magic the day before. Everyone was deep in conversation, but his father broke away to welcome him.

'Ah, Seamus, I am pleased to see you have recovered from your activity yesterday. The king's advisor on magic tells me you must be more careful in the future as you came close to doing yourself some serious harm. I am told using magic can drain a person's energy, and it seemed you used a lot of yours during the battle.'

Seamus stopped dead in his tracks. He never thought he would hear his father talking so openly about the using magic, and especially not his own son's use of it. How ironic it happened now when the gods had taken it from him. He decided there and then, that he would tell no one what had happened. So he merely shrugged, and frowned. 'I am feeling better, thank you.'

'Good. Good. I was just showing the others where I believe you may find some information on early magic that might help you in your fight.' He showed Seamus a roughly drawn map of a library. It seemed familiar, but through the fog of his brain, Seamus could not place it.

'There are some very old papers your aunt knows of. We did not have a chance to go and get them when we evacuated to Port Marden, but from what she said, there should be a wealth of information there.'

'Ahh… Father?'

'Mmm…' Damon added some notations to his diagram.

'You know over the next few days I will have no choice but to practice and use magic if I am to learn how to defeat a god. And I cannot guarantee no one will see me use it. You know what I am saying.' Seamus watched his father carefully to gauge his reaction.

Duke Damon stopped writing, but did not look up. The others sheepishly searched around for something else to be busy doing. Eventually, he raised his head to look his son in the eye.

'I know what you are saying, Seamus. It is the only way forward. I am more convinced than ever having spoken with your friend Emer.'

'People will know what I am. There will be no going back. I will no longer be able to be your heir.' Seamus' stomach churned as he admitted out loud what he had known for some time.

'No, Seamus, you will not.' Duke Damon shook his head sadly. 'But we must do what is right for now, and worry about the future if—when—we get through this.' Damon moved to face his son, and put his hand on his shoulder as he stared him in the eye. 'I want you to know this. I am proud of you, and I am proud of the courage you are showing. Whatever happens, I will not turn away from you.'

Seamus was embarrassed to find tears in his eyes as Duke Damon took him into a hug, and he was ashamed he had put his father through this, especially now when his powers had deserted him. His thoughts were interrupted as the door banged against the wall and King Terion entered.

'Oh, good. I worried I would be too late for the farewells. You have everything you need?' He waited for each of those assembled to agree before he moved on. Seamus merely stood there, dazed. *We are leaving? Where are we going?*

'Good. There is a small fishing boat waiting for you at the harbour. They will sneak you across and leave you at the docks. You will have to find your own way up to the town and to safety.

'Just so we are clear, because I understand there was some confusion on your recent mission, Daniel, you are in command. I know Aliah outranks you, a fact she may remind you of to make sure she gets her way, however I need her to concentrate on whatever she has to do, not to be worrying about everything else. Is that clear?'

Daniel stepped forward. 'Yes, Your Highness. And I have letters from the duke to his commander outlining my responsibilities.'

Aliah's face clouded over, and Seamus held his breath waiting for the explosion. When it came, it was small compared to some he had witnessed.

'When all this is over, Father, you and I are going to have a very long discussion about my future position, as heir *and* in general.' She forced out through gritted teeth.

'I would not have thought otherwise.' The King smiled at his daughter before turning back to the assembled group. Aliah's foot tapped her frustration, but she managed to contain her temper, something she would not have done when Seamus first met her.

'Dominic, Emer, and Liam you are responsible for ensuring our Wizard and Warrior come to no harm. One of you must be with them at all times.' The three guards nodded their agreement. Aliah went to speak, but Terion held up his hand.

'Aliah, I am aware you are the Warrior, and I know that you are more than capable of looking after yourself, as is Seamus. I am also capable of defending myself, but I have guards who follow me everywhere at all times. It is only sensible to take precautions to ensure you are present when we need you to battle this god.'

Aliah sighed, and Seamus was pleased she was not going to argue with her father on this point. He agreed with King Terion. If they were to concentrate on what they needed to learn to defeat a god, they could not be forever looking over their shoulders, worrying about everyone else. Besides, the prophecy had said they would all need to work as a team to defeat their foe.

'Has anyone heard anything from Walter and Amelia?' he asked. 'We have a lot of research to do, and our two best minds are not even with us.'

'Nothing as yet...' the king responded, only to be interrupted by Emer.

'I had contact with my father last night, and he said they have set out from Sanctuary and should arrive here soon.'

'That is good. We will send them after you as soon as they get here. Now, are we ready?'

'We have a few more things to organise, and Seamus needs to bathe, change, and pack,' Daniel informed the king.

'I have to meet with the commander of the forces from your Sanctuary, so I will say my farewells now.' King

Terion walked over to his daughter and wrapped his arms around her.

The good byes were quickly said, and a servant appeared to lead Seamus back through the corridors to his room. As he walked, he realised he had no idea where they were actually going, although there was a niggling thought at the back of his mind that he might just know after all, but he could not fully grasp it. Anyway, he had much more important things to worry about.

Gaius stood cowering behind Millard as the god figure in front of them drew up to twice the height of a human male. The thundering of his voice caused the waves to rise, which in turn caused the ship they were on to dip and swirl in the ocean. Millard seemed unconcerned by the god's wrath at their inability to stop that brat Aliahanna and her friend Seamus.

'It was not the right time to defeat them magically.' Millard spoke firmly to the god, as if he were placating a wilful child.

'Not the right time? NOT THE RIGHT TIME?' The god shouted so loudly Gaius' teeth chattered together from the shock. 'In your opinion, when exactly would be the right time? When they are about to kill you?'

'No, of course not. But we do need to be sure we know the full extent of the magical threat against us before we attack. We do not want to be caught out thinking we have won, only to find these two are mere annoyances and we still have our real foe to take on.'

TRIALS

The god shrank back to human size and moved forward until he was nose to nose with Millard. Even though his form was not solid, his ghost-like persona reeked of power and was more frightening than a human could ever be. Still, Millard did not flinch away.

'You do not understand the importance of the two you let escape.' The god was even more scary when his voice was so low. It resonated through every fibre of Gaius' body as he spoke. 'These are the only two who can stop me, and if I lose, so do you. How will you win over and rule your precious Aria without my support? *Bah!* I should never have trusted a mere human to help me.' He turned away and his form floated to the bow of the boat.

Millard tensed and Gaius sensed his fear that his plans to rule Aria were slipping though his fingers. He moved as if to follow the god, then stopped, thinking better of it. Gaius took a breath and whispered in his master's ear. 'He still needs us, master. He cannot act upon the real world in his present form. He needs us to act for him, and to bring him through to this plane of existence.'

Millard smiled, but before he said anything, the god whipped around and fixed his gaze on Gaius. Gaius, whose stomach did somersaults every time the god noticed him, again shrank behind Millard.

'You are right, boy. I cannot act in your world like this. Maybe the two of you can still be useful to me.'

A flash of light blinded Gaius, and he shuddered as something began rifling through his body and his mind.

'No,' Millard shouted close to his ear. 'Get out of my head.'

'I do not know why I did not do this sooner. My last

body was definitely warrior-like. But, oh how good it is to taste powerful magic again. Now, I will be unstoppable.'

Back in his room, Seamus knew he should prepare for wherever they were going, but instead, he sunk down on his bed and once again tried to reach for his powers. Still nothing. With a worried knot in his stomach, he lay back and closed his eyes. *Why are you punishing me? What did I do wrong?*

Seamus found himself back in the cave with the seven gods, who were seated on chairs as if sitting in judgement.

'You have had some training, and you have used your powers to help achieve your calling. But you have also used your power without thought. We are concerned about those times.'

Seamus thought hard. When had he used his power without thought, or without good reason? Thinking back over the last few days there was nothing, until he came to the farewell outside the Sanctuary.

'I gagged Eon with air because his whining, annoyed me,' Seamus responded.

'That is indeed one of the times. Magic used for your benefit alone is not magic used wisely.'

'But it was only a small incident,' Seamus argued.

'Small it may have been, but if we allow you to act thoughtlessly with small things, what is to stop you acting without thinking with bigger magical feats? Yesterday you did just that, and endangered thousands of lives.'

Seamus looked at the Gods, trying to think of what

he had done that met that description. He stroked his chin. 'Do you mean when I moved the ships?'

'We do.'

'But I controlled my magic, I used only what was necessary to move the ships away. No one was hurt. I may even have saved lives by stopping the battle when I did.' Seamus could not see what was wrong with his actions.

'That is correct, and that is the only reason why you have been given the chance to explain yourself.'

'Then what did I do wrong?' Seamus was really perplexed.

'You saw what was happening and you reacted. You decided you were the solution without stopping and considering whether you should do anything, or whether there was another course of action.'

Opening his mouth to argue, Seamus stopped. He could not fault what the gods said. He had considered all possible courses of action, before deciding the best way was to cause King Spearon to collapse, removing the commander from the battle. He had not given the same consideration to his actions when he decided to move the ships to stop the fighting. He dropped his head in shame. This decision of his might have killed thousands.

'You are right, I am not ready to wield this power.' He took his wand from his pocket and held it out to the gods. No one moved forward to take it.

'We have taken into account no one died, and we had all agreed before bringing you here that if you understood the importance of the lesson, then this time we would be lenient. But remember, the most important learning from all of our training is not how you should act in any given situation, but whether you should act at all.'

'Seamus. *Seamus.* Seamus, wake up.'

'What?' he asked groggily.

'Seamus. Come On. We have to go.' Aliah stood over him, hands on hips, dressed in clean travelling clothes that included a divided skirt, sturdy boots, and a thick warm coat.

'What? Why? I only just got to sleep.' He wearily rubbed the sleep out of his eyes, swung his legs over the side of the bed, and sat up. *Thank goodness someone put sleeping clothes on me last night,* he thought to himself. *Aliah and I would be feeling pretty uncomfortable now if they had not.* He smiled at that thought, only to be jolted by Aliah shaking him by the shoulders.

'You are not listening to me. You were only meant to bathe and change, not to have a nap.' Her blue eyes were glaring at him.

'Sorry,' he mumbled. 'Still feeling a bit woolly headed after yesterday.' He shook his head to clear it, remembering it was not morning, and he was supposed to be getting ready to leave for somewhere, but had been distracted by... oh, yes... *the gods.*

'Seamus.'

'Sorry. You were saying?'

'Some of the witches working in the hospital tents came and met with father this morning. They overheard some of the wizards talking about our arrival, and were saying Gaius would need to hear about it. Those wizards cannot be found this morning.'

'Sorry? There are witches working in the hospital tents? Women have not been allowed to practice magic in any official capacity in Aria for generations.' Seamus dragged a hand through his hair.

'Gah! That is what you took from that story? You really are impossible sometimes.' Aliah turned on her heel and headed for the door, but stopped before she actually opened it.

'A local coven of witches came and offered their help healing the injured. Against the advice of the Wizard's Council, my father agreed. With half the wizards from the Wizard Isle defecting with Millard, we would have been severely short of people able to tend the wounded otherwise.'

Seamus stood. 'You learnt all of that in a short space of time.'

'What time do you think it is?'

'Late morning. Or possibly a little later. After all, I only had a short nap when I returned to my room.' He guessed.

'You slept through most of the day before we had our meeting, and you have just dozed again. It is early evening.' Aliah was clearly exasperated.

Seamus tried to pull himself together and think clearly. 'So, while I slept you all decided we have to go somewhere away from where the wizards expect to find us, to learn what we need to know? And you want to leave by cover of night?' Seamus nodded his head, appreciating the planning that had gone into this. 'That is smart. Where are we going?'

'Hand.'

'Are you out of your heads?' Seamus thundered as he leapt to his feet, suddenly realising why the plan he had seen in the Council Chambers had seemed so familiar.

'That is the closest place for the enemy fleet to land, given where I sent them.'

'Please do not yell at me like I am an imbecile,' Aliah clearly enunciated each word to make a point as she turned to face him again. 'While you were sleeping, Emer flew over the island. The enemy command is camped on the far side of the island. Port of Hand is still protected by the mountains between, and relatively safe. There is a garrison in Port Hand guarding the city walls, looking after those who were not able to evacuate, so we will not be alone and will be relatively safe.'

'Oh,' Seamus responded feeling a little silly, but he was still annoyed they had made such a big decision without him.

'So why Hand?' he asked, trying to be open minded as to why they would choose such a silly place to retreat to, and going though other options for a hiding place in his head. *Maybe Amelia's farmhouse?*

'Seamus, please pay attention.' Aliah sighed, he had been wool gathering again.

'Sorry, you were saying...'

'We had to consider three things. Firstly, we needed somewhere no one would expect us to go. Secondly, we needed somewhere where we can research what we need to do to defeat a god. And, lastly, it needed to be somewhere easy to defended from attack, where we can practice what we learn before we face the god.' Aliah stood in front of him, hands on hips, patiently waiting for Seamus to process everything.

'Oh. Right.' Seamus had to admit they had chosen the perfect place. 'I had best get ready then.'

'At last. Dominic left you some things on the end of the bed, along with a pack.' She indicated a pile poking out from the bedclothes.

'Thanks, Aliah, I will not be long.'

She turned to open the door. As she placed her hand on the door handle, he could not help himself. 'Aliah? So you do not think it is great they actually let female magic users work with the wounded?'

'Grrr.' Aliah slammed the door behind her.

Grinning, because he had managed to get Aliah to react, Seamus readied himself to leave. When he was nearly ready, he cautiously reached for his magic, and sighed with relief when he found it where it usually was.

A few moments later, he tightened the straps on his pack as he joined Aliah in the corridor. She started off without saying a word. He caught up with her and asked, 'Where are we going?'

'There are some tunnels underneath the city that lead to the docks. We will be able to leave unseen from there.' They walked along in silence, until Aliah touched his arm to stop him.

'So we are really going to do this? We are going to try and win this war together?'

Seamus laughed. 'No, there are soldiers to fight this war. Our job is to fight and defeat a god.'

'Oh well, when you put it that way, I have nothing at all to worry about.' Seamus caught the note of fear behind her levity.

'I am worried too.' He admitted. 'In fact, I am scared out of my wits, especially after yesterday.'

'Then why are we doing this?' Aliah asked the obvious question.

Seamus chewed on his lip for a moment before answering. 'Because no one else can.'

'I am not sure we can either,' Aliah whispered, almost as if she did not want to admit her fear.

'Nor am I. It seems so overwhelming even just saying we need to defeat a god.' Seamus' stomach did a somersault as he spoke the words out loud. 'I mean, we barely stopped him from overrunning Port Marden. He destroyed a ship full of men in anger because we challenged him. Then he laughed at us. I am not sure I even know where to begin.'

Aliah was quiet for a moment, then he heard the familiar swish of her plait being flung back over her shoulder, and he knew things were going to be fine.

Aliah the warrior was back, and she had an idea. 'We start at the beginning, we take it one step at a time, and we remember we are not in this alone.' Aliah slipped her arm through his.

Seamus grinned as he caught her mood of defiance. 'And if we do it right, they might even write an epic ballad about us.'

They managed a laugh as they continued through the tunnel towards the docks.

ABOUT THE AUTHOR

Vivienne has been writing books since she was fifteen years old, but only friends and family were allowed to read them. Forced to give up work because of family commitments she was encouraged by friends and family to finally put some of her writing out there for others to read.

In the real world after leaving university with a BA in History and Politics she worked as a Personnel Officer, an Office Manager, a Project Manager, a DBA and IT Manager then as a Business and Data Analyst, adding an MSC in Information Systems along the way. In her world she continued to write.

Born in Invercargill (New Zealand), she has lived in; Dunedin (New Zealand), London (England), Petersfield (England) and currently lives with her husband and son and their dog Trouble and kitten Lola in Sydney (Australia).

For future releases and current news you can find Vivienne at **www.viviennelfraser.com.au** or on Facebook at **www.facebook.com/vivienneleefraser**

ACKNOWLEDGEMENTS

The community that helped cultivate this book to full growth has grown from *Beginnings*.

There is always Sam, my inspiration for writing Young Adult fiction, who was confident enough this time to give me ideas on how I could improve my story. My editor Heather Bosevski, who always has been questioning and clarifying and inspiring me to make my story even better. You make editing fun with your comments throughout.

This time I was lucky enough to have a beta reading group: Sandra Korres, Mark Fox, Avis Williamson, Gary Halder and Amanda Harle. Thank you all so much for taking the time to read my part-formed book and for helping me make it better. Your questions and comments had me learning along with you.

My books would not look as beautiful as they do without the talents of Kim Last from Kila Designs who imagines my covers and typesets my books, and Anna Basey who does the illustrations. A special thank you to Jim Simpson, who produced a new map of Aria for me.

I could not write this without mentioning my constant writing companion, Trouble. When everyone else is out and I am alone in my fictional world Trouble is always there forcing me to break with his need for ball throwing. I should also thank Lola, but her contribution is more in the way of standing infant of my screen demanding attention.

And lastly, but never least, I thank my lovely husband Jim who supports all of this and respects my writing as the hard job it.

Thank you also to the people you for reading my book. I feel humbled that you take time out of your busy lives to read the thoughts that germinated in my mind and grew to fruition in these pages. I hope you return for Battle, the final book in this trilogy.

You can keep up with Wizard and Warrior news
on Facebook @wizardandwarrior